GILLARD'S STING

GILLARD'S STING

Margaret Duffy

This first world edition published 2020
in Great Britain and 2021 in the USA by
SEVERN HOUSE PUBLISHERS LTD of
Eardley House, 4 Uxbridge Street, London W8 7SY.
Trade paperback edition first published
in Great Britain and the USA 2021 by
SEVERN HOUSE PUBLISHERS LTD.

British Library Cataloguing in Publication Data
A CIP catalogue record for this title is available from the British Library.

ISBN-13: 978-0-7278-9054-2 (cased)
ISBN-13: 978-1-78029-714-9 (trade paper)
ISBN-13: 978-1-4483-0435-6 (e-book)

This is a work of fiction. Names, characters, places and incidents
are either the product of the author's imagination or are used fictitiously.
Except where actual historical events and characters are being described
for the storyline of this novel, all situations in this publication are
fictitious and any resemblance to actual persons, living or dead,
business establishments, events or locales is purely coincidental.

All Severn House titles are printed on acid-free paper.

Severn House Publishers support the Forest Stewardship Council™ [FSC™],
the leading international forest certification organisation. All our titles that
are printed on FSC certified paper carry the FSC logo.

FSC
www.fsc.org   FSC® C013056

MIX
Paper from
responsible sources

Typeset by Palimpse
Falkirk, Stirlingshire
Printed and bound in
TJ Books Limited, P

ONE

I had just about got over a local woman screaming at me, 'What's it like being married to a mass-murderer then, eh?' when she saw me in the village high street, as she was deemed to be mentally unbalanced. Privately, I had other terms for her conduct as I'm dubious about modern thinking that nasty behaviour can be explained if a medical term is slapped on it and you ought to feel sorry for whoever it is.

No, if I was honest, I hadn't quite got over what had happened, but I forced myself on this early spring morning to sit down and take stock of my life. It had already occurred to me that with regard to my husband Patrick Gillard there was every possibility that once the State was in possession of an asset there was a reluctance to relinquish it. He had recently resigned from the National Crime Agency after a case where his family had been targeted by criminals, some wanted by international police forces, led by a man called Simon Graves. In spite of the fact that he had taken a supposedly 'safe job' for the NCA within the Avon and Somerset force, Patrick, outraged, had conducted a highly unofficial one-man invasion of the criminals' London HQ where, after they had resisted arrest and opened fire on him, he had shot dead several of them, including Graves. Patrick had been lucky not to be charged with manslaughter. The inquests into all the deaths and the considerations of the police complaints department had been lengthy, involved and very stressful. Finally, the verdict was that they had been lawfully killed. Whether his resignation, amazingly not demanded by anyone who mattered, would result in the criminal fraternity feeling all jolly or if they would even notice would, I felt, remain a mystery.

Some years previously, when he left the army, Patrick had worked for D12, a department of MI5, and it had become clear to me that he was still, very quietly, on the payroll of that organization, although D12 itself had been disbanded.

With this in mind I had been half-expecting – perhaps slightly dreading – a visit, or at least some kind of communication, from an MI5 man by the name of Charles Dixon. But nothing happened, so I made no reference to Patrick about it and almost forgot about this enigmatic little man with the whispery voice whom we had met for the first time several months previously in connection with the Graves case. Patrick reckoned that he had a far more senior position than we had originally thought but the man had given no clue as to his role, or even for which department he worked. As I said, enigmatic.

I write crime novels with a spattering of romance under my maiden name Ingrid Langley and had recently had a novel published, finishing it comparatively easily after the distractions of working as a 'consultant' to my husband for the NCA. He used to refer to me as his 'oracle' and some of my ideas and gut feelings over the years had resulted in progress with cases. His role had officially been that of 'adviser', all these quotation marks necessary. That this had entailed his being armed with a Glock 17 might also indicate that the job had been more hands-on than the title suggested. Definitely. The presence of the weapon had been due partly to the fact that we're still on the hit lists of criminals and terrorist organizations. This is on account of Patrick's activities in stowing them and their hitmen – oafs for hire, call them what you will – either in prison or snugly in body bags, and this had not made surrendering the handgun easy. Not as far as his wife was concerned anyway. I no longer felt altogether safe.

Seemingly undeterred after resigning from his 'desk job', Patrick had taken the job of claims investigator for the Bath branch of a national insurance company. They must have thought he possessed the right attitude. Not all that long afterwards this bore fruit when he had a couple of successes with cases involving people who had deliberately made false claims. One of these featured an aggressive character who, it turned out, had pulled down a section of his own garden retaining wall because he wanted it rebuilt but saw no reason to pay for it himself. He had gone on to bully his elderly neighbour, the roots of whose trees he was insisting were responsible and, also later, left the previous, female, insurance company employee who had visited him feeling very threatened. For this triumph Patrick had quickly been promoted to 'trouble-shooter', although this wasn't reflected in his salary or on any paperwork that I clapped eyes on.

All this activity on his part was very safe for his family, of course, and there were no complaints from him. But I have known Patrick for a very long time. This happened when he was instructed by his father – he and mine were friends – to help me with my physics homework. The attraction had a lot to do with this head boy's black wavy hair, grey eyes and wonderful sense of humour. But what was in front of me now was a man being a good husband and family man while trying to brainwash himself into being happy. He wasn't.

Still in introspective mood but with a lot to do in the house, despite employing two home helps, I carried on sitting in the living room and thought about the woman's outburst. During our years of working together first for MI5, then the Serious Organised Crime Agency, which was later absorbed into the NCA, there had been horrible moments. I had shot, and killed, thugs for hire in self-defence. There had been times when I thought Patrick would die, that we would both die, and as already stated, the occasion quite recently, when our family, the children and Patrick's mother Elspeth, had been targeted by criminals. But there had also been laughter, enormous fun and, for me, the joy of working with someone I love.

And now? Despite abuse from a local lunatic, I was left with what I can only call a virtuous emptiness. Rightly or wrongly, probably the latter, I felt that I could tell everyone that we were now 'normal', not engaged in undercover assignments during which we had seriously, *seriously*, tested the boundaries of what was lawful in order to get results. Patrick has always broken rules. But we had put mobsters in prison, rescued some of those at the mercy of them – particularly trafficked women – and that had made it all worthwhile.

I told myself that we could go on active, exciting holidays, trek in Nepal, take the Orient Express to Venice, journey along the Silk Road . . .

'*Really?*' shouted an inner voice.

OK, no. I got on with organizing the household.

We have five children: Matthew and Katie, Patrick's late brother's children whom we adopted after he was killed, and three of our own, Justin, Vicky and baby Mark. They are lovely young people but take up a lot of our time even with the help of a nanny and two home helps. Elspeth lives with us in an annexe to our old rectory home in Hinton Littlemoor, a village in Somerset. John, Patrick's father, who recently died, had been rector of Saint Michael's Church here and Patrick had bought the rectory when the diocese put it on the market and planned to rehouse the couple in a bungalow on an ugly new estate at the bottom of the village.

Still with MI5 in mind, I had a surprise then when I answered a ring at the front door on a chilly morning a few days later – it was early April – and there stood Patrick's old NCA boss, Commander Michael Greenway. He hastened in, almost before I had invited him to, and stood in our wide hallway in the manner of someone who would prefer not to be out in the open for reasons other than it being cold out there. It is important to mention here that he is a big man, still built like the rugby football player he once was, and is taller than Patrick who is six foot two.

'I'm not here, you haven't seen me, and if anyone asks you think I'm abroad on a fact-finding mission to the States,' he said, running his hands through his thick fair hair, perhaps in an effort to tidy it. 'Is Patrick around?'

As this kind of opening remark is usual for him – he hates anyone other than his immediate family knowing where he is when he's outside the London HQ – I wasn't at this stage unduly worried.

'He's at work,' I told him. 'Didn't he tell you that he'd got a job?'

The man sort of wilted. 'God, yes, so he did. Is there any chance that you can contact him? I really need to have a chat.'

It occurred to me that he must have Patrick's private mobile number, and then I remembered he'd changed it for security reasons when he resigned.

It turned out that the man in my life was in the office writing up his findings on a claim, something he assured me he could do at home. That he turned up around twenty minutes later rather reinforced my views on a certain matter. Please see paragraph six.

Meanwhile I had plied the commander with coffee and biscuits as he'd admitted that he'd left home without having breakfast. The house was quiet, the three older children being at school, and Vicky and Mark at toddlers' club with Carrie, our nanny. Greenway had seemed in no mood to break the quietness to engage in conversation, which was a little strange, so I had left him with his thoughts and elevenses and got on with something else. But I too had been closely involved with the NCA and definitely wasn't going to stay away when Patrick got home.

The first thing the commander did when the two had shaken hands was to key in the code to open his black leather briefcase and remove a Glock 17, shoulder harness and ammunition. He placed them on the low table before him.

'It's yours,' he said to Patrick. 'I want you to have it back.'

Patrick shook his head. 'I'm no longer entitled to carry a weapon.'

'I've been ordered to give it to you.'

'Why?'

'We're worried that after years of being able to protect yourself and Ingrid from any number of criminals you've brought to justice, you're now no longer able to do so – and I haven't said a word to anyone about the knife you carry most of the time.'

'*We're* worried?' Patrick queried. 'Who's "we"?'

'I can't give you all the details I know you want.'

'And you know damned well that I won't tolerate any kind of smoke and mirrors stuff!'

The commander sighed. 'That's what I told her.'

'There must be other reasons, important to the NCA, for giving me back the gun,' Patrick persisted.

After a short silence the commander said, 'I also told her I wouldn't get anywhere with you unless you had the full story.'

'I take it the person you're referring to is the director.'

'Yes.'

Patrick glanced at me and then said, 'What's it all about then?'

'Well, as you might know, the NCA's been allotted an extra forty-eight million pounds to enhance law enforcement response. Also, more NCA officers are being recruited who will focus on serious and organized crime and provide extra investment for data and intelligence assessment capabilities. Whatever the hell *that* means in practice. We're apparently also going to endeavour to persuade one-time operatives to return. As far as you're concerned it's just for one job.'

'Which is?'

'A contract to locate someone to enable him to be arrested, which the Met's been unable to do for lack of evidence for quite a long time. But you get to keep the Glock for as long as you like, and its authorization, whether you're successful or not. And you'll be able to carry on with your new job.'

Without hesitation, Patrick said, 'As you're well aware I resigned because the personal risks came too close to home. We almost had to move house. No.'

'It's highly unlikely that those kind of risks will be attached to this job.'

'Who is this person?' I asked, not wanting there to be any grey areas right now.

'A senior cop who's just retired and gone right off the map. His boss, now an assistant commissioner, had him in his sights but couldn't collect sufficient evidence against him before he retired due to what he rather quaintly described as the "cunning" of the man involved. It would appear that he was in the pay of mobsters in London. It's felt important that no serving police officer should go after him and—'

'Why not?' Patrick interrupted to ask.

'To keep it under wraps.'

I tried again. 'What's his name?'

'John Brinkley. Commander, as was. I believe you've both met him.'

Patrick groaned. 'We have indeed. He used to be the Metropolitan Police's Liaison Officer for D12, the department of MI5 where Ingrid and I worked, before it folded and he went on to head up a new department in the Met, and ought to have come with a government health warning. He was devious to the point of being dangerous to those who worked under him. On one of the last occasions I saw him he was such a picture of well-groomed fat-cat self-satisfaction that I told him he smelled like the inside of a knocking shop. He worried me actually. Starting to have his hair blow-dried seemed to affect what was going on inside his head.'

Greenway brightened slightly. 'Does that mean that you might change your mind?'

'No. I'd be very suspicious of any accusations of actual criminality against him.'

'I'm suspicious too. But I understand that his old boss has quite a dossier of information against him.'

'OK. I'd like to see it.'

'So would I, but I don't think getting it out of the Met would be that easy. That's down to you.'

Gazing at the ceiling for a moment, Patrick said, 'It occurs to me that I don't owe the NCA anything. Also, I seem to recollect a case where a man by the name of Mladan Beckovic assumed a false identity and got himself into the Metropolitan Police. He already had a criminal record for murder at home and came over to the UK hoping to track down those who had murdered his father in Bosnia quite a few years previously. They were known to be in London. DCI James Carrick – the reason for his involvement in the case slips my mind right now – and I planned to arrest Beckovic at a night-club and, having pretended to be an old chum of his, I had arranged a time to meet him. I deliberately gave you the wrong time as I didn't want you to be there. But you guessed I'd do something like that, got yourself into the place early as a replacement bouncer – God knows what happened to the real one – and thoroughly dusted up the pair of us in a fit of pique thus risking the entire job. For which you've never apologized.'

Without warning he had crashed the pair of them together like cymbals with no chance to defend themselves or take evasive action. At the time I'd thought he'd done it to help preserve his own cover as James and Patrick had been acting drunk and were 'fighting' in the road outside to preserve theirs. Despite everything, Beckovic had been arrested.

When Greenway said nothing, Patrick continued, 'Another

point in my saying this is that I've learned to be careful when dealing with senior cops, Brinkley especially. Not only that, what you're suggesting has all the makings of a very large can of worms. Why has the NCA become involved?'

'I understand it's because we're working on cases involving the mobsters in question.'

Patrick shook his head. 'Let the Met dig their own dirt and find him.'

There was a short silence and then Greenway got to his feet. 'I'll tell her you're thinking about it.'

I went with him to the front door, but he paused on the threshold and dug in an inside pocket for his wallet. Extracting a small plastic card from it, he said, 'Almost forgot. He'll need this. It's the authorization for the weapon in case any cops stop him.'

'I have a question,' I said. 'You've just said that you can't see there would be risks involved, so why does he need a weapon in order to track down John Brinkley? The man might have merely retired to Frinton.'

'You never know.' He smiled a little sadly. 'Ingrid, I do understand, but it was a shame Patrick felt the need to resign. I really miss working with you.'

So was that the pair of us he missed or just me?

'If I hear anything useful I'll be in touch,' he said as he left.

I returned to the living room, gave Patrick the authorization card, which was in fact a proper NCA warrant card with his photograph on it, and, having realized that there was something in the office that he needed for the case with which he was involved, he went back to work. I put the weapon and the things that went with it in the wall safe and pondered. The commander had been very casually dressed in sweatshirt, jeans and a jacket that had seen better days. That wasn't like him at all as he usually leans to being formal. The thing that really bothered me about his visit was that I had never before seen the commander look distracted and nervous. It bothered me to the extent of voicing my worries when Patrick got home that evening.

'I would have expected him to air any personal concerns with us,' Patrick said, fixing himself a tot of whisky.

'Perhaps not after you'd told him you'd only trust a senior cop when hell froze over.'

'Ingrid, I wasn't *that* rude. Didn't he say anything to you? You used to have a certain rapport with him.'

OK, I did once quite fancy the guy. Once. For about ten seconds. 'No, he didn't.'

'What does the oracle say?'

I regarded my husband steadily. 'She says you're trying to shift the responsibility of making a decision about this on to her.'

'I thought you'd say that.'

He obviously felt the need to consult someone else as, a little later, he suggested that we ask James Carrick and his wife Joanna, who was once his CID sergeant and has now rejoined the Avon and Somerset police as a WPC at Frome, if they would like to have a meal with us that evening at the village pub, the Ring o' Bells. This occurs on quite a regular basis anyway, the Carricks living only a few miles away in an old farmhouse they've restored, so I was more than happy to contact them.

The Ring o' Bells is situated across the village green from Saint Michael's Church and the rectory – 'a short stagger's worth' as Patrick puts it. Elements of it are very old, especially the cellars, and there is local argument as to whether it was originally constructed as accommodation for the men who built the church. Our deeds suggest that they were quartered in a building on the site of the rectory, the present one being the third. The inn, long and low, with a massive oak tree at the rear and creepers on the walls, is now an almost organic part of the village.

When the four of us met in the saloon bar, very traditional with shiny brass, copper and bits of horse harness, James Carrick regarded my husband appraisingly. 'Not getting shot up by mobsters regularly seems to be suiting you,' he went on to say, his Scottish accent crisp.

'Greenway's trying to change all that,' Patrick told him.

'They want you back!'

'For a contract. And gave me back the Glock.'

James said something in Gaelic – he always swears in Gaelic.

There was then the serious business of the men choosing what they were going to drink, the pub having several guest beers, and Joanna and I uttered hollow laughs when they settled for Jail Ale, which is brewed on Dartmoor near the prison and turns up here occasionally. They then remembered our glasses of white wine, which were still on the bar.

'What?' Carrick asked Patrick. 'Or, rather, who?'

'John Brinkley – newly retired commander of the Met. Apparently his former boss has a file on his misdemeanours along the lines of taking bribes from criminals.'

'I don't think I ever met him. Does that gel with what you know about him?'

Patrick sampled his pint. 'Well, he was a conniving bastard and would do just about anything to schmooze with higher authority. He wasn't a particularly good cop either. But soil his hands taking money from low life? Somehow I doubt it.'

'So the Met's kept it under wraps until now to ensure that there hasn't been the scandal of a serving officer being implicated.'

'Precisely. I have an idea they don't want to investigate it themselves for the same reason. Greenway said he'd been told that it was because the mobsters involved are on the NCA's radar so they ought to do it.'

'D'you believe that?'

'Right now I don't know what to believe.'

'What about Complaints?'

'Not mentioned.'

'Greenway was twitchy,' I observed. 'I've never seen him like that before.'

'That's a most significant detail,' Joanna said thoughtfully, flicking her long titian hair off her face. And to Patrick, 'Why the weapon, though? Bribery so you and your family will feel safe again? Do they expect you'll get entangled with the mobsters in question? Or do they want you to kill him?'

'And that's the most significant thing anyone's said so far,' Patrick told her soberly. 'I confess that I'd thought of the first two, but not the third.'

'The NCA doesn't tend to murder retired Met officers,'

I pointed out, hoping that I didn't sound too sarcastic. 'But the order to Greenway did come from the director.'

'Which raises two questions,' Joanna said, getting the bit between her teeth. 'Did it *really* come from her? Is this man Brinkley actually in danger from dodgy serving cops? And is the commander under some kind of duress from another quarter? My guess, Patrick, is that if he was you'd be the first person he'd approach.'

'Then why not come out with it right at the beginning?' her husband enquired.

'Reluctance to get Patrick involved again in something he clearly doesn't want to be? Ashamed of admitting that he's under pressure – that he's scared? Perhaps he had intended to say something and then couldn't bring himself to.'

Joanna is very good at her job.

'It might be worth letting it brew for a bit,' I suggested.

'Good idea,' Patrick said. He chuckled and said to me, 'Remember when Brinkley offered me a job in his new department when D12 folded, saying it was in "a sort of a branch of a branch" – so we referred to him as "His Twigship"?'

If we had known the real story behind what was going on, we wouldn't have laughed.

In practice the ploy of 'letting it brew' metamorphosed into the affair being placed firmly on the backburner. The reason for this was the foot or so of snow, with deeper drifts, that was dumped in our little valley a couple of days later. Most of it had been blown off fields by a ferocious and icy north-easterly wind. Snowbound, the primary school was closed and the narrow lanes out of the village were impassable, even by a Range Rover. Patrick tried to set off for work on the first morning but the five-foot drift on the bend just past the church defeated him. All we could do was wait for a snow plough to arrive but the village would not be a priority.

On the fifth day the road was cleared by a group of local farmers with snow ploughs on their tractors. All other human activities apart, this was a relief to those who, latterly, had been trying to feed their families on a strange collection of what is referred to in this household as 'UFOs' – Unidentified

Frozen Objects found at the bottom of the chest freezer. This
was food I had frozen when I had cooked too much, but the
labels had fallen off. There were a few surprises but nobody
went hungry.

At last, life returned to near normal and I was able to sit
down in my writing room, which at one time had been Patrick's
father's study, with a view to planning my next novel. But the
only plot I could think of concerned a retired Met police
commander who had apparently disappeared and was wanted
for questioning in connection with possible past iffy goings-
on, a one-time NCA operative asked to find him, and another
commander who shouldn't be nervous but was. The stuff of
crime novels indeed.

John Brinkley. I hadn't worked closely with him as Patrick
had done, and I'd found him pleasant enough but basically
unhelpful. Nevertheless, I was sure that Patrick's summing up
of the man was accurate and not engendered by resentment
after his disastrous handling of a couple of cases. But I couldn't
imagine him in the pay of criminals, serious or otherwise. Did
a commander need the money? Did he have a secret gambling
addiction? Was he being blackmailed? Would someone so
fastidious about his appearance be interested in consorting
with low life? And on the same subject, would he have the
first idea on how to dress down in order to blend in at
the kind of clubs and strip joints some mobsters frequent?
On the other hand he might be chums with the kind of career
criminals who can be found at private gatherings at Royal
Ascot or in high-class West End restaurants.

Flippantly, a bad fault of mine, I thought that perhaps I'd write
the book in order to find the answers. Then, more seriously,
wondered if we ought to look for Brinkley anyway, the NCA or
no. Was he in trouble? Was the case his one-time superior officer
was making against him on the level? And, most important of
all, what on earth was going on with Michael Greenway? There
were far too many questions with no logical answers.

'Confession,' Patrick said when he got home that evening.
'I emailed Greenway and said I'd consider looking into this
business of Brinkley but only on condition that I got to see
the file with the evidence against him.'

'Because it stinks?' I hazarded.

'Something's not right.'

'Where does he live?'

'He once told me that he had a house in Dorset and a bedsit in Hammersmith for during the week.'

'Which presumably have been visited by interested parties and he's not at either.'

Patrick shrugged. 'All very vague, innit? What's for dinner?'

Life went along in fairly routine fashion. It rained, heavily, the snow cleared from the roads but for dirty heaps in corners where the winter sun never penetrates and, in the garden, the first snowdrops began to peep through the leaf litter. Except for Mark, all the children went down with colds which they promptly gave to their parents and grandmother. The only bright spot, if it could be described as that, was that Patrick was made Colleague of the Month. When we had both stopped falling about with laughter over this he went on to tell me that the prize was an all-expenses-paid weekend trip for two to London.

'Sorry, but what makes you so popular?' I had to know.

Patrick said, 'Apparently that bloke who pulled down his garden wall and tried to claim on his neighbour – the company reported him to the police for attempted fraud and threatening behaviour – had adopted a false identity and was wanted having escaped from a prison van some years ago. It's all there in the company magazine complete with cheesy grins. "Eagle-eyed ex-cop employee spots escaped convict." I didn't, he just looked downright shifty. So, loads of publicity for the company. I'm just praying that it doesn't get into the media so all my old chums see it.'

'When are we going to London?'

'This weekend?'

'No, you promised to take Matthew clay-pigeon shooting on Saturday.'

'So I did. Next weekend then. I intend to have a snoop round Brinkley's bedsit.'

'OK, I'll hit the shops and meet you somewhere afterwards.'

He gazed at me, a little smile twitching his lips. 'Sure?'

'Sure.'

Not at all sure actually.

The bedsit was on the top floor of an Edwardian semi-detached house in one of the tree-lined residential streets of which London has thousands. I knew the first of these details because we had just climbed three flights of narrow stairs circumnavigating parked bikes and buggies on the landings. It crossed my mind that it was a good place for a senior police officer to live if he wanted to be anonymous, to disappear into the madding crowd. But then again Brinkley hadn't been like that; he had rather flaunted himself and his rank. Another enigma. Perhaps I was overthinking the situation.

We had travelled to the capital by train. Driving would be pointless as Patrick's 'prize' had included first-class rail tickets. Even if he hadn't spotted a potential criminal who had pulled down his own garden wall, I'm sure this is precisely where we would have been this weekend. One complication was that Commander Greenway had emailed to say that he was out of office on leave for a fortnight so there had been no reaction to Patrick's conditional agreement to make a few enquiries nor his requirement for the appearance of the file in question.

I had been wondering where Patrick would get the relevant addresses from, but it appeared that he still had contacts within the NCA who had obtained the information for him. We had been pleased to discover that this place was for sale with no one in residence. Therefore, all we had had to do was approach the estate agent and ask to have a look round. Naturally they were reluctant to allow us to do this without someone from the agency being present, so Patrick was forced to show the warrant card that Greenway had given him – utterly surreal in the circumstances. No, I kept telling myself, he wasn't back with the NCA. This was all completely off the record and I don't like working in these circumstances any more than he does.

We had been told there was a security system but the alarm had not been set, this particular estate agency having been plagued in the past by vendors who had set it, having previously said they wouldn't, and then couldn't be contacted.

And yes, I had come along, mainly out of sheer curiosity.

'Please look on the internet and see if his other property is for sale as well. It just might be,' Patrick said as he inserted a key in one of the locks on the front door. It was known that he lived in Tor Drive, Glastonbury, Somerset, but there was no house name or number. He added that at some stage Brinkley must have moved as he had been sure he lived in Dorset.

'I happen to know that full addresses aren't listed anyway,' I told him. 'Are there any more details?'

'Try detached houses – he was a detached-house sort of bloke.'

I decided to work on it later.

The bedsit – it was large enough to be described as a small apartment in the particulars – was fully furnished, the decor tasteful but faded. The living area we immediately entered through the front door was light and bright with quite large windows on two sides. There were two sofas, one of which obviously converted into a bed, and near to that a door giving access to a bathroom. A tiny kitchen – no cooker, just a microwave – was in an alcove on the other side of the room. Everything seemed to be clean as well as tidy, although there seemed to be a lingering fusty smell.

We decided to be professional and donned nitrile gloves, quite a store of which I had filched from Patrick's office at the NCA's HQ before he left.

'There's hardly anywhere to store anything,' Patrick muttered, having investigated a cupboard that was stuffed to the doors with various belongings.

'Have you ever lived in a bedsit?' I enquired.

He shot me an amused look. 'Barracks and then small flats. Then I shacked up with you and you had a cottage. Good move.'

'So you only married me because of the house?'

'Natch.' He chuckled. 'And sex, of course.'

'But we'd been doing that already.'

'Yes, but Dad was getting on at me.'

'I never knew that!'

There was another large cupboard with sliding doors that we hadn't previously noticed and this was used as a wardrobe. The clothes within were all what I would call men's town wear: expensive suits all carefully stored in plastic covers, casual trousers, shirts, mostly white, and a couple of bath robes. Shoes in what looked like their original boxes were on the floor. A small chest of drawers by the sofa bed contained underwear and socks.

All very normal for a home that was used Monday to Friday. Obviously he hadn't moved out.

'No outdoor clothes,' I commented.

'He's not a person to walk round the parks in the rain but chuck a coat in his car,' Patrick said. 'There's probably a garage,' he added to himself, examining another key on the ring.

I wandered into the tiny kitchen, the decor trendy shades of grey, and opened a few cupboard doors. There were hardly any pots and pans, next to nothing in the way of non-perishable food, and a tabletop fridge was empty and switched off. The fusty smell was quite strong here. A blocked sink drain, perhaps. I said, 'If he left this place when he retired and put it on the market, why didn't he take his clothes and furniture?'

'Perhaps he and his wife intend, or intended, to use it for the odd weekend in town and then changed their minds.'

I looked in the rubbish bin, one of those tall ones with a push-down-to-open lid. The smell, a thousand times worse, rose out of it and I instinctively backed away for a moment before looking closer. 'Did you say that people, the police, I mean, have already checked for Brinkley here?'

Patrick was gazing out of the window, perhaps trying to locate garages. 'I don't know for sure, but would have thought so. Why?'

'They would have found a headless rat surely.'

He came over, had a look and shrugged. 'That's been dead for quite a while. Perhaps it was freshly dead when someone was last here and they didn't look in the bin.'

Exactly the kind of pragmatic remark an ex-military man would make when he wanted his lunch and his thinking processes were as good as switched off. I said, 'OK, if Brinkley was still living here then and found a headless rat outside, would he put it in the kitchen bin? No. If he was sent one in the post by nasties unknown, would he put it in the kitchen bin? No. Would a neighbour who hated his guts and is in possession of a key put a dead rat here to try to compromise any sale taking place? Possibly, but surely it would be easier to do nothing and hope he sells and moves out fast. Would someone threatening him get in somehow and dump the rat to pile on the pressure so that Brinkley didn't feel safe even in his own home? Quite likely.'

'That has a lot going for it,' Patrick said slowly, perhaps still thinking about garages.

'What are you going to do?'

'What would you do?'

'There are so many unanswered questions. Has his wife disappeared as well? If not, is she at home in Somerset?'

'Shall we find that out before we do anything else?'

We persevered with our search for any kind of evidence as to where Brinkley might have gone carefully, not yanking stuff out of drawers but leaving things exactly as we found them. MI5 had taught us that. I was happy to leave the rat right where it was, but should we tell the estate agent about it even though the stench would eventually give away its presence? Did the wretched thing represent evidence in connection with the disappearance of the flat's owner? We could hardly demand that the property be declared a crime scene. I wasn't even sure if Patrick had left a message for Commander Greenway to tell him what we were doing. Was anything official? Was *anyone* looking for the man?

'I wish I'd gone shopping now,' I said when we'd finished without finding anything else and gone on to discover that the garage was completely empty. 'The can of worms has been opened.'

'I don't think it was ever closed,' Patrick observed quietly.

TWO

It transpired that being Colleague of the Month entailed meeting what Patrick called a 'top company wonk' for drinks and photographs in the hotel bar at seven that evening. I was hoping that would be better organized as when we had arrived the hotel told us that our booking had been cancelled. No further details were given but there were profuse apologies for the mistake and we were able to have a room. I had been invited to drinks as well and for that reason had packed a decent dress, black, not full length but with a few glittery bits on it. My black Jimmy Choos go very nicely with it and it was a pleasure to have an opportunity to wear them, something that doesn't happen very often.

The pleasure was short-lived.

The wonk, Cyril Hampton, was a fat, balding man who was wearing a suit that was approximately two sizes too small for him, a grubby shirt and told me to call him Cy. His breath smelled horrible and he wasn't at all sober. He asked me about myself and, having discovered that I was an author, freaked out alarmingly with jowl-wobbling joy – more good publicity for the company – and insisted on even more photographs. These were being taken by a young woman described as an assistant who didn't seem too happy with her assignment. I told myself it was publicity for me too when I was asked to pose with him, one of his chubby arms tightly and proprietarily around my shoulders. He seemed reluctant to reclaim it.

'Do you want me to kill him?' Patrick whispered in my ear when I'd finally succeeded in prising myself free.

Having already had two G&Ts because we had arrived far too early and then been presented with another by Cyril, who had been late, I'm afraid I shrieked with laughter.

From this point the evening went precipitously and drastically downhill. I discovered to my horror that we were having dinner with this man. The assistant, who hadn't been introduced, was banished and didn't look at all pleased about that either as the dress she was wearing suggested she had been expecting to stay. Cyril insisted on sitting close to me at the table and contrived for his left thigh to press against my right one. I was expecting at any moment for his hands to start to invade my space as well. When they did, at an early stage during the first course, and in truly awful fashion, his podgy fingers groping between my thighs, I got to my feet and as he turned his head to look at me, smirking, slapped him resoundingly around the ear. My slaps tend to be dynamic, which caused him to jog his soup bowl with an elbow and it landed in his lap. He yelled as the hot liquid hit him and was still yelling in the distance as I walked out.

'Sorry if I just got you the sack,' I said, fighting back tears as Patrick caught up with me.

'What did he do?'

I told him. Then, alarmed that he would detonate, I hissed, '*Please* don't do anything drastic.'

'I think you've already done that rather nicely,' Patrick replied, gazing back the way we had come. 'I'll report the bastard.' He kissed my cheek but his eyes were glittering with anger. 'I noticed an Italian restaurant just along the road. Madam, would you care to join me?'

'This wouldn't have happened if you'd come on your own,' I persisted, quite devastated that by reacting as I had I'd probably cost him his job.

'So we find out that he's a complete shit now instead of later.'

'Yes, but why do things like this always seem to happen to *us*? Ignoring the business of the dead rat for a moment, you get a job and almost immediately locate an escaped criminal and then I'm assaulted by one of your new bosses. Why can't we be ordinary, normal people?'

'Ingrid, there's no such thing as normal,' Patrick said. And then seeing how upset and angry I was, he added, 'Look, I was offered three jobs and only went for this one because it meant I was based in Bath. *And* I'll get my army pension soon.'

He took my arm, we left the hotel and ate in the Italian place.

I calmed down even though Patrick, who I know better than he thinks, did not.

The next morning, Sunday, was a cold but beautiful day. We started our online search for Brinkley's Glastonbury home by searching for properties for sale on Tor Drive – assuming, of course, it was on the market in the first place. If he was at home after all then our job would be done. Three properties looked promising. One was a semi-detached house with three bedrooms, the other two detached with four and five respectively. They were for sale with different agencies. I contacted all three and left messages. Even if they were open on Sunday morning, it was too early for anyone to be there yet.

Going on Patrick's intuition, it was decided to start first with the agent advertising The Gables, the one with five bedrooms. It was for sale for just under a million pounds and came with an acre of garden, mostly grass, and a small copse.

We had abandoned our official itinerary for today, hired a car and headed for Somerset instead. The programme laid out for us had included a visit 'for coffee' to a senior manager's house (Cyril again?), then lunch at a local pub (with Cyril?) followed by a tour of a company-sponsored monkey rescue centre (my idea of hell). I banished the suspicion, correct as we were to later find out, that the whole thing was a nasty joke.

When we arrived at the agency it turned out to be open, even on a Sunday. A woman was sitting at a desk trying to look busy in an otherwise uninhabited office. Patrick produced his warrant card and asked if the name Brinkley was on their list of vendors. It wasn't. This was a setback, but he went on to ask if we could look at The Gables. For some reason, looking at her, I immediately thought of Margaret Rutherford's Miss Marple. Something to do with the multiple chins perhaps.

'I'll have to lock up and come with you as there's no one living there,' she told us, her whole collection quivering.

'And you are?'

'Gloria Froome – Mrs.'

'Thank you. Is it a couple who live there normally?'

'Yes, a man and a woman.'

'Have you met them?'

'No, the initial work was done by one of my colleagues. I only work at weekends.'

'What names did they give?'

She fetched a file from a nearby cabinet and looked it up. 'Oh, it's just a Miss Ann Shipton. She must have mentioned a partner but hasn't given their name so perhaps the house is her property.' Gazing at us over her reading glasses, the woman went on: 'She would have to give proof of identity of course, a passport and utility bill which we would take a copy of and put in this file. But nothing like that seems to be here yet so perhaps they're pending.'

'Any idea where she's gone?'

'I think that's confidential, don't you?' she snapped.

Patrick said, 'This is a police matter and I'm trying to keep it low-key. The confidentiality will come from *me*.' He had spoken with commendable patience but had given the impression that there was a thin line between that and some kind of tectonic plate activity.

'Don't you have to have a search warrant or something?'

'We're not going to search the place – just have a look round.'

'All right, I'll let you go without me but you will leave it tidy and bring back the keys, won't you? There's a viewing tomorrow morning. And no, I haven't the faintest idea where she, or they, have gone.'

'No forwarding address then.'

'No.'

'I might have to talk to your colleagues. On second thoughts, do you know which of them spoke to her?'

'No. How could I possibly know that?'

'Is there anything in that file in front of you in someone's handwriting that might give you a clue?' When she just sighed, Patrick patiently added, 'We're trying to trace a missing person.'

'And you don't want to be charged with withholding evidence, do you?' I said, not at all patiently.

Mrs Froome went pink, perused the file and then said, 'Yes, it's Phil's writing. He's the boss.'

Patrick said, 'Be so good as to phone him.'

It was on the tip of her tongue to argue but she caught my eye and picked up the phone.

Patrick had quite a long chat with the manager and then, after being given the keys, the code for the alarm system and directions of how to get to The Gables, we left.

'You're in good form this morning,' my husband observed when we were in the hired car, which I was driving. Our own Range Rover has specially adapted controls since Patrick's lower right leg is of man-made construction following serious injury during his Special Forces days in the army. Made in the USA, it cost roughly the same as a medium-sized family car and gives him near-normal freedom of movement.

'I hope that wasn't sarcasm,' I retorted.

'Merely an observation, my dear.' And then he laughed. He knows I hate being called that.

'What did the manager say?'

'He said that she was nervous, fidgety, kept looking over her shoulder when the door to the street opened. She told him that her partner was away and she didn't like being in the house on her own – it gave her the creeps so she was going away for a short while. He half-jokingly asked her if she thought it was haunted and she hesitated and then rather angrily said no of course not.'

'Did he know if she was going off to be with her partner, whoever it is?' I enquired.

'She didn't say anything about that and he hadn't liked to ask.'

'Patrick, I think we ought to be a bit careful.'

'The oracle's freaking out, eh?'

'No, but be fair, everything's been a bit strange so far.'

Everything carried on being a bit strange. The house turned out to be Gormenghast Castle writ small, an amazing red brick edifice with turrets, twirly chimneys and large wrought-iron gates.

'This place isn't quite John Brinkley, a woman called Ann Shipton or no,' I said.

'Try the other two agencies,' he suggested.

There were still only recorded messages from these – clearly they didn't work on Sundays.

Patrick said, 'OK, I suggest we take a look at the other two properties from the outside and come back tomorrow. I'll phone in sick. But first . . .'

'You're going to have a snoop round this one?'

'Why not?'

I love looking round houses.

Perhaps the manager of the agency we had just visited knew more about the house than we had thought. I was prepared to eat my hat if it wasn't haunted. Perhaps built by someone with a love of all things Gothic, it had been further embellished by whoever lived in it now, as surely the two black-painted skulls – real? – hanging in the glassed-in porch were not original. The hall we entered was oak-panelled, seemingly throughout, the dark wood making it very gloomy. I gazed around as Patrick sought out the alarm control panel. He ran a faint beeping to earth in a cupboard, thankfully before all hell broke loose.

'Three corpses and a headless horseman in there,' he reported when he rejoined me.

'I really can understand the woman not wanting to be here on her own,' I said, a bit shivery and not in the mood for jokes right now. And after all, Glastonbury did have a reputation for ancient myths and legends.

It had certainly chilled down, a lot, since Miss Shipton had left – that is if she had ever turned on the central heating at all. We wandered around looking for any clues that might give an insight into her partner, but whether this had ever been John Brinkley I thought highly unlikely. A large room with a bay black-curtained window on the ground floor contained a long refectory-style table with a chair resembling a throne at one end. Posters of rock bands and several more depicting other popular music genres that were mostly a mystery to me were arrayed on the walls. What I thought must be a full-sized gallows stood in one corner. I had a closer look and there was a trap door painted on the bare floorboards. Interesting. Patrick glanced at it and shrugged Gallic-style.

Another room, again with a bay window and more black

curtains, was on the other side of the hall and appeared to be used as an office. Oddly, a 'desk' had been created by over-turning two ancient tea chests, positioning them about three feet apart and placing a couple of planks sawn to size across the top. More posters with runes, more skulls and symbols on them and a strange wall-hanging featuring women with black lips and facial tattoos were the only 'decoration' except for an ornate candelabra holding several thick candles that had been used, heavy wax dribbles down their sides. There was evidence of the impending move, flat-packed cardboard boxes leaning on the walls of both rooms.

At the rear of the house was a kitchen that was completely different in that it was very modern, its size suggesting that a couple of smaller rooms had been knocked into one. There were stainless-steel appliances, everything comprehensively and expensively fitted out. One could cook dinner for quite a lot of people here.

'This is catering standard,' I mused to myself. 'I wonder if she ran the place as a small hotel.'

'Or ran murder weekends for Goths?' Patrick queried.

'You always get annoyed with me when I'm being flippant,' I countered.

'I wasn't.'

'Sorry, this place is giving me the creeps too. Are we looking in the bins here – bearing in mind that they'll probably be built-in somewhere?'

'Do we think that Brinkley ever crossed the threshold of this house?'

'It isn't logical. But if there were events like murder mystery weekends here he might have been brought in by the Shipton woman as some kind of tame, decorative cop for screwing afterwards.'

'Eh?'

'You said you weren't being flippant.'

We didn't say any more on the subject, just sighed and sought out the bins. It turned out that there was one for general rubbish that swung out from a cupboard beneath one of the two sinks, and a more comprehensive group for recy-cling and so forth in a utility room next door. Other than a couple of newspapers and some other wastepaper in one they were all empty.

Except for the skulls there were no rats or anything else that crime novel editors just love calling 'sinister' in the blurb.

Upstairs – the decor of which didn't fit the Gothic theme – the only potentially useful find was some men's clothing in a wardrobe. I cross-questioned myself as to whether it was wishful thinking on my part to come to the conclusion that they belonged to Brinkley but remained undecided. I consulted Patrick.

'There's a slight smell of scent or aftershave,' I told him. 'And the expensive suits and shirts are about his size after he put on weight.'

Some cops, acting, part-time or otherwise, are good at remembering how people smell. This one is. He has detected my proximity in the dark before now thanks to the perfume I was wearing. On one occasion this was useful as we were in the middle of a violent fracas with criminals and someone had turned the lights out. I seem to remember that we were the only two left standing. He's not a man to lavish designer scents on himself though, happy to wash in anything and slosh on the first toiletries to hand when his thoughts are elsewhere – even something of mine that's wildly unsuitable for a bloke-ish kind of bloke.

'I would say,' Patrick said slowly, emerging from the wardrobe where he had been half submerged among the clothes, 'that these could easily be Brinkley's. He used to wear the same or a very similar aftershave or body spray to this. But obviously there's no proof and I don't think I have the mandate to remove anything for DNA testing, even if his DNA's in records.'

I said, 'We've been to his flat and he's not there and we've been here, which is also for sale and the vendor, apparently nervous, has gone away without, as yet, leaving a forwarding address. Was Brinkley her boyfriend? She mentioned a partner to the estate agent manager. I know Brinkley was married, so has he left his wife? Is she still living here? Or are we being highly unprofessional in trying to link these details?'

Patrick threw up his arms in a gesture of impatience. 'It's

all conjecture. I suggest lunch, a think and then find the other two properties.'

The next house was instantly crossed off our shortlist when we discovered that it was undergoing a huge renovation that appeared to have come to a halt. Opened bags of cement as solid as boulders were strewn in the ungated drive, a pile of bricks nearby had long grass growing through it.

'Probably a one-man project that ran out of money,' Patrick commented. 'This isn't Brinkley's style either.'

The 'think' over the White Hart's vegetable soup – it was too cold for salads and the massive roasts on offer were not what we'd wanted – hadn't produced anything worthwhile, so we decided to carry on with our search in Tor Drive. The last one appeared to be right at the far end of it as one of the photos depicted it from across a field. Rather than drive around looking, I went over to one of the barmen, showed him the picture on my iPad and asked him if he knew where it was. Not being a resident of Glastonbury, he didn't recognize it and called over the landlady. Tall, as thin as a rail and with red hair piled untidily on the top of her head like a ginger bird's nest, she gave me a broad smile.

'Oh, that's John's place and I only know that because folk have been asking the way as it's for sale,' she immediately said. 'Someone said that he's gone away. You'll need to speak to the agent tomorrow if you're interested in it. Lovely house, mind, and I can understand if you're impatient to see inside.'

'John Brinkley?' I queried.

'That's right. Friends of yours, are they?'

I didn't answer, merely beckoned to Patrick who showed her his warrant card. It transpired that Brinkley and his wife were, or had been, regulars at the pub, which was on the edge of the town, their house being around a ten-minute walk away. There didn't appear to be a reliable source of the information that he had 'gone away'; all the woman could do was repeat that 'someone or the other' had told her. The wife, Sarah, was assumed to be still at home. The pair were deemed to be 'rather reserved' and 'didn't put themselves about'. We were given directions of how to find the place.

Patrick was quietly pleased, a little smile on his lips, something I noticed when I shot a sideways glance in his direction as I drove along Tor Drive, which had now turned into a country lane. There had been quite a lot of snow here too, piles of it remaining in dark corners and, I soon discovered, concealing the ditches at the sides of the road. I almost drove into one while reversing to allow another car to pass, the car tilting alarmingly for a moment or so before I got it going forward again. This Ford was no Range Rover and I vowed to be more careful.

'This is more like it,' my husband said when we drew up outside a detached house with large stone eagles on the pillars on each side of the entrance gates. These were closed and I noticed a security camera mounted in a nearby tree. There was also an entry system and without further ado Patrick got out and pushed some buttons. He spoke to someone over an intercom for what seemed a long time. At last he came back to the car and the gates swung slowly open.

'Sarah doesn't want to see us,' he said. 'But I exerted a little charm, explained that I was a one-time colleague and she said we have ten minutes.'

'Was she rude?' I asked.

'Yes – and had possibly been hitting the bottle.'

'Have you met her before?'

'No.'

The house wasn't visible from the entrance, being obscured by shrubs and trees, but as we rounded a slight curve in the drive it came into view. Described by the estate agent as imposing – no lie – it was also ugly, stone-built and sort of Victorian with more recent bits added and out of the same stable as the property ostensibly belonging to the oddly departed Miss Shipton. I was careful to avoid the strangely placed stone plant containers, the contents of which, last summer's bedding plants, were predictably dead. As we got closer I saw that there was the same general air of neglect at the front of the house, the previous autumn's leaves lying in rotting piles where they had been blown.

I parked next to a small white saloon car of some kind and we stepped out on to the gravel drive. Patrick, I saw, had slipped into his professional mode of hyper-awareness when arriving at a strange and potentially hostile place, and was gazing about, even eyeing what could be seen of the rooftops above our heads. This made me wonder how rude the woman had actually been to him, but I said nothing so I would not break his concentration.

The front door opened before we had even reached it and someone who was presumably Sarah Brinkley came out. She wasn't quite steady on her feet.

'I've never heard of you,' she snapped, speaking to Patrick. 'We've done some entertaining over the years and I've never clapped eyes on either of you. How do I know you were a colleague of his?'

Patrick held up his warrant card. 'National Crime Agency these days,' he said. 'And I was the last person he'd entertain as we fell out rather badly.'

'You said you wanted to speak to him. But as I told you, he's not here.'

'May we come in for a few minutes?'

'No, I don't think so.'

'What are you frightened of?' he asked very quietly.

Flustered, she stammered, 'Well, n–nothing – nothing. But you never know, do you? There were all sorts of horrible people he brought to justice during his career who might want to get their own back.'

'Mrs Brinkley, I'm a retired lieutenant colonel in the one-time Devon and Dorset Regiment. There's no need to be scared of *me*.'

'And who's she?' This with a contemptuous flick of her head in my direction.

'My assistant.'

'And why the hell are you working on a Sunday?'

'Because in the real world, cops work on Sundays.'

She shivered and clutched a thin cardigan more tightly around herself. 'You'd better come in. It's bloody freezing out here.'

The three of us, plus a Glock 17 and an Italian throwing knife, went inside.

There was not much time to assimilate my surroundings as

we followed her to a large living room towards the rear of the house, but first impressions were that her taste, and no doubt that of her somewhat forthright husband, was anything but phoney Gothic. The wide hallway that we crossed had a polished floor with thick and modern expensive rugs, a small one which I was convinced I had seen on the John Lewis website. A couple of pieces of antique furniture were at the sides of the room, a buffet sideboard and a writing desk, the former with a splendid arrangement of flowers on it that were probably silk.

The room we entered was in a similar vein with the addition of large dark-blue or black – I find it hard to differentiate between the two – leather sofas and chairs. Sarah Brinkley waved us wordlessly to a sofa near the fireplace in which a log fire crackled. She needed it; otherwise the room was rather cold and the assistant decided to keep her coat on. It is our working arrangement that I am introduced thus as Patrick never wants me to be in the firing line, sometimes literally, should those on the other side of the law get nasty with *him*.

Happy to be ignored, I studied the lady of the house. She was probably in her fifties and didn't look very healthy, her complexion somewhat grey. Her eyes, small and of indeterminate colour, regarded Patrick narrowly while she carried on clutching the dark-blue cardigan to herself tightly, her knuckles white. She was scared all right.

'How long has your husband been away?' Patrick asked.

'Tell me first why you want to know,' the woman demanded.

'I've been asked to find him.'

'Because an assistant commissioner, his boss, wants to pin a corruption charge on him now he's retired. I call that spiteful.'

'What's this man's name?'

'No idea.'

Speaking carefully, Patrick said, 'The man I knew as Commander John Brinkley wouldn't have associated with or done any kind of business with criminals.'

Furiously, Sarah said, 'That's all very well, but as far as I'm concerned if he has been and now has some London mobster on his tail as well as the Met then it serves him right.'

'Please tell me about the London mobster.'

'Oh, I don't know the bloody man's *name*, just that he has a manor – that's the right word, isn't it – in Barking, east London.'

'Are you worried about your own safety – received any threats?'

'No, of course not. I don't suppose this crook even knows I exist. Look, I can't tell you any more so please go away. I'm selling up and taking myself off somewhere where I can forget all about it.'

'And forget about your husband?' I queried.

She transferred her attention to me, and if looks could kill I would have been as dead as last year's Christmas turkey. 'Yes, and him,' she spat.

Patrick made himself more comfortable. 'So you're not actually concerned for *his* safety then?'

'No, not since he got himself involved with some woman by the name of Shipton.'

'Ann Shipton?' I queried.

'How d'you know about her?'

I ignored the question and said, 'Like you, she's nervous, and her house is up for sale too. Did he live with her?'

'God knows.'

'Could they have gone off together?'

For a full twenty seconds she appeared to think about what she was going to say. 'No, I *think* she's gone back to her boyfriend. He calls himself a wizard. Glastonbury's thick with those who like to call themselves wizards. My friend Babs, who's a real gossip, said something about the woman having fled from him in the first place as it wasn't a Harry Potter sort of thing but more like worshipping the Devil – rituals and stupid stuff like that.'

'Do you know his name?'

'No.'

'And your husband just walked out without saying where he was going?'

'Yes, and took hardly any of his clothes. Lately I hadn't noticed what he was wearing anyway, didn't care, so God knows exactly what. The only things that I know are missing are those he wore for gardening, not that he ever did much out there as we pay someone – who incidentally hasn't turned up for ages – plus his walking boots and an old rucksack.'

'How long is it since he went?' Patrick asked.

'It must be just over a fortnight. Look, I don't have the first clue where he is. Please go!'

'And he hasn't contacted you at all?' he persevered.

'No, and he won't. We had a hell of a row.'

'About the woman?'

'You're a persistent bastard, aren't you? What the hell else d'you think it was about?'

'Did he take his car?'

'Yes, although it was found at the railway station the next day.'

'Who by?'

'The people who run the car park, I suppose. He'd left the keys in the ignition and hadn't put a ticket on it.'

'Yes, but how did they know it was his?'

She sighed with exaggerated patience. 'He used the train a lot to go to London when he was working, so I should imagine one of the station staff recognized it. Someone phoned me but I had to pay a fine before I could bring it home.'

'At what stage did you report him as a missing person?'

'I haven't. I don't want him back. I despise him now.'

'That's hardly the point, is it? Have you made enquiries around the family?'

'There isn't one.'

'The Met know he's missing though. How do you explain that?'

'No idea. Perhaps he kept in contact with old colleagues. His job never interested me. My mother hated the thought of my marrying a cop – in her view it was a squalid choice of career. She was right.'

'Who put his London flat on the market – you?' I asked.

'Yes, me. It's actually in joint ownership. Why should he have it anyway?'

You'll need his signature on a few bits of paper though, I thought.

'May I have a look at his car?' Patrick asked.

'What on earth for?'

'It's something I'll be asked if I've done.'

She rose and without saying another word led the way outside, only pausing to take a coat from a cupboard in the hall. We followed her to a range of three garages towards the back of the house where she waved in the general direction of the middle one, remembered that it was locked, went over to remedy that, the key being in a pocket of the coat, and then turned and, in by no means a straight line, stalked off. Moments later the front door slammed.

Patrick had a rare fit of giggles. This proved to be catching but we finally managed to get ourselves back under control and Patrick opened up the garage. Inside was a diesel Jag, perhaps the same one I knew Brinkley used to own, perhaps not.

'Yes, I suppose station staff would know who a car like this belonged to,' Patrick muttered, grasping the driver's side door handle. 'If this sets off the alarm I'm not going to demand to have the keys as I have a feeling there's nothing of interest inside. I shall just walk out of here and leave her to deal with it.'

It did go off, very loudly, so we left the devoted wife and went to find somewhere to have a warming and reviving cup of tea.

THREE

'She's the sort of person who leaves a nasty taste in your mouth,' I commented. 'And she told us nothing.' I had a funny feeling about the woman but it was nothing that could be put into words.

Patrick took a sip of tea and grimaced. It wasn't a very good brew. 'Yet she's scared.'

'I'm finding it very difficult to feel sorry for her. Do you think she's telling the truth about not knowing where he is?'

'Do you?'

'I'm not sure.' I thought about it for a minute or so and then said, 'She was a strange mixture of not caring a toss about him and yet angry that his boss wants to prosecute him for allegedly consorting with the enemy. Worried about the potential shame attached to that, I suppose. But the bit about him going off with his gardening clothes, a pair of boots and a rucksack suggests he was planning on hiking. To disappear into the blue yonder?'

'It's possible. Greenway's the boffin on the Met and we can't ask him who this AC is as he's on leave for a fortnight. Handy for him, isn't it?'

'Isn't there anyone else you could contact?'

'Not that I know of now. I don't want to stir up what might be a muddy pond either.'

'Surely there's no need for us to come back to Glastonbury tomorrow.'

'But I shall still throw a sicky. I want to go and find Ann Shipton and her wizard.'

'I suppose you could always Google Somerset wizards,' I said gloomily, preferring the thought of going home.

Patrick wiped his fingers on a paper napkin and found his phone.

'I wasn't serious,' I said.

'No, but you might have a point.' There were a couple of

minutes of perusal and then he said, 'Wizards in Somerset clear drains, repair broken windscreens, sweep chimneys, go to Oz, and are guides on historic Glastonbury trails. No black magic as far as I can see. But I shall find him.'

Like his late father, Patrick has absolutely no time for people who practise what are called 'the dark arts'. Some years ago we came across a career criminal, a wanted murderer, who more than dabbled in Satanism. Patrick hadn't prevented one of his subordinates, Terry Meadows, who had been half killed by the man, from shooting him from point-blank range. He got into a hell of a lot of trouble over it.

But would finding the wizard and Ann Shipton take us any nearer to John Brinkley?

The following morning we paid a second visit to the estate agency handling the sale of The Gables. The manager, Phil, whose full name was Philip Sanderson, was there and although obviously busy he seemed pleased to talk to us. He was a tall man with greying dark hair neatly cut and wearing one of the best pin-striped suits I had ever seen. Nevertheless, the general impression he gave was of someone slightly old fashioned.

'As I said on the phone, I'm afraid all she told me was that she was going away for a short while,' he said in response to Patrick's enquiry, after we had accepted an invitation to draw up chairs to his desk.

'Apparently she has a boyfriend who seems to call himself a wizard,' Patrick continued, stowing away his warrant card. 'Do you know who he is?'

'Lazno Hiershal. I think he's of interest to the police.'

'It would be extremely useful to me if he was. For what reason, do you know?'

'Look, I can't be too sure about it, but you get to hear a lot of gossip in this job.'

'Let me worry about that,' Patrick said. 'What I do with information given to me is my responsibility and your name won't be mentioned.'

After a short pause, Sanderson said, 'I get the impression from what people tell me that he's a local bad boy. You know, behind quite a few local crimes, mostly small – if any crime can be described like that – but as slippery as a fish. Never any direct leads back to him because of various layers, so to speak, of others who do the dirty work – thugs, drug addicts and others he has a hold over.'

'It's a well-known pattern in cities and large towns,' Patrick informed him. 'But I wouldn't have thought that Glastonbury would have anything like that. Where can I find him?'

The man shook his head. 'Even if I knew, and I don't, I would be reluctant to tell you. Walls have ears and I have a family.'

'I take it that isn't his real name.'

'Goodness knows.'

'So where does the wizard bit come in?'

'I'm not sure. But The Gables is a bit alternative, isn't it? The pair of them held parties there – drugs and unpleasant goings-on.'

'So how did you hear about him, Mr Sanderson?'

The estate agent flushed. Then, reluctantly, he said, 'I wasn't going to mention it. I have a daughter in her mid-teens, Katherine, who everyone calls Kat. She ended up at one of these gatherings when a friend took her along. This was supposed to be a birthday party at someone's house and my wife and I were furious when she rolled up at four thirty the next morning stoned out of her mind. She's under eighteen and should know better. We gated her for a month.'

'Did she tell you what took place there?'

'No, and we didn't ask. Didn't want to know, frankly.'

'Would it be possible for us to talk to her?'

'I'd rather you didn't.'

'We're trying to discover the whereabouts of a missing retired senior police officer.'

'Sorry, but I can't see the connection.'

'He was having an affair with Miss Shipton.'

I said, 'I could talk to her. Just the two of us.'

Sanderson looked shocked. 'Surely not at a police station. She'll think I've reported her after her behaviour.'

Finding that remark a bit odd, I said, 'No, of course not. I could meet her at a place of her choice. A bistro or café for example. But it'll have to be today.'

He thought about it as I willed Patrick not to put any more pressure on him. These people had done nothing wrong.

'Does it have to be today?' he finally asked. 'I think she's revising for exams.'

'Preferably,' I replied. 'I have a family too – five of them.'

'Oh. In that case . . . I'll phone her.'

This he did and, whether the young lady in question was glad to be dragged away from her revision or not, she agreed to meet me at Sadie's in the town. Sanderson told us where it was and that it was a tearoom – so perhaps Kat hadn't wanted to meet us where she might bump into friends. We made our way there, ordered coffee and took separate tables not too far away from each another so Kat wouldn't feel intimidated. This proved to be a good idea, as when she arrived she looked around thirteen years old. She was dressed in quite childish fashion too, in jeans and a top with stylized flowers printed on it, making me wonder if her mother still bought her clothes for her.

I introduced myself, told her that I worked part-time for the National Crime Agency, and then said, 'I have an adopted daughter at home called Katherine, Katie for short. She's mad on horses. Are you?'

This Katherine looked nothing like her namesake, being dark-haired like her father and a little on the plump side. Her eyes were dark as well and right now they were gazing at me warily.

She said, 'No, I'm a bit scared of them really.' She licked her lips nervously. 'Dad said you wanted to know anything I could tell you about the house where that party was. The one that Bev took me along to. I didn't want to go. People talk about the place at school.'

'No one's blaming you for anything,' I assured her. 'What would you like to drink?'

She opted for a milkshake.

'Dad said there were two of you,' Kat said.

'He's over there,' I told her, indicating Patrick. 'We didn't want you to think this was an interrogation.'

Patrick gave her a little wave and stirred his coffee, his interest seemingly on his phone.

'He looks all right though,' said Kat in a whisper. 'And he's a cop too?'

I nodded.

'I love the cop shows on the telly.'

'Would you like him to come over?'

She shrugged. 'Why not?'

I gestured to him to join us.

'Patrick,' he introduced himself by saying and sat down.

Her milkshake arrived. It had a big dollop of cream on top and the motherly part of me, quite a small percentage actually, made me worry fleetingly about the number of calories in it.

'They put stuff in my drink,' Kat said after an appreciative taste. 'I only asked for a glass of wine. I'm not even allowed to have that at home. But it tasted funny and then I felt dizzy and a bit sick.'

Patrick looked at me, worried, and I said, 'D'you think anyone assaulted you while you were there?'

'You mean *sexually*?'

'Yes,' I answered carefully.

'No. I'd know, wouldn't I?'

'You might not have realized until afterwards.'

'No. I don't think anyone touched me.'

'We're looking for a man called John Brinkley.'

'What's he look like?'

'He's quite tall and well built. Around fifty years old but looks younger. Dark hair going thin, well dressed.'

She shook her head. 'No, they were all young people. The local roughs really. I didn't stay very long.'

'But you didn't get home until four thirty in the morning.'

'Oh. No, I didn't, did I? Bev stayed but I went. Her brother had given us a lift there on his way to go clubbing so I had to walk home. I sat in a little park for a while because I felt funny, fuzzy. Must have gone to sleep but still felt funny when I woke up. My bag had been stolen but there was hardly any money in it. Mum and Dad were livid 'cause they'd given it to me for Christmas and it was expensive.'

The one who would have been ready to toss a hand grenade through the front door of The Gables if our Katie got involved in anything like that, rather than concern himself with handbags, took a fierce mouthful of his coffee and said nothing.

I asked, 'Do you know Ann Shipton?'

'No, but I think Bev does. That's why we went.'

'Was she there?'

'She was when we got there but she went off somewhere, which we thought was a bit funny. Bev thinks she's got another boyfriend but doesn't know who.'

'And Lazno?'

'Her bloke. He was pouring the drinks and smiling at everyone. A bit creepy if you ask me. Someone said he could call up the Devil but I didn't believe it – that kind of thing's rubbish.'

'Whose birthday was it?'

'Dunno.'

'How long ago was this party?'

She thought for a few moments and then said, 'A couple of months.'

'Kat,' Patrick said very softly, 'I'd like you to promise me that you'll never go near Ann Shipton or this man again. She may be perfectly innocent but he's a criminal, something I've just confirmed by looking on police records. Also, I really want you to keep this conversation, especially what I've just told you, between ourselves. Will you do that?'

She nodded then said, 'Even keep it from Mum and Dad?'

'No, as your dad knows we're talking to you. Our real interest is the man Ingrid mentioned. You didn't see him there and that's the end of it.'

'OK,' Kat said lightly. 'Oh, I've just remembered. Bev's brother knows Lazno and that's how she got the invite. I think he does jobs for him.'

'What's his name?'

'Eddard Crake.' She spelt it. 'I think his real name's Edward. Eddard's a character in *Game of Thrones*. But everyone still calls him Ed and he gets really mad about it. Bev says he's a pathetic git.'

Patrick gave the girl his card. 'Please ring me if you think there's anything else I ought to know. And also if you're in any bother with these people. Any time, day or night. Do you know where I can find this Lazno or Ed?'

'Not Lazno. No one ever knows where he is. But Ed

sometimes works as a builder's labourer. In the car he said something about the new supermarket going up. You can't miss it, it's at the end of the High Street where the old bus depot used to be.'

We thanked her and asked if we could take her home, but she said she'd call into the agency to see her father.

'Kat said you looked all right,' I said to Patrick with a laugh when we were walking back to where we'd left the car.

'I do make an effort not to look like a serial killer in English tea shops.'

'D'you think it's worth pursuing the Lazno and Eddard side of things?' I queried.

'It's easy to get side-tracked, but the former might know where we can find Ann. And to find him we'll probably have to talk to Ed, who may or may not be at this new supermarket site.'

We were in luck. One of the muddy and cold-looking workmen pointed to an individual laying concrete blocks for what looked like the outer wall of the car park. He stopped what he was doing when he saw our approach.

'Eddard Crake?' Patrick enquired.

'Who wants him?' the man muttered, straightening his back.

'Police. We're looking for Lazno Hiershal and someone said you knew him.'

Crake laughed. 'Cops is always lookin' for Lazno. Never find him though. He's far too smart.'

'I understand that you do jobs for him. What kind of jobs?'

'Well . . . odd jobs . . . building jobs. This and that.'

'Where do you meet him?'

'I don't. He texts or phones me.'

'These jobs then. Are they at his house?'

'No, never. He don't trust anyone to know where he lives. He rents out houses and I do repairs that need doing.'

'Do you know where he hangs out? Pub, clubs, places like that?'

'No. Bad things happen to folk who know stuff about him.'

'We're actually interested in speaking to Ann Shipton, his girlfriend.'

'She ain't no more. The silly tart had a fling with someone else and thought she could go back to him. He threw her out.'

'When was this?'

'Last week.'

'Do you know anything about this "someone else"?'

'Just some posh bloke. Look, I don't know nothin' about it. It's best not to.'

'D'you think Lazno might have got his revenge on him? Did he ask you or some of your chums to sort him out?'

The last question had been uttered on a zephyr of breath, the speaker smiling in horrible fashion.

Crake, a slight individual with a strange complexion and hair colour that I belatedly realized were probably due to cement dust, took a fresh grip on the trowel he was holding and then visibly decided not to subject his questioner to any kind of warfare, verbal or otherwise. 'No,' he finally said.

'He appears to have gone missing,' Patrick added.

'Nothin' to do with me.'

'Do you know where Ann Shipton is now?'

'No. How the 'ell would I?'

'Does Lazno call himself a wizard to frighten impressionable people into doing jobs for him?' I asked.

The man looked at me for the first time and then shrugged. 'No idea. Can I get back to work now?'

We left him to it, having learned next to nothing.

'I can picture it,' Patrick muttered. 'If illegal immigrants from places where superstition is rife, North Africa, for example, are working for him, probably for a pittance or nothing at all, that might be the hold he has over them. But that's not what we're here for.'

'He'd loathe someone like Brinkley,' I pointed out. 'Especially if it came out that he was a retired cop.'

'You think I should go and find him?'

'With all due back-up,' I replied, noting the personal pronoun. 'Perhaps a visit to the local nick would be helpful?'

'Can't do any harm, I suppose,' Patrick muttered.

It turned out to be not at all helpful. Avon and Somerset Police in this neck of the woods, it transpired, had been working on an elaborate and time-consuming sting operation for months designed to arrest Hiershal and the last thing they wanted was the National Crime Agency on board. Politely informed of this by a DI and then again by his DCI boss, Patrick got nowhere. I had stayed in the reception area. This was very disappointing of course, especially as he was given to understand that they had a good idea where Hiershal lived but refused to give the information even after he'd explained the purpose of his assignment. But this was not an occasion to throw his weight about.

'I reminded her that we – the NCA, that is – would be expected to lend a hand should they need help,' Patrick said when he joined me. 'She wouldn't even give me an idea as to the timescale of their plan or what it entailed.'

We went looking for a source of more coffee.

In a most amazing café, loaded down with forties' and fifties' memorabilia, Patrick said, 'Once upon a time I would have gone undercover and laid my hands on this Hiershal character. God, how I want to do that, parcel him up and take him to the nick.'

I wanted to suggest gently that he shouldn't agonize over past glories, but I didn't, saying instead, 'You said earlier that you'd looked him up on police records. Does he operate just in this area?'

'No, also in Exeter and London. He's not involved in small crime at all but protection rackets, fencing stolen property, including high-end cars. He also has personal form for GBH and driving under the influence of alcohol. A man of many talents, but the law's only really caught up with him twice and he's done two stretches in the slammer, for five and two years with a three-year interval in between.'

'He's a tempting target but not necessarily anything to do with John Brinkley. But we could go and have a real search of The Gables for anything that could give us a lead.'

'I'd need a warrant – probably should have had one the first time.'

Trying not to nudge a small black and white television off a shelf far too small for it, I whispered, 'We'd leave it really tidy though.'

'You've talked me into it.'

In order to get the keys again we had to drive past the place. Having just done so I performed what amounted to an emergency stop and whipped the car into a parking space.

'I didn't bring any sick bags with me,' said Patrick, not moving his lips much. He's not a very good traveller and suffers very badly from seasickness.

'Sorry, but there are two cars in the drive.'

'You might have driven into someone not keeping your eyes on the road.'

Ye gods, he really had gone greenish-white.

'Open the window and take deep breaths,' I said. 'I've been told that my peripheral vision is excellent. There's a silver vehicle and a red one in the drive.'

He got out of the car and walked the short distance back, presumably taking deep breaths, then went from my sight.

Muttering about men, their behaviour in general, I followed him. When I caught sight of Patrick he had paused to look at the cars before heading for the front door. As I approached he rang the doorbell – I heard it from where I was – and after this several things occurred very rapidly. There was a shriek and a bang from within, the door was seemingly wrenched open, and a woman came running out and straight into Patrick's arms.

'Calm down!' he shouted as she fought to get free.

'He's going to kill me!' the woman shrieked, still struggling.

'Calm down,' I said, running up. 'This one won't.'

'Eh?' She gazed at me myopically.

'Police,' I said. 'You're safe.' Her face was reddened and bruised.

'Oh, God,' she gasped before bursting into tears. She just managed to whisper, 'But he'll kill you too!'

'Ann Shipton?' Patrick said in her ear, still having her in a fairly tight hold.

'Yes.' She gulped. 'But . . .'

'Who's inside?'

'My one-time boyfriend. The pig tricked me into going back to his house and then kept me there . . . against my will. He – he kept raping me and says he wants the money I get from this house as punishment for leaving him. I – I escaped but he followed me here.'

'Is he armed?'

'I – I don't know.'

'Is his name Lazno Hiershal?'

'How did you know?'

'If I let you go will you stay with this lady here?'

'I'm so frightened,' she sobbed.

That was probably a no then.

'And he smashed my glasses!' she wailed.

But it appeared that Hiershal was coming to us, a power-fully built man suddenly appearing in the doorway. He had a knife. I grabbed Ann Shipton as Patrick released her and hoisted her away a few yards. The next time I looked in that direction – the woman's long hair in as many colours as the flag of an African republic almost blocking my view – I was in time to see Patrick lunging into the house. There was shouting followed by a commotion – I became aware that Miss Shipton now had her arms around *me* – followed by the sound of what could have been a large bag of rocks being tossed down a flight of stairs.

Patrick appeared, shrugging his jacket straight, and called across to me, 'D'you still carry tree ties around with you when we're on a job?'

'No, cable ties.'

'Even better.'

Due to this mind-blowing and highly unexpected occurrence Patrick got his wish, lugging the now-conscious Hiershal into Glastonbury police station having arrested him for assault, suspected rape, resisting arrest and carrying a bladed weapon. Not only that, it became obvious when she suffered from delayed shock that Ann Shipton had been seriously knocked about by the man just before we arrived at the house and she was taken to hospital as a precaution.

The reaction of those at the nick was predictably guarded. The 'suspect' having been taken to the custody suite, we were shown into an office and a woman of ample proportions and attitude came in and seated herself behind the desk. She introduced herself – to me as Patrick had met her earlier – as DCI Sue Manning.

'I'm furious,' she said. 'I told you to leave him to us when you came in earlier. You've buggered up our investigation.'

'Then perhaps you had the wrong sort of investigation,' Patrick retorted, as usual ignoring the fact that he only has the nominal rank of constable to enable him to arrest people. 'And I'd like you to know that I'm not remotely interested in that man and I arrested him because he was threatening and had seriously assaulted a potential witness in the case *we're* working on. You saw the marks and bruises on the woman's face. They weren't all inflicted today. Would you rather we'd gone away and left him to kill her?'

She made a gesture of peace. 'No, of course not. It's just that . . .' She didn't seem to know how to continue.

Patrick said, 'As I explained earlier, we're looking for a retired Met commander by the name of John Brinkley. He's gone missing and the Met want to find him to press corruption charges. Personally, and having worked with the man, I find any guilt in that direction very hard to believe. The corruption might lie elsewhere. If that is the case – *if* – then we might have a scenario where a one-time senior cop is being hounded not only by his ex-employers but by certain London mobsters. I think you'll agree with me that that would be an intolerable situation.'

'Yes, of course,' Manning murmured. 'I take it you want to interview Hiershal.'

'I do, but it's really Miss Shipton I want to talk to as she was seeing Brinkley and I have an idea he might have lived with her for a while. His wife said she doesn't know where he is and although I'm inclined to believe her there is a lingering doubt in my mind. He's not at his flat in London and she's put it on the market.' Any other thoughts he had on the subject, including the business of dead rats, Patrick kept to himself.

'And you suspect that Hiershal might have taken out his resentment on this man.'

'In the correct jargon, ma'am, I merely want to eliminate him from enquiries.'

'There are emerging bruises on Hiershal's face too,' the DCI said somewhat accusingly.

'After I made him let go of the knife, he bolted up the stairs, and when I went after him he took a swing at me and overbalanced,' Patrick told her smoothly. 'Nasty things, stairs.'

FOUR

At this point some real thinking was done and Patrick was permitted to interview the accused virtually straight away. They got a solicitor for him from somewhere. This came in the form of a Mr Rufus Stringfellow, his qualifications unknown and his name fitting him well as he was extremely thin. Patrick's 'assistant' was also deemed to be vital to the proceedings, by Patrick that is, and we traipsed into interview room two. The solicitor must have known something about his new client as he had requested additional back-up should there be any attempts to escape. As a result of this a burly constable escorted in our suspect and then positioned himself by the door. I could understand the caution on Stringfellow's part because, as previously noted, Hiershal was a big man, something that had not stood him in good stead when he had taken his tumble – having been upended by Patrick? – down the stairs.

Red-faced, probably with anger, and sweating, Hiershal fixed Patrick with a surly glare and said, 'I'm going to get you for this, you bastard,' thus demonstrating that he wasn't yet one of Mensa's cherished own. I had already guessed that this might be the case as there was very little space between his bushy eyebrows and unkempt hairline. He was rubbing his right wrist, no doubt where it had been wrung to make him drop the knife.

I had my notebook and pen, not to write down all that was said – which I could if necessary as my shorthand is still fairly good – but just salient points of interest to us.

DCI Sue Manning came in, pulled up a spare chair and said, 'I'm here to observe, that's all. Carry on.'

Patrick gave her a big friendly smile and formally opened the proceedings, adding for Hiershal's benefit that it was being recorded. No doubt the man would be aware of that as he had been in this situation several times before.

Patrick said, 'I've already made it clear to the officers here that I'm not interested in you, nor am I about to charge you in connection with any criminal activities you've been involved in locally. Neither am I connected with the case of your having seriously assaulted Miss Ann Shipton.'

'I never touched her!' Hiershal bellowed. 'She's a damned liar if she said I did.'

'So she fell down the stairs too? Severely bruised, mate, where you hit her several times. But, as I was saying, that isn't my case. What I want you to do is tell me all you know about her recent boyfriend, John Brinkley.'

'What about him?'

'He appears to have gone off the map.'

The man shook his head but he was watching Patrick carefully, perhaps glad that he was on the ground floor.

'Have you met him?' Patrick prompted.

'No.'

'You must have been very angry when she left you for him. Didn't you do a little snooping to find out a bit more about the man?'

'Someone said he lived down the other end of Tor Drive, that's all.'

'And even more angry when you discovered that he was a retired cop.'

'Was he?' Hiershal responded dully.

'I was told that Miss Shipton left you because of your wizarding antics.'

'I call that a derogatory remark.' Stringfellow sniffed.

'OK, I'll rephrase that,' Patrick said. 'She left you because you persisted in turning everyone who didn't do as they were told into toads.' Before the solicitor could again interrupt, he went on, 'No? Well, perhaps you just use it to threaten superstitious and vulnerable people in your employ and that was what Miss Shipton found unacceptable.'

What *had* the woman seen in this vision of tattooed and unwashed ghastliness? I asked myself. I said, 'I think you did know about Brinkley and could even have met him. In your eyes it couldn't have been worse, could it? The biggest insult. She left you for a one-time police officer with a big house, a lot of money and a Jag. No contest, was it?'

Hiershal said nothing but still kept glancing at Patrick, who I guessed was exuding not-so-tightly controlled malice.

'So you decided to sort it out once and for all and – what shall I say? – frightened him off,' I persisted.

'He weren't the sort of bloke you could frighten.'

'You have met him then.'

'Oh . . . er . . . no. She told me about him.'

'To wind you up.'

'Yes. But I didn't do nothin'.'

'Yet you took it out on her after you tricked her into going back to you.'

'No, I didn't, and it wasn't me. *He* did that when she told him she was leaving him and coming back to me.'

'You're lying,' Patrick said in disgust. 'Some of those marks on her face were caused today.'

I said, 'Why did she leave him?'

'He left her. Did a runner. And after that she was scared of being in the house on her own.'

'Because of finding dead rats?'

The man registered surprise. 'Yeah, that's right, bleedin' dead rats. Without heads. Stinking enough to make you throw up. In the kitchen bin and cupboards, even one in her bed. It freaked her out. But it weren't him. He'd gone by then.'

It looked as though we were getting somewhere.

'And you didn't do it?'

'Nah, I hate anything like that – dead things. Turn my stomach.'

'Any ideas as to who might have been responsible for it?'

'Not one.'

Patrick said, 'Miss Shipton said you were threatening her because you wanted the money from the sale of her house.'

'I was mad at her when I said that.'

'Why did you go there? Just to say hello?'

There was no reply to this.

'To check that Brinkley hadn't come back?'

'In a way.'

'And if he had been there?'

'Well . . . nothing.'

'You *were* carrying a knife.'

Perhaps subconsciously Hiershal rubbed his wrist again. 'I have to protect myself.'

'I'm sure you do.' Patrick looked over to the DCI. 'Ma'am, I have no more questions. For what it's worth my opinion is that this man is guilty as charged but can't be of any more help with my enquiries.'

We departed.

'Brinkley's not here in Glastonbury, is he?' I said. We were on our way to West Mendip Community Hospital, hoping to speak to Ann Shipton.

'Probably not, no,' Patrick agreed.

'So far, all we've discovered is that there's a definite sequence of events. Frightened people and dead rats. Someone knew quite a lot about him: where he lived, who he associated with.'

Patrick's thoughts appeared to have gone elsewhere. 'I must go back to work tomorrow.'

'If I haven't lost you your job.'

'I have every intention of losing that fat idiot his.'

At the hospital we were told we could not interview Miss Shipton as she was deemed to be too unwell. This was inconvenient of course, but we had to think of her welfare.

Back in the car, I said, 'Why don't you go home by train tonight and I'll see if I can speak to the woman tomorrow?'

Himself looked dubious. 'I don't think that oaf Hiershal would have had an opportunity to use his phone but he probably has friends locally, so if you don't mind I'd rather not leave you here on your own. I can arrange to return the car to Bath and we can get a taxi straight home – now.'

I didn't argue. At one time, in my younger days perhaps, I might have done.

Fact: John Brinkley wasn't in Glastonbury. I told myself this in an effort to move my own take on the investigation forward. There was no reason for him to be there. His girlfriend had left him and a local mobster, admittedly who had now been arrested, had been likely to make his life uncomfortable if he stayed. The marital home was a no-go area and up for sale. Where would he head off to with his London flat on the market as well, even if he knew it was?

Patrick had gone back to work and filed a complaint, with full details, against Cyril Hampton. There was some confusion and it transpired that Head Office had been told we would not be going to London as Patrick had been taken ill with the flu. A couple of days later he learned that no one had heard of Hampton and he certainly didn't work for the company. There were sincere apologies from those in charge.

Curiouser and curiouser.

It was obvious that the situation wouldn't end there, but as it was Friday, my mood was buoyant. At the appropriate time I gave the three youngest their dinner – Matthew and Katie have theirs a little later with Elspeth on Fridays – as I'd decided that Patrick and I would have a meal at the Ring o' Bells. We needed to talk.

Forced to dress as though going on a polar expedition merely to cross the village green as it was snowing again, it was a real pleasure to enter the old inn with a massive log fire crackling in the open grate in the public bar. Having shed outer layers and bought drinks we went through into the other bar, now mostly used as a restaurant, where I had booked a table. There was another log fire, a smaller one, in here. And so were the Carricks, seated at a table looking at menus. Judging by Joanna's quietly glittery dress, this was an occasion to celebrate.

'Hi!' they chorused.

'We won't interrupt,' I said, aghast that I seemed to have forgotten their wedding anniversary, but as I spoke they were moving their things to make room for us, their table seating four.

'We've got the cold weather blues,' Joanna said. 'So we decided to pretend it was someone's birthday, or James had been promoted, or whatever.'

'And our London weekend was a disaster,' Patrick said with a laugh.

They looked shocked as he explained.

'You could get that character for sexual assault,' James said to me when Patrick had finished. 'Who the hell was he and what was the point of the deception?'

'I intend to find out,' Patrick said.

'I ken you were looking into this Brinkley business.'

We gave them the rest of the story. Patrick's mobile rang and he went out into the lobby to answer it. When he came back, he was looking pensive. 'That was Greenway. Yes, I know, he's supposed to be on leave. He wanted to know about progress on finding Brinkley and of course all I could tell him was that it appeared someone was harassing him and it was almost certain he wasn't in Glastonbury. That didn't satisfy him at all and he told me to get on with it.'

A nasty, creeping idea entered my mind like something snaky. I had thought that the oracle was in semi-retirement but apparently not. To Patrick, I said, 'Did you think of asking him the name of this assistant commissioner who's supposed to have evidence against him?'

'Yes. Someone called Luke Wallingford.'

'Never heard of him,' Carrick muttered.

'Did you tell Greenway about our impending weekend in London?'

'Yes, but only jokingly. Colleague of the Month and all that. He laughed. Why?'

'Who else knew about it?'

'Well, the bods at the office obviously.'

'Anyone jealous enough to organize something nasty like that? They'd be able to contact Head Office easily to tell them that you were ill.'

'There's only one fairly poisonous female but it would be so easy to trace any call back to her as you have to state your name, security pass number and branch when you phone.'

'Was this Hampton character staying at the same hotel?' Carrick asked.

'No idea,' Patrick answered.

'You could ask the Met to check.'

'I don't have the authority.'

'Greenway gave you a warrant card, didn't he? An authorization number's on that.'

'But right now, steak and kidney pie and chips,' said Patrick, whose gaze had been on the specials board.

The following morning the building of a snowman had to be supervised and, after a snowball fight instigated, as usual, by Justin – on which Patrick had to blow the final whistle after it predictably got out of hand – the younger members of the family, mostly worn out, flopped in the living room and said they were hungry. 'Helped' by Mark, who is toddling now and had made a short-lived foray outside and, to his horror, promptly taken a header into a modest snowdrift, I had spent part of the time making a huge potful of thick soup.

'I got on to the Met and they discovered that there was no one booked into the hotel by the name of Cyril Hampton,' Patrick reported as he assisted in doling out lunch. 'But a couple of members of staff remembered him on account of a lady guest boxing his ears. I don't think the soup can have been all that hot as he didn't complain of having been scalded. Apparently he did make quite a lot of noise though, and demanded compensation despite an offer to have his suit cleaned. But in connection with the suit he left a name and address. He's Denny Whitman and he lives in Stratford.'

'So tomorrow?' I asked, having a very good idea already.

'Tomorrow I shall haul him out of bed and ask him about himself. There might just be a connection with the Brinkley business.'

I assumed that this was wishful thinking but with Patrick you never knew. We were both aware of course that he couldn't pursue this from the angle of the man having assaulted his wife, that is, reduce him to what I'd once heard James Carrick call 'mince and tatties', as that would breach police protocols, seriously. No, what we needed to do was find out who had set up the deception.

The next day the pressures of family life meant that I stayed at home as I really cannot expect Elspeth and Carrie to have to cope with the family on Sundays. For one thing, everyone expects a big roast dinner which we always have in the evening as I find the children then sleep better. Patrick having not turned up by six, I delayed the meal for a little while, getting a bit concerned. Then, twenty minutes later when I was serving up, I heard the front door close.

'Nothing serious,' I heard Patrick say somewhere out in the hall.

Elspeth came in, shepherding Vicky and Justin, sat them down at the table and then came over to whisper, 'I think he's been in a spot of bother.'

'What sort of bother?' I whispered back.

'I'm not sure, but he was moving rather slowly.' She placed a hand on my arm. 'It might frighten the children if you go rushing off.'

Justin dropped his knife and fork, which he had been waving around, with a clatter. 'Daddy's been in a fight,' he said in a loud voice.

Katie and Matthew came rushing in, the former announcing, 'Mum, I think Dad's a bit hurt.'

I asked them to start their meal before it got cold, put my own dinner and Patrick's back in the oven and took off my apron. I met Carrie, looking alarmed, in the doorway carrying Mark.

'Yes, I know,' I said before she could say anything.

Patrick was in the bathroom, appearing to be a bit lost. 'Where's the key to the cabinet?'

'Where it usually is,' I told him and went into our bedroom where it's kept in a small drawer. 'Painkillers?' I enquired, returning.

He sat on the closed toilet. 'Yeah . . . please.'

I was going to give him two codeine tablets but changed my mind as he would probably want a stiff whisky as well and mixing the two was not a good idea. So it would have to be paracetamol. 'What the hell's happened to you?'

'That bastard must have known I'd follow up what went on at the hotel. I got to the house, a small terraced place that appears to have been split into two flats as the upper one's for sale. It seemed deserted, front door locked. But the back one must have been open and as soon as I got to it some yobs shot out and jumped me.'

'Take the pills,' I reminded him, handing over a toothbrush mug full of water.

'Oh . . . yeah.'

There were telltale red marks on his face and knuckles plus a cut lip but I got the impression that what was really hurt was his pride.

'I'm not fit any more,' he muttered, having downed the painkillers.

Perhaps not – he hadn't been to the gym recently, although had been taking the boys swimming. Katie can swim but doesn't like the water very much and Vicky won't go anywhere near it, not even at the seaside.

I said, 'Did you report it to the police?'

'No, just left three of them in wheelie bins and the other one ran off.'

'Four of them!'

'It was touch and go for a couple of minutes.'

I stroked the redness on his face. 'Your dinner's in the oven.'

'I look a mess. I'll shower and have a tot first.'

But in the end he didn't, just tidied himself up a bit and made his way downstairs a couple of minutes later. I'm sure Elspeth was biting her lip, determined to make no comment, yet, but Katie felt no such qualms.

'Dad, I thought you weren't in the police and doing dangerous things any more,' she said quietly.

'I'm not really,' he answered. 'Just doing a little job for them.'

'I bet it's a job that no one else wants to do,' she snapped.

A bright child, is Katie.

Patrick gave her a big grin. 'I got some funny looks on the train.'

'Surely those men can't have been waiting around in case you decided to check on the address,' I said over next morning's early tea.

'That had occurred to me,' Patrick said. 'I reckon they were dossing there anyway. My problem was that I didn't feel up to taking a look inside the house afterwards where more of them might have been hanging out. On reflection I should have informed the Met.'

'It's not too late.'

He passed his mug over for more tea and without saying anything I gave him a couple of painkillers. 'No, and I'll ask Carrick to run Whitman's name through records. This has gone way beyond the pair of us being the victims of some kind of stupid con.'

'But *has* this anything to do with the Brinkley business?'

'What else?'

'I know Greenway wants you back – and even possibly the director – but would they go to such lengths and to get you personally and emotionally involved?'

'Ingrid, those yobs weren't undercover cops.'

'Are you sure?'

'Sure. I would have disposed of them a bit more tidily if I'd thought they were.'

'But who the hell else knew what you were doing?'

'Someone, or more than one someone, in the Met.'

A minute or so later he stiffly got to his feet and went off to get ready for work. I sat there for a little while thinking how roughly life was treating him and then hurried to organize the children's breakfast. The day rattled along at the usual pace and I only really paused mid-morning when my mobile rang. It was James Carrick.

'I can't get hold of Patrick so he might be in a meeting,' he began after we had exchanged appropriate greetings. 'He asked me to check up on this Cyril Hampton/Denny Whitman character. Unless it's a big coincidence it looks as though the latter's one of the names used by a confidence trickster whose victims have variously described him as "slime bucket", "unprincipled slob" and other things that I won't bother you with.' Adding that he would try to contact Patrick later, he rang off.

After a while I made coffee and found myself wondering about the woman who had been with Slime Bucket. She had given every impression of taking photographs. If she had – to give authenticity to the proceedings if she was in on it too perhaps – had she deleted them or had there been a real purpose behind it? I pondered and then grabbed my mobile.

He was back in circulation.

'Question,' I began. 'That photographer at the London hotel.

Was she with Hampton or genuinely from the company and someone forgot to stand her down? She was wearing a dress suitable for evening and seemed very disappointed, furious actually, when he sent her packing as I think the arrangement was that she would stay for the meal.'

'I did catch a glimpse of her a couple of times after she ostensibly left. I'll find out,' Patrick said. 'Right now.'

It turned out that the photographer, Rachel Blakeney, worked for the agency that the company used for promotion and advertising purposes. Ms Blakeney had complained to her boss about the incident but had not deleted the photographs she had taken, wondering if they might be 'evidence', her intuition telling her that something wasn't right. She had done quite a few similar jobs for the company in the past and had never heard of Hampton, apparently coming to the conclusion that he ought to have been drowned at birth. I immediately decided that this lady was my friend.

The photos she had taken were to be emailed by the agency to Patrick's insurance boss who had been horrified at his employee's battle-worn appearance and wanted to send him home on sick leave. Patrick had told him that he would rather keep busy. He was called back into the man's office at three that afternoon when the photographs arrived and that was when things became really interesting.

Sufficiently suspicious to hang around almost out of sight, Ms Blakeney had taken more pictures than her brief required. There was an absolutely wonderful action shot of me slapping Hampton, who had his back to the camera, and another of his subsequent reaction to a mushroom soup bath. Then, when I had left the dining room, followed by Patrick, another man – tall, bald and with an exaggerated, rather arrogant way of walking – came into view and sat at the same table. This sequence of events had been captured in several shots. There was one of Hampton frantically mopping his lap with his napkin while the other man, his face turned slightly away from the lens, laughed – loudly, Rachel had noted to the head of the agency. Then he had patted Hampton on the shoulder and walked out, still highly amused.

I saw all this for myself some time later after Patrick received permission to send them to me. During the day I had been doing some thinking and the more I thought about it the more Commander Greenway's behaviour appeared downright odd. An ex-operative of his had a new job and in exchange for having his handgun returned to him was supposed to drop everything and do something else. No contract, nothing official, seemingly no pay and Greenway had promptly gone off on leave. I had to admit that it wasn't like him so reasoned he must be acting under orders, again from the Director. Or, he was fearful.

'I have every intention of finding out who that second man is,' Patrick said when he came home looking cold and tired, the gleam of the chase nevertheless in his eyes.

'But the hunt for Brinkley? I queried.

'Next weekend – and I'm damned if I'm going to use my annual leave or sick leave as I ain't sick to look for him – it might be worth going back to London. Brinkley's a London cop and knows the city inside out.'

'Are you going to send those photos to Greenway?'

'I already have. I know he likes to be kept in the picture but might not be bothering with anything work-related right now.'

I carried on cooking the dinner. Not much in the way of writing was happening. I had no real ideas for a new novel unless it was about a retired cop who packed up his past life and set off to walk to Scotland to get a job on a ferry or in a haggis factory.

'Brinkley went off with what his wife said were his gardening clothes and a rucksack,' I reminded Patrick after dinner when the youngest children were in bed and we were sitting in the conservatory with Katie and Matthew, the latter reading, Katie frowning while trying to learn to knit by making a scarf. I'm not much help with that and guessed she would soon be heading in Grandma's direction.

'You think he might be hiking?' Patrick said.

'It's a good way to disappear from urban riff-raff.'

'It's a good way to disappear from us too.' He rose. 'I'll find out if we can talk to Miss Shipton yet.'

'There's a hole in it!' Katie suddenly exclaimed and hurled the knitting on to a nearby chair.

'I'd stick to ponies if I were you,' Matthew said in a pompous older-brother voice. 'Or knit things with on-purpose holes in.' He laughed.

'I hate you!' Katie yelled and hurled herself at him. She'd landed a couple of punches before I could intervene, then burst into tears and ran out.

'Matthew, that wasn't funny,' Patrick remonstrated, having returned on hearing the rumpus. 'You're to apologize when you next see her.'

Matthew slammed down his book and marched out rubbing his shoulder where she'd hit him.

'They do sometimes have these spats,' I said to Patrick, who was looking concerned, as we heard Matthew's bedroom door slam, Justin asleep in there or no.

'We don't want them to become stressed because of what happened to me though.'

No, we didn't.

Miss Shipton, it transpired, was being discharged from hospital the following morning. Realizing that Avon and Somerset Police would want to interview her, Patrick contacted them and left a message for DCI Sue Manning at Glastonbury police station to the effect that we needed to talk to her as well. There was no response to this until breakfast the next morning when he received an email from the lady herself telling him that contact had been made with the assault victim who had every intention of heading out of the country for a while. However, she had consented to be interviewed on condition that she was picked up from the hospital. If we wanted to talk to her we would have to be at the police station at nine thirty as the woman was meeting a friend who was going away with her.

'She's dead scared,' Patrick commented. 'I hope they're keeping that bastard Hiershal on remand.'

'I'll go and talk to her,' I said. 'I can drop you off at work on the way if you don't mind being there rather early.'

He gazed at me soberly. 'Please take care.'

It was still cold but the roads were dry and I made good time. I parked in the town centre and although I was early walked immediately to where the police station was situated. Everywhere was quiet – Glastonbury probably usually is – but I did keep an eye on two young men wearing hoodies who loitered, smoking, hands in pockets in a shop doorway opposite the nick.

Patrick had contacted the DCI to tell her that I was coming and would be on my own so when I arrived all I had to do was provide proof of identity. I was then asked to wait and seated myself in the reception area. The posters on the walls were of a rural nature; exhortations to keep dogs under control after local cases of sheep-worrying, warnings of increased break-ins at stables and farms, notifications about the licensing of shotguns.

Quite quickly, my name was called and I was shown into an interview room. Ann Shipton, looking wan, unhealthy really, bruises still evident, and showing her age which I guessed to be around forty-five, was already present. She was accompanied by a DS I had not met before who introduced himself as Stephen Newton. Newton was youthful, sporty looking and had a fresh complexion – the sort of person who makes me feel middle-aged and sort of inert.

'Oh, it's you,' said Miss Shipton starchily, not about to thank Patrick and me for getting her out of a very nasty situation. 'I've had to wait around, you know.'

I glanced at my watch and said, 'Actually, I'm early.'

'This is just a chat,' Newton assured her. 'Miss Langley's from the National Crime Agency and wants to talk to you about someone you used to know, John Brinkley.'

'John? What about him?'

'We need to know where he is,' I said.

'What's he done?'

'Nothing as far as I know. We just want to find him as he seems to have disappeared.'

'I can't help you. He walked out on me and that's the last I heard of him.'

'When was that?'

'Not all that long ago but I couldn't tell you the exact date.'

'Do you mind telling me why he went?'

'Yes, I damned well do. It's none of your business.'

Newton cleared his throat. 'Miss Shipton, I have to tell you that when a retired Metropolitan Police commander who has worked in areas connected with serious organized crime goes missing then questions tend to be asked.'

I was wondering how he knew so much about it but my thoughts were disrupted by Miss Shipton shrieking, 'John? A cop! Get on! He said he was in banking.'

A little tingle went down my spine. 'Did he give you any reason for his departure?' I persisted. 'Had you had a row about something?'

'No, nothing like that. But he did say that I wasn't his sort.'

True.

'And he gave you no hint of where he was going?'

'No, and I didn't care. I don't care a toss about him now.'

'Did you think he'd left you for someone else?'

'No idea. Perhaps he went back to his wife.'

'Did it have any connection with your past friendship with Lazno Hiershal?'

'You've really been snooping around, haven't you? Well, he hated the parties he had. People call it black magic and turn their noses up but it's just a bit of fun really. I had them at my house as well and that was where they met.' She sniffed. 'Hate at first sight really.'

Hiershal had lied then, when he said he hadn't met Brinkley.

'Perhaps the reason for Brinkley going off was that he hated your so-called parties too,' I continued. 'Drugs, was it?'

'Only sometimes,' the woman answered defensively after a short silence.

'Do you have a mobile number for him?'

'I did but I got rid of it when he left.'

'What was the purpose of that gallows in one of the downstairs rooms?' I went on to ask.

'Oh, we used to have mock executions.'

'Not real ones?' Newton asked lightly.

'Don't be stupid.'

He had a point though. I mentally filed that.

I said, 'The kitchen in your house resembles those in small hotels and restaurants. Why was that?'

'Can't a woman have a decent kitchen?' she snapped.

'I got the impression that your parties might have stretched to a couple of days with paying guests. Murder mystery weekends? The catering arrangements would have to comply with local hygiene laws or you would have been closed down.'

'What of it?'

I changed the subject. 'Do you think Hiershal can have had anything to do with Brinkley's disappearance?'

'God knows, but John did chuck him down the stairs. They had a blazing row at the last party I gave and John called him a fat rat and the next thing I knew Lazno was in a heap down in the hall. I've never heard such language.'

I almost smiled when I remembered how Patrick had kept up this good work. But why hadn't she mentioned it before?

'Tell me about the real rats,' I requested.

'You know about that too then. I reckon it was Lazno in revenge for my leaving him and taking up with John. I found them in all sorts of places. Gave me the horrors and that's why I'm selling the house.'

'Hiershal said he doesn't like dead things.'

'Then he's a liar. It doesn't seem to bother him with people.' She clapped a hand over her mouth. 'I shouldn't have said that.'

I noted that also but felt it was for the good cops in Glastonbury to investigate and said, 'And you haven't heard from Brinkley at all? No phone calls? Nothing?'

'Nothing. Have you nearly finished? Only I'm desperate to leave this bloody place and I still don't feel too good.'

'Many thanks and you've been most helpful,' I told her. 'One more question: does the name Luke Wallingford mean anything to you?'

'Oh, yes. He's a mate of Lazno's. I have an idea he came to one of the parties – Lazno's, that is, but they're not mate mates, if you get me. I think he's supposed to be a bit upper class. But if that was your next question, I've never met him, have no idea what he does for a living and as far as I know neither did John, but that's just a guess. It was before I met *him*. Even before, I *think,* John came to Glastonbury.'

I thanked her again and rose to leave.

'Was that useful to you?' DS Newton enquired when the pair of us were in the corridor.

'Very,' I said.
'So who is this Luke Wallingford?'
'Right now, I'd rather not say.'
'But is he someone we ought to know about?'
'Probably not – not just yet anyway.'

FIVE

What she had said was completely staggering. I didn't know what had made me ask the question – it had come to me right out of the blue. Also, Brinkley had told Miss Shipton that he was in banking. Why not tell her the truth? One reason I could see for the deception was that he knew she was connected with crime or criminals and had no wish for her to be aware of his one-time career, perhaps because it would lessen his chances with her. No, that didn't ring true at all as I had known him to be a fastidious man and, frankly, she was what my grandmother would have called a baggage. Far more likely was that he was interested in her criminal friends. Patrick had checked up on her in police records with no result so unless she was using a false name she was innocent – even though I was worried about those 'parties' with gallows as an added entertainment. And it appeared that Assistant Commissioner Luke Wallingford knew Hiershal and, more importantly, might well have known him before Ann Shipton had said she met Brinkley, which rather supported her tentative guess that Wallingford had been in the area first. What the hell was *he* doing? People in his position wouldn't be out 'at the coal face' working undercover to obtain information about suspects and the Met's remit hardly stretched to Glastonbury anyway.

I was very careful as I returned to the car, keeping to the main thoroughfares even though several of the little by-lanes were signposted to the car park, which seemed to be in the middle of everything. There was no reason to stay in the town; I had plenty of things to do at home. But when I reached the main entrance to the car park, I could see in the distance what looked like the same two youths I had seen in a shop doorway. They were leaning on the Range Rover, still smoking.

I went back into the high street remembering that among

the boutiques and so forth selling dream catchers, broomsticks, crystals and plastic dragons was a motorbike dealer and repair shop. In my experience men connected with motorbikes tend to be on the . . . well . . . chunky side, and as I didn't have my personal bodyguard with me this was not a time for silly feminist heroics. I have a family to look after.

'Madam!' exclaimed a five-foot-six charmer who looked as though he had come straight off the set of *Strictly Come Dancing*, light blue satin shirt and all.

Slightly despairing, I explained my problem, not mentioning anything about the NCA.

'No probs,' said charmer. He sashayed into the back and yelled, 'Dave!'

'Wot?' roared what sounded like a Highland bull.

'A lady here wants you to pulverize a couple of yobbos she doesn't like the look of lurking by her motor.'

I hadn't worded it quite like that.

'No probs,' replied the bull.

A very tall black man wearing overalls appeared, wiping his oily hands on a rag and grinning. He threw the rag at charmer and the pair of us left the shop as I apologized for stopping him from working.

'No probs,' he said with another grin.

He had to do absolutely nothing. When they saw him the two hurriedly melted into the scenery.

'They look very much like folk I know about,' my saviour said.

'Who are they?' I asked.

'Bad boys. The Wilkins brothers. There are actually three of them and they'd all boil their grannies down for glue for the price of a packet of fags.'

I thanked him and left.

'It puts a completely different angle on everything,' Patrick said that evening. 'And what she said about Wallingford must be true, for why would the woman lie about it if she didn't know who he was, had never met him and presumably had merely heard him mentioned?'

'And this is the man who's supposed to have a file on

Brinkley's illegal activities and yet it looks as though he might have been in Glastonbury first.'

'An assistant commissioner simply doesn't socialize with the likes of Hiershal never mind any black-magic rubbish,' Patrick went on furiously. 'I'll check up on your yobs, the Wilkins brothers.'

This he did and found out that the three of them, James (Jamie), Robert (Robbie) and Kenneth (nicknamed Hairy because he was) had all been in trouble with the police since being old enough to throw a brick through someone's window. All had been sent to young offenders institutions and when released commenced a career of crime, mostly in nearby Shepton Mallet, dealing in drugs, stealing top-of-the-range cars to order and mugging people smaller and younger than themselves for their phones. Robert Wilkins was reckoned to be the most dangerous of them, serving three years in prison for burglary and GBH. There were mugshots of them but as the two I had seen were wearing hooded tops it was impossible for me to identify them. Patrick reckoned they were part of Lazno Hiershal's mob of useful idiots.

The rest of the week went by in the usual rush and then it was Saturday morning. Nothing had been discussed about going to London and I couldn't see how Brinkley could be tracked down by visiting his old haunts, whatever they were. I wasn't sure if Patrick even knew the names of any of his former colleagues who could perhaps be traced and questioned. But Carrie was due to have the day off so I wouldn't be going to London anyway.

Patrick came in, carrying Mark, perhaps drawn by the smell of frying bacon. He was on his mobile and it didn't take much brain to realize that he was talking to Commander Greenway. Finally, he said, 'No, I'm not doing anything more with this until I get the file. Then, and only then, I'll tell you about the very large spanner in the works we've just discovered.'

There was then a rather abrupt ending to the call.

'He wants results – again,' Patrick said, putting Mark in his highchair. 'Does this child always go to bed with quite a lot of Vicky's soft toys and teddies?'

'She gives them to him in case he gets lonely in the night,' I said.

'I practically had to search for him under them. And one of the cats was asleep in his cot too.'

'He's too big to be smothered by a cat.'

'But isn't it rather unhygienic? And if he pulls her tail she might scratch him.'

'Possibly, but it gives his immune system something to do even though they're both regularly treated with flea and worm stuff, and it's Pirate 2 as Patch is out. She's never been known to scratch anyone. Anyway, you know I'm a lousy mother and I haven't eyes in the back of my head never mind that someone must have left the nursery door open.'

Patrick gave me a look, peeled a banana, cut some of it into slices, gave them to Mark on a saucer and ate the rest himself. I got on with cooking mushrooms and tomatoes to go with the already cooked bacon and put Mark's egg on to boil. Matthew, Justin and Katie appeared and seated themselves around the table, and for some reason it went rather quiet.

'Sorry,' Patrick said.

I blew a kiss to him.

'Mum, are you going to have any more babies?' Katie piped up.

'No,' I said.

The file – together, amazingly, with an NCA parking pass, another carrot to persuade Patrick to get results? – arrived by special courier quite late the next day and Patrick took it to work with him the following morning to read in quiet moments and in his lunch hour. During the afternoon he rang me.

'I haven't finished reading it yet but it's interesting stuff,' he began. 'So far the one thing we can relate to is that Lazno Hiershal was born in Poland and has a brother by the name of Zeti who lives in London. They both have criminal records – something we were already aware of regarding Lazno, and the author of this, who appears to be Luke Wallingford, the AC, seems to know all about them. There's a note that they might be stolen identities. He claims that he's been investigating Brinkley personally for some time because when he himself was a mere DCI his team hadn't been able to pin Zeti down for years and he suspected that there was some kind of insider assistance going to him, in other words tip-offs from the Met. He seems to have become rather angry about it.'

It had sounded like a feud to me, right from the beginning.

Patrick continued, 'I'm not convinced of any of that and there's no real evidence except for a list of monies from obscure sources paid to Brinkley, culled from what is said to be his bank account records but how Wallingford got hold of those isn't revealed. They might not even be genuine. See you tonight.'

He then had to get on and do the job he was being paid for as he didn't have time to read any more of it.

'It's sort of convincing,' Patrick continued that evening. 'But the fact that he's admitted he became slightly obsessed by not being able to nail Zeti Hiershal makes me wonder if that's affected his judgement.'

'But does the file contain real evidence that would hold up in a court of law?' I asked.

'In my opinion, no. But I still haven't finished reading it.'

'Would you like me to have a go?'

'By all means. Make a note of anything that strikes you as important and it'll save me from doing it.' He chuckled and went away to fetch it.

Handing something like this to an author has the effect of it being seen from a completely different viewpoint. When you've had quite a few books published and gone through all the processes of copy-editing and proofreading it is inevitable that what you first notice are what I'll call the nuts and bolts of the thing. Also, typos leap off the page. The section I started reading dealt with how Wallingford had gone to Glastonbury as he had received a tip-off that Brinkley was there (who that tip-off was provided by was not given). This immediately threw up that Miss Shipton had told us Wallingford had been there first, not that anything she said could be considered absolutely accurate. Wallingford then went on to give a somewhat grandstanding account of how he had gone undercover to present himself as an upmarket fence who admired Zeti's brother Lazno's tactics in connection with the theft of antiques and antiquities. (No one had yet said anything about that to *us*.) Brinkley, Wallingford was convinced, now he had retired, had gone from providing information to going into business with both of them. The evidence was to follow.

I turned the page and beheld a photograph taken in a pub or club of four people standing by a bar. Ann Shipton was unmistakable with her multicoloured hair and Lazno Hiershal was also easily recognizable. The somewhat weedy younger-looking man on his left might be his brother Zeti but the fourth was definitely John Brinkley. All were obviously enjoying themselves. A caption beneath the photo stated that it had been taken at a 'dive' in Bristol during a weekend trip, since closed down as the place was a front for a brothel using trafficked women. The names of those guilty of this weren't mentioned. This wasn't evidence either: the photo could have been taken anywhere.

After a little while I became aware that Patrick was sitting opposite me on the other sofa regarding me with a small smile on his lips. This was a distraction as, lean, elegant, his wavy dark hair now more than tinged with grey, he's still the sexiest man I've ever met.

'Well?' he asked.

'I haven't finished yet,' I said.

'First impressions then.'

'I'm fairly sure this wasn't written by a cop. No acronyms and no jargon, which as we know the military and police are steeped in. It flows and is creatively written, probably by a professional.'

'Perhaps he writes fiction in his spare time.'

'Perhaps,' I acknowledged. 'But that doesn't necessarily mean that he'd write what amounted to a report in the same fashion.'

'Or dictated it to someone.'

'Perhaps.' I passed over the file open at the page with the photograph.

'That's Brinkley all right,' Patrick murmured. 'But what's it supposed to prove?'

'That he socialized with them? We already knew that – if one counts a couple of so-called parties, that is. But Wallingford did too, although one imagines not at the same time.'

He gave it back and I read a bit more. Finally, tired, I had to call it a day. I said, 'Apparently there's a group of three of Wallingford's one-time colleagues looking for Brinkley. Quietly, in their spare time as they have other jobs now, it says.'

'Why put that in the file? Surely it's a bit clandestine. Yes, it is when you think about it, especially if they're carrying weapons.'

'So even though we haven't quite finished going through it have we both decided that, so far, it's dodgy?'

'Dodgy. And not proper evidence. Even the Complaints people will expect something better than this.' Impatiently, he got to his feet. 'I have an idea this man's playing with us.'

'Or it's not the genuine file and merely tries to explain why he was in the company of such people?' I suggested. 'Does he actually have any evidence? Or is it that he just hates Brinkley's guts? Or worse, is it to cover up his own actions?'

'And he might eventually say when he finds him that Brinkley was armed and resisted arrest so his Met chums had no choice but to shoot him?'

'Patrick, that's a horrible thought. That leads me to think that Greenway wants him found, by you, before they could do anything like that.'

'If so, he might not dare put it in so many words, not even to me.'

'That would be stupid.' After a few moments of silence, I added, 'What can you do?'

'I've unfinished business with Cyril Hampton, or Denny Whitman, whatever the bloody hell his name is. He still needs his head screwing off.'

'I really don't think you ought to revisit that place.'

But he just looked at me. He was going.

'And the other man,' I added. 'The tall, bald one with an arrogant way of walking at the London hotel that night. He gave the impression, laughing like that, that he put Whitman up to it and thought it funny when it went wrong.' I broke off and shrugged, fed up with guesswork.

We were in bed later when Patrick whispered, 'I intend to ask for two weeks' unpaid leave to settle this once and for all. As I intimated before, it's not right to ask for sick leave as I'm not sick.'

Almost asleep, I think I just muttered something. Unpaid leave from a job to tackle another that he wasn't being paid for either?

Hands were straying over me in knowing fashion. Knowing that I find it impossible to resist him.

The leave was granted, probably due to the fact that the whole wretched business had started off with the company's 'prize' of the weekend trip to London. There might, I reasoned, be a little corporate feeling of guilt. I resolved to get on with writing while I could, as with regard to raising five children some of the food might grow on trees but everything else doesn't. It was a surprise then when Patrick asked me if I wanted to go with him, caveats attached.

'As in?' I queried.

'The usual. Keeping out of danger, doing what I ask and not getting the giggles at tense moments when I'm trying to concentrate.'

'A lot of women would call you a pompous pig for saying things like that.'

'They're probably right. Pompous pigs might be the ones whose nearest and dearest stay in one piece.'

'*And* you once grabbed my wrist and gave me a real talking-to when my imagination went into overdrive and I thought of something funny.'

'I don't remember that. Did I hurt you?'

'Yes.'

'Did I apologize?'

'Yes.'

'Well, what are you going on about it for then?'

It's difficult to win arguments with this man. Instead I said, '*Should* there be any trouble, I don't have the Smith and Wesson any more.'

'It's in the wall safe in the living room.'

'But you said you were going to return it!'

'I didn't in the end as it was yours.'

'OK. I'll come.'

*   *   *

Stratford hasn't been the same, in a very good way, since much upgrading work was done for the 2012 Olympic Games with the creation of the Queen Elizabeth Olympic Park and the Westfield Stratford City mall. However, the facelift had passed by the area where the man we had first known as Cyril Hampton lived – either that or it was due to be demolished for more redevelopment. Whatever the truth, the residents appeared to have given up the struggle against littering, graffiti and tattered plastic carrier bags in trees, perhaps waiting for someone with more energy, time and money to come and sort it out.

'There, that one,' Patrick said, not pointing. 'The one with the estate agent's board outside. It's the upper flat that's for sale and, after what happened the last time I came here, I can only assume that he lives downstairs.'

'He might not be there,' I observed.

'No matter, we can have a snoop round and wait for a while to see if he comes back.'

I was thinking that on the grounds he had expected to encounter an overweight numpty on the first visit Patrick had relaxed his guard. Even though he had prevailed he had paid dearly, but perhaps merely vying with people who went in for knocking down their own garden walls hadn't done him any favours. Looking at him now I knew that it wouldn't happen this time.

There were so many unanswered questions. Who had set up this man to do what he had? How had anyone known our programme for that weekend other than those working for the insurance company – and also Commander Greenway, as Patrick had told him? Greenway had close connections and cronies in the Met, for that was where he had started off. When was he due back from leave? I put the question to Patrick as we crossed the road.

'I don't know exactly but I'll have to find out,' he answered, concentrating on what was ahead of him.

By the look of it the house hadn't had a coat of paint for years and window cleaning had been left for the rain to do, something that hadn't been too successful. The inhabitants had also seemingly come to the conclusion that piles of rubbish in a front garden saved them from cutting the grass. We made our way down the path towards the front door where another went off to the right and down a sideway, the house being on the end of a terrace. I fully expected Patrick to repeat what he had done on his previous visit and go round the back. Not so.

The bottom-of-the-range plastic front door flew inwards like a piece of cardboard as he shoulder-charged it then hit the wall and the small piece of patterned glass in the upper section fell out. I trod on it and skidded as I ran in after him, the little pause as I regained my balance meaning that I wasn't actually present when Hampton/Whitman was hoiked out of his armchair and then slammed back into it. I just heard the sound effects connected with the latter as the springs protested.

'Remember us?' Patrick yelled at him. 'I'm the one whose wife you sexually assaulted, and if you don't tell me right now who paid you to be at the hotel that evening to engineer that scam I'm going to wring your effin' neck!'

This was absolutely nothing to do with being a cop – temporarily, of course.

The man had been in the middle of his elevenses, the contents of a mug of tea or coffee now all over the front of his already grubby sweatshirt, a couple of biscuits on the stained carpet. Unshaven, eyes goggling, mouth quivering, he stared at the pair of us like a freshly landed carp. Then, when Patrick made another grab for him, he shrilled, 'It was a joke! A joke! You know, like . . . like . . . a kissogram. No harm done.'

I intervened before Patrick really lost it and said, 'Advice. If you don't tell him the truth he probably will wring your neck.'

He struggled to his feet courtesy of the man standing over him. 'Look, I'm . . . I'm sorry,' he blurted out. 'Really sorry. I'd had too much to drink . . . much too much to drink. But I'd been told to keep you entertained for the evening and during the next day, Saturday. I'm an actor. It was just a job.'

Patrick slammed him back into the chair. 'Who paid you?'

'Just a man I met in a pub.'

'Which pub?'

'The Coach and Horses round the corner.'

'What was his name?'

'He didn't say.'

'Describe him.'

Hampton shrugged. 'Ordinary . . . not as tall as you . . . dark hair cut short. That's all I noticed really.'

'You're lying. After Ingrid slapped you and we left, a tall, bald man came over to you and seemed to think the situation highly amusing. Who was he?' When Whitman remained silent, he continued, 'The photographer took a lot more photos than you imagine. She was furious due to your behaviour and thought they might be good evidence. She's quite correct on that. Who was he?'

'Oh . . . oh . . . just a friend of mine. We'd been supposed to meet for a drink and I'd forgotten about it.'

Speaking quietly but venomously, Patrick said, 'I don't believe a word of that either. Another point: I came here to question you just under a week ago but was attacked by several yobs. Who were they?' And when the other again remained dumb, he shouted, 'Talk!'

'I – I heard about that and it was nothing to do with me,' Hampton stuttered. 'They were squatting in the flat upstairs and wanted by the police.'

'They came out of *your* back door.'

'They must have broken in. Stuff was missing from my fridge. Yes, that's right, the lock was broken when I got home.'

'You gave a different name, Denny Whitman, to the staff in the hotel when they offered to have your suit cleaned. Why was that?'

'It's my real name.'

'Why the Cyril Hampton charade then?'

'Er . . . well . . . as I said, I'm an actor.'

Patrick stood back. 'Get your coat.'

'Why?'

'You're going to the nearest nick.'

'You can't arrest me,' the man blustered.

'I can. I've just remembered that I'm a cop.'

And he did.

*　　*　　*

It was a good ploy. Patrick could no longer investigate this himself as it involved the pair of us personally. There was also a need to put the case, if it could be described as such, on an official footing. Put another way, it meant we could offload our suspect on to someone else and get on with looking for Brinkley. But before that Whitman had to be interviewed – by that someone else.

Those at Stratford nick expressed surprise and some displeasure at having him dumped on them but, during the afternoon, Whitman started to talk. A factor may well have been the demeanour of the DS interviewing him. I spotted this man in a corridor after he had been fully briefed by Patrick and immediately wondered if he too was helping with enquiries into some crime or other until enlightened by my working partner.

We were grateful of course for the prompt response to the NCA's request and went off to have a bite of lunch – someone quietly warned us about the inadvisability of eating in the canteen – while Whitman was questioned. When we returned the DS involved invited us into a vacant interview room. We seated ourselves and, perhaps on account of his big dark eyebrows, I found myself wondering if angst was his default position or he really was annoyed with us.

The DS, whose name was Harry Benton, looked at me. 'How do you fit into all this, lady?'

Did I *really* have to explain my role? I said, 'I worked with Patrick for MI5, again when he was with SOCA, which as you know was subsumed into the NCA, and am now lending a hand on this case. What did you make of Whitman?'

Benton beetled his big black brows at us fleetingly and said, 'He's a right little toad. He's got form. Did either of you check him out?'

Patrick nodded and said, 'A DCI friend of mine in Bath did.'

'He's a confidence trickster by profession and served eighteen months quite recently – the kind of shit-face who swindles old ladies out of their life savings in lonely hearts scams or by posing as an investments expert. He soon decided to cooperate when I told him he'd be back inside real quick if he didn't. I understand he told you that a man in a nearby pub gave him the job of meeting you that evening. That bit has the makings of being true as he then went on to say that he was the tall, bald man you asked him about. He got paid in advance and admitted to drinking quite a lot of it – has a drink problem does Denny. He said he'd never seen the bloke before – it's his local – and hadn't been told his name. I don't quite believe him on that.'

'I'll explain a bit more,' Patrick said. 'Until quite recently I'd retired from the NCA but have been given a contract – with all the correct permissions, I hasten to add – to find a certain Met commander, also retired, who appears to have gone missing. His old boss has a file against him alleging corruption. I've read it and it doesn't hold water. I used to work with the guy in question and although he was a nightmare, forever bragging, doing anything to improve his own image, even at the expense of his staff, I just can't see him taking money from mobsters in return for losing evidence, or whatever.'

'Can you tell me who this man is?'

'I'd rather not, if you don't mind.'

'So whose side are you on, Gillard?'

'On the side of cops who don't pay little toads to pull a fast one on me. What else did Whitman say?'

'Only that he'd screwed up and drunk too much.'

'I called at Whitman's place quite recently and was set upon by four thugs. He said they'd been squatting in the empty flat upstairs and had broken into his place too, to steal food. Did you hear anything about that?'

More brows were beetled. 'Yes, a woman phoned in, freaking out, to say that dead bodies were sticking out of wheelie bins outside her house. When it was checked out the corpses had vanished, and the woman then said that when they'd started moving she'd locked all her outside doors. I think I'd have done that a bit sooner. Would that have been anything to do with you?'

'Guilty. I was trained to look after myself. Whitman said they were wanted by the police.'

'Yeah, but we don't normally use wheelie bins to get them to the nick. We found three of them in a local churchyard looking a bit sorry for themselves. They said they'd been beaten up by a gang.'

'The other one ran off.'

'What are *they* saying about what occurred at Whitman's place?' I asked.

Benton's whole face frowned. This had the effect of making him look thunderous. 'I don't *think* there's a connection with what you're working on. They're all as thick as two short planks and have been causing local bother ever since their parents chucked them out for being the filthy little gits they are. They admitted breaking into the flat upstairs but said they'd only been there for a day and a bit. Hungry, thirsty and broke – the water had been turned off – they said they'd got into Whitman's place to try to find something to eat or drink. My guess is that alcohol was quite near the top of their list. They swear they were hiding from another local hoodlum – we know all about *him* – who they owed money to. That's who they thought you were, Gillard.'

Patrick didn't quite snort. 'They must have been really twitched then if they laid into the first bloke to approach the back door. I could have been coming to read the gas meter.'

'Yeah,' the DS said, making the word last a long time.

'Who's the local hoodlum?'

'A waste of space calling himself Freddy Higgins. This force and his enemies know him as Friggin Higgins or Friggers. We're pretty sure his name's on the recent attempted murder of a bloke who works in a betting shop, the attack reputedly on the grounds that a horse he'd backed didn't win. You simply wouldn't believe some of these people.'

'Perhaps he called in what he was owed by that bunch.'

'And got them to give you the once-over? It's possible.'

'What does Higgins look like?'

'Off the top of my head . . .' Benton began and then got to his feet and left the interview room. He returned quite quickly with a laptop, put it on the table and turned it so that the screen faced us. 'Know him?'

We didn't.

'He's associated with a man calling himself Zeti Hiershal, another waste of space.'

'We do know about him, though,' Patrick told him. 'Brother of Lazno Hiershal who runs all kinds of scams in Somerset.'

'Do I take it then that this retired commander might not only have what one is forced to call the law on his tail but any number of small and big-time mobsters, including Lazno Hiershal, whose domains might come tumbling down if and when he's found and arrested and starts to tell all?'

'That's very neatly put,' Patrick said.

SIX

'Although we might be finally driven to it, I think chasing our tails right now going after this succession of low life, Higgins or even Zeti Hiershal, is a distraction,' Patrick said that afternoon, echoing my own thoughts. 'It's not helping us to find Brinkley. I still think he might be here though, in London. It might be fruitful to talk to Luke Wallingford, call on him at work without giving him any notice.'

The fairly new structure on the Embankment that is now the Met's HQ is still called New Scotland Yard but is a far cry from the iconic building that featured in so many early police dramas both in the cinema and on TV. From the outside the new building could almost be mistaken for a top-class hotel. I was looking forward to seeing what it was like inside but this almost didn't happen as I no longer have a warrant card and there was a protracted security check before I was eventually issued with a visitor's pass on a lanyard.

While this was going on, Commander Wallingford had been contacted and apparently after hesitating had agreed to see us. But not for long as he said he was due at a meeting. I asked myself if cops like him ever did any actual policing or if their daily round was more like that of a company director.

After a journey to what appeared to be the top floor but one, there was then quite a long walk along corridors, again similar to a large hotel, and we finally arrived at room number 413. It was ajar.

'Come in,' a man called in response to Patrick's tap on it.

There were a few moments of mutual appraisal after appropriate greetings and then we were invited to seat ourselves. We were indeed in a meeting or lecture venue, chairs arranged in rows before a medium-length table at one end with further chairs on one side of it facing the room. The man we had come to see was seated in one of these and he waved us to the others. I decided to take one that was on the end of the table so I didn't have to crick my neck in order to watch him and Patrick did likewise at the other end.

'I've been undertaking a little research on you,' said Wallingford, speaking to Patrick. He was in uniform and I supposed in his late forties. His grey hair was cut very short at the sides in the kind of style that makes men look either businesslike or ruthless depending on the rest of their facial features. This coupled with steel-rimmed glasses and a chiselled sort of face meant that he rather leaned towards the latter. Despite the fairly affable greetings this man couldn't be described as friendly.

'And?' Patrick asked, not about to be overly chummy either.

'You retired from the army as a lieutenant colonel, were then recruited by MI5 to work in a department called D12 and then worked in various police departments, the NCA being the latest. Bit of a loose cannon, are you?'

The fact he's still connected with MI5 hadn't seemed to have reached the Met's grapevine then. Good.

Patrick smiled and said, 'I've only served in one police department before this, SOCA, which as you know no longer exists as a separate entity. And I've always been described as a loose cannon – even by my own father. But I've never tried to undermine the outfit for which I'm working.'

Wallingford ignored that and said, 'No stranger to the complaints people either, are you?'

'No, when suspects resist arrest and open fire on me I tend to retaliate – and I'm a very good shot.'

'And now, officially, you've retired from the NCA only to be given some kind of under-the-counter contract to look for John Brinkley. I'm not quite sure why.'

'*Officially* I've been given a contract to look for Brinkley. I'm not quite sure why either, unless it's because I usually get to the bottom of things.'

There was an awkward short silence while I wondered why Patrick hadn't mentioned that his instructions had come from the director of the NCA, and then Wallingford said, 'Years ago he was on my staff. I thought he was suspect then and now I know it. You've read my file?'

'Yes, it's superficial and wouldn't stand up in a court of law.'

'I'm not prepared to have all the details out in the public domain.'

'I'm not the public domain,' Patrick pointed out.

'They still might fall into the wrong hands.' He paused and then said, 'I've done a lot of work on this, even contacted – undercover, of course – the criminals with whom he associated.'

'The Hiershal brothers?'

'And others in London.'

'Ingrid and I have tracked down Ann Shipton, the woman Brinkley went out with for a while. She'd been living with Lazno Hiershal, the pair of them apparently throwing wild black-magic-themed parties. She'd left him. Apparently Brinkley walked out in disgust, perhaps when she again started having booze-ups, with trimmings, at her house, which – and I'm still guessing here – was where he was living by then. It's now up for sale, one of the reasons behind it being that she'd been plagued by rats – planted dead rats. He's also left his wife, if she's to be believed, and that house is on the market as well. So is his flat in London and we found a dead rat there. Care to have a stab at explaining any of that?'

'Well, it's obvious that some of his criminal cronies are trying to rid their manors of him.'

'I'm asking myself why Lazno Hiershal set himself up in a respectable Somerset town in the first place.'

'That's easy. To get away from us, the Met.'

'And his brother Zeti, the one who you had no luck in pinning down? He's still knocking around in the capital, isn't he?'

'Regrettably, he is.'

'Someone mentioned Barking in connection with this.'

'That's it.'

'No strong evidence?'

'Silenced witnesses, several secret addresses, the usual thing.'

'And still getting tip-offs so when you think you've got him, suddenly, like Macavity, he isn't there?'

'Yes,' Wallingford answered heavily.

'But Brinkley's retired. How would he be in the know now?'

'Look, I'm not sure you have the authority to question me like this. You're only a bloody constable when all's said and done.'

'So I can arrest people, so yes, it's quite handy sometimes. Have your investigations gone a bit further than dabbling around and writing crap files?'

'You're making dangerous insinuations.'

Dangerous to who? I wondered.

'Have a go at this then,' Patrick went on. 'Since I resigned from the NCA and took a job in Bath at an insurance company, Ingrid and I were given a weekend trip to London. Someone found out about that – and it could only have been a police connection as I'd mentioned it only to my old NCA boss – and the weekend was sabotaged. Without me knowing the company was told I was ill and we couldn't go and a petty crook was hired to wreck it further. Any comments on that?'

'No,' Wallingford said.

'I checked up on the petty crook. He has a record and his real name is Denis, known as Denny, Whitman. When I went to where he lives I was set upon by four yobs who obviously had every intention of seriously injuring me. I seem to keep hitting a wall of hired louts.'

'You're still implying that I'm involved in this,' Wallingford said stonily.

'You might well be, or someone you know is. You indicate in the file that some of the members of your old team are looking for Brinkley. Perhaps the man's armed and dangerous, who knows? He might resist arrest and fire on those who run him to earth – who may well be illegally armed as well. Very sad, of course.'

Wallingford's already pale complexion went white and he shouted, 'This is intolerable!'

Again, Patrick smiled. 'I'd really like to know what you have against this man. He's gone, retired, it's water under the bridge.'

'There's nothing personal in it at all. I just loathe corruption.'

'Despite new rules being introduced in 2006 thousands of police and civilian staff have not been properly vetted. Serving members should be checked every ten years, including their partners, family and friends. Why wasn't something discovered about Brinkley when he was in the job?'

'I can't be expected to answer questions like that. He took money to suppress evidence so Lazno Hiershal's brother Zeti was cleared of murder – and that wasn't all.'

'Have they checked on you lately?'

'I want you to leave,' the AC said in a cold whisper.

'We will. But I suggest you quickly produce some credible evidence, with proof – if there is any.'

Very quietly, the man said, 'I'm warning you, Gillard, tread on my toes and you'll regret it.'

'The NCA has you on its radar,' Patrick told him, having the last word, and we left.

I'd said hardly a word, merely being a witness to a declaration of war, and we'd learned nothing useful. I wasn't happy about any of that.

'I detect disapproval,' Patrick said when we were outside in the street.

'Indeed you do,' I replied.

'You often rely on intuition. What's that telling you?'

Yes, what's been referred to as my cat's whiskers. I said, truthfully, 'Not a lot actually.'

'He's bent – I know he is.'

'And you've stirred up the man to what end?'

'Just to show him that the NCA's working on it.'

'Sorry, I think you should have left him to brood. He knows you have the file and that what's in it wouldn't stand up in court. He might intensify his one-time team's search for the man and then what would happen?'

Patrick remained silent.

'Another thing is that I can't understand his utter loathing of Brinkley,' I went on. 'I know that corruption happens in all walks of life, but this is deeply personal. One explanation is that Brinkley was checking up on *him* and he has a lot to hide.'

'It would explain why it appears Wallingford got to

Glastonbury ahead of Brinkley, but as we've said more than once before, that's only on the say-so of Ann Shipton.'

'Do we need a change of direction?' I asked.

'Short of trawling around London for the next three years to no avail, what do you suggest?'

'We need to go right back to the beginning. Greenway was nervous the day he came to see us. He came through the front door as though he didn't want to be seen. That's not like him at all. He's gone on leave. Is he at home, do you know?'

'No idea. He rings me on his mobile.'

'You might have to ask him about it outright.'

He just got the messaging service.

'And, knowing Brinkley quite well, I'm asking myself would he, having retired, bother himself with messing around with people like the Hiershal brothers?' Patrick queried aloud. 'No, he wouldn't, he'd sail off into the sunset. But would he do so to bring down his old boss, whom he didn't like, possibly for several different reasons, if he had a good idea he was corrupt? Yes. It doesn't really gel from Wallingford's point of view. For one thing, he's so senior it isn't his job to involve himself with what must be regarded as pretty unimportant low life, yet he's been knocking round with undesirables in Glastonbury, Bristol and, as he admitted himself, in London. Why? He has every facility at his fingertips not to have to investigate this personally. The reason he might not act officially is that his case – if it can be described as such – against Brinkley won't hold water and that's why he's relying on old chums who may well have been fed a pack of lies.'

'And Brinkley's gone to ground.'

'Ingrid, we must find him.'

'To hand him over?'

'Not necessarily.'

'Did you ever meet the director of the NCA?'

'Yes, but not the present one. And in case you're thinking that's what we ought to do next, I agree up to a point but I'd rather get hold of Greenway first.'

'Then let's get hold of him.'

Patrick's mobile rang and, hearing just one side of the conversation, it became obvious that it was Kat, the teenager

we had spoken to in Glastonbury, and that she was worried.
Patrick listened gravely for a couple of minutes and then
said, 'If you go home are there relatives or friends you could
stay with while your parents are away?' The answer must
have been in the negative for he then said, 'Not even some
distance away?'

A muttered answer and then the sound of her crying
came over the phone.

'Please stay right where you are,' Patrick then said. There
was a pause and then, 'OK, right. Don't worry. Ingrid and I
will come and fetch you. We're in London anyway. Have
another coffee and we'll be there as soon as we can.'

'Where on earth is she?' I asked.

'Heathrow, Terminal Five. She was going skiing with her
parents but there was a huge row between the two at the
airport. Apparently this was supposed to be a make-or-break
holiday as her mother's been having an affair, ended it and
they've tried to patch things up by going on a family holiday.
But the woman had several G&Ts at the airport and that's
when it started. Kat got upset, they shouted at her to behave
and she stormed off saying she would go home, forgetting
that her dad had all her euros for safekeeping and she only
has a little cash in sterling, not enough even for something to
eat right now. God, are her parents bloody irresponsible or
what?'

'Is there a relative she can go to?'

'Yes, a grandmother, but she lives in Devon. She also said
that something's happened that might help with our enquiries
but whether it was in the hope it would act as a carrot for us
to get her out of her predicament I don't know . . .'

A very subdued Kat was hunched in a corner in a Costa
coffee shop and had obviously been crying again. Patrick
went off to fetch us all a drink and a very late lunch. I sat
down opposite Kat.

'I'm sorry, I've caused you such a lot of trouble,' she
whispered.

'Not at all,' I told her. 'But we must let your parents know
that you're safe.'

'They don't care. I'm adopted, Mum can't have children. I don't think they've ever liked me. Dad even said that I'm not like anyone in the family.'

Tears again threatened.

'That might not be such a bad thing seeing what's happened today,' I observed gently. 'But shouldn't you be at college?'

'It's still a revision period. Sorry, I can't remember your name.'

'Just call me Ingrid.'

'Ingrid, I *can't* go home. Bev's brother, Ed, came round the other evening, told Dad he was a friend of mine and they let him in! I got rid of him really quickly and then got told off because he's so rough. They wouldn't believe me that he's not my boyfriend. Since then I've seen him hanging around when I go out. I'm getting really scared and I'm sure it's all because I went to that horrible party. And, what I promised to tell you . . .'

'Yes,' I prompted when she stopped speaking.

'That man you said you were looking for. I *might* have seen him.'

'Where?'

'I go to a gym on Wednesdays and as I was walking past a pub, the King Arthur's Arms, I saw Ann Shipton. I think it was her but only saw her face for a couple of moments, just the really wild hair colours. They were going in. She was with a man and as I went by I heard him say, "It wasn't a good idea to lie like that, was it?" And Ann, the woman, whoever – she looked a real mess actually – snapped back, "I just had to get the bloody police out of my hair." Sorry about the swearing but that's what she said. The man had a nice, educated sort of voice – hardly her sort.'

'Did you see his face?'

'No, not really – and he had a hat on.'

'What sort of hat?'

'The kind of thing sailors wear – don't know what they're called.'

'What else was he wearing?'

'Oh, just navy blue or black clothes – or even brown. I couldn't really tell the colour as it was dark and the street lights aren't very good there.'

Why the hell didn't one of her adoptive parents escort, or drive her, to the gym? I wondered.

Patrick returned with a loaded tray which turned out to be chicken salad and slices of fruitcake all round. I offered to go and fetch the drinks but he went off again, perhaps to give me a longer time to talk to Kat. I further learned from her that the man she had seen was tall rather than well-built so, unless Brinkley had lost weight – perfectly possible – it was unlikely that she had seen him. But, as Kat had stated, it had been after dark and the lighting was poor.

'I'll send you the money for this,' Kat said. 'I've got some at home.'

I shook my head. 'No, it's all right, you deserve the rest of your day to be a bit better than it has been so far. D'you think you could stay with your grandmother?'

'You're really kind, thank you. I could phone her. She's always saying she doesn't see us – Mum doesn't like her much 'cause she's Dad's mum, but I do.'

'Have your lunch first.'

It turned out that Grandma would be delighted to have Kat staying with her. She tried to phone her father but the phone appeared to be switched off and she was too angry with them to leave a message. Patrick promised that he would speak to him later to assure him that his daughter was quite safe but didn't add that the man would get a verbal roasting, something I was quite sure about. Then we drove Kat, plus her suitcase, to Budleigh Salterton in East Devon, getting home, having stopped for a break, at just before midnight.

'It could have been anyone the woman was with,' Patrick said gloomily the next morning. 'If it was even Ann Shipton in the first place. And why would Brinkley go back there – let alone into a pub with her?'

'Would you like some toast to go with that marmalade?' I asked, always amused by his love of the stuff.

Unusually, the joke fell flat and he said, 'I'm not of a mind to go haring off back to Glastonbury on the strength of what Kat told us. It might be more profitable to dig into the background of Luke Wallingford.'

'Could it have been him the Shipton woman was with?'

Still glum, Patrick shrugged.

'Did you ever see Brinkley wearing a Breton hat?'

'No, it probably wasn't his kind of thing.'

'Please rethink my last but one question.'

'I suppose it could make more sense,' he conceded after a few moments' thought.

His mobile, not normally on the kitchen table at seven in the morning, rang and he impatiently snatched it up. It was impossible to tell from the short conversation that followed who was calling, only that Patrick agreed to meet whoever it was.

'That was Dixon,' Patrick said.

'Charles Dixon, the MI5 man? What did he want?'

'To meet me. This morning. He's in Bath for what he said was a meeting at an MoD establishment in the city. To be honest I didn't think there were any left. The Empire Hotel was converted into flats years ago and Foxhill, Ensleigh and Warminster Road have all relocated to Abbey Wood in Bristol. I suggest you come as well – you've been involved right from the beginning.'

'So where are we meeting him?'

'At the Francis Hotel – where he usually stays.'

This was interesting as I have only met Dixon there once, with Patrick, when he had made no reference to his habits. But then again, he worked for a security service, didn't he?

As previously noted I'm very prone to flippancy and this proved to be the case this time. We met the rotund little man in the same lounge at the hotel and, stifling a giggle, I was prepared to swear that he was wearing the same suitable-for-work suit, even the same tie: a bit like a genie, just rub the magic lamp and he appears. He rose politely when he caught sight of us, perhaps because I was present, and we all shook hands.

After a little conventional conversation and coffee had been brought, Patrick said, 'What can we do for you?' I thought this was him getting off on the right foot. What exactly *was* his relationship with MI5? I felt I ought to know.

'I might be able to assist *you*,' Dixon replied in his whispery voice. 'But I'm hoping for a little help in return.'

Patrick and I smiled non-committally.

'I'm aware that you're looking for John Brinkley,' Dixon continued. 'I know this because he's had connections with us other than when he was D12's liaison officer. When you left your main employment with us some years ago and went to work for SOCA you became involved with a scheme whereby senior service officers could apply to join the police without starting right at the bottom. I'm assuming you did that for the very good reason that you were hoping to live and work nearer to your family.'

'That's correct,' Patrick said. 'It didn't last very long though – the scheme, I mean.'

'No. But it's where you again bumped into Brinkley, who had been put in charge of a Met branch with which you became involved. I understand there was a clash of personalities.'

'You could say that.'

'Well, possibly unknown to you, Brinkley handled some cases which we were working on as the criminals involved mixed with people we regarded as a risk to national security. I need to talk to him, urgently.'

I wondered if Patrick was now asking himself if the man had screwed up on those as well.

'That's why I'm concerned as to what's happened to him,' Dixon went on. 'Not only that, he has a lot of information about certain mobsters, London-based mobsters. In other words, the man's what could be described as hot property.'

'Not to mention his ex-boss gunning for him,' Patrick said.

'Did you find Wallingford's story convincing?'

What didn't this man know?

'No, I didn't.'

'Neither did I.' He added, with a wry smile, 'But he has a personal axe to grind – he hates the man.'

'And on the strength of that has been mixing with the very same suspects that he's accusing Brinkley of doing.'

'To obtain evidence?'

'That's what he says. I'm not convinced about that either. Tell me something, do you know how Mike Greenway fits into all this?'

'He doesn't. He's been told to stay out of it.'

'Mr Dixon, I'm getting nowhere with this. Perhaps I ought to put you in the frame with what we've discovered already.'

Which he did, succinctly and without referring to any notes, but it still took about five minutes.

'Typical layers of law-breaking with faceless criminals at the top,' Dixon commented a trifle sniffly. 'Not that it really affects MI5. Now, you've been asked to find Brinkley and I would like you to add us to that list of those interested. Only I'd like you to deliver him to *me*. I have an idea that might be more agreeable to you.'

'It depends what you're going to do with him,' I interposed.

'I think it's called debriefing,' Dixon said blandly.

'And then he'll sort of disappear and no one will miss him?'

He looked a bit put out. 'I sincerely hope not.'

'As you know, Patrick's last case before he resigned from the NCA concerned Julian Mannering, a one-time knighted banker and friend of North Korea. He ended up mysteriously being hanged and the verdict was suicide.'

'I can't comment on that,' said Dixon, predictably.

Er – well, he was right there when it happened.

There was a short silence and then Patrick said, 'I'll keep what you've said in mind, but I can't promise anything. If Wallingford's one-time chums get to him first, Lord only knows what'll happen.'

'You might need to deal with Wallingford first.'

'That's Complaints' responsibility.'

'They usually get involved *afterwards*.' That with an admonishing finger.

'You mentioned that you might be able to assist us.'

'Yes, for one thing, I think you'll find that Brinkley's in London.'

'I'd already guessed that.'

'Word has it – and I'm talking about informers' gossip here – that he has a couple of small jobs to keep his head above water. This is because on some pretext or other his wife transferred almost all the money in their joint bank account into one in her name.'

'If you have people working on this who can discover these kinds of details, why don't you get them to pick him up?'

'Getting a production order from a magistrate on the grounds that the bank account holder is wanted in connection with a criminal offence isn't the same as having people on the ground in the capital. I simply don't have the staff.' He didn't add, 'That's where you come in.'

'Is there anything else we ought to know?'

'Only that he's got hold of a firearm of some kind. So be careful.'

SEVEN

'For someone who was pretty lousy at his job, Brinkley seems to have an awful lot of baggage,' I grumbled. 'And Dixon's so damned devious.'

For this I got an enigmatic smile.

Nettled, I went on. 'Patrick, I really think you owe it to me to tell me exactly your present standing with MI5. From where I am it looks like you're errand boy, Man Friday and unpaid erk all rolled into one.'

Note 'nettled' rather than 'furious', and this because he was actually looking particularly scrumptious this morning, wearing black jeans with a black silk shirt and grey silk tie topped with a black waist-length leather jacket. A good follow-on from his panache in bed the night before.

Patrick solemnly put a scant spoonful of sugar in his coffee, stirred and then said, 'As you've probably guessed I'm paid a retaining fee. It's going into a savings account for the children. There's nothing underhand about it – all the details are in a file in a drawer in your desk where we keep our banking stuff – and I haven't mentioned it because I thought it could end at any time. In return for this I'm required to assist where necessary. Up until now this hasn't strayed much beyond being asked about cases that I – we – dealt with for D12. When Daws, the previous head of D12, retired to his castle to grow roses and write scathing letters to *The Times* about the state of the roads, he shredded a lot of paperwork so there are significant gaps in the info. What he did wasn't strictly permissible, but I'm not going to complain as some of it involved cases where *I'd* definitely bent the rules.'

I couldn't complain either as I leave the household money side of things to him and tend not to go into the said drawer unless it's to refer to my own bank account. And I wasn't surprised at what he had said about the late colonel, who had been the fourteenth Earl of Hartwood, as he had been a law unto himself.

'So Dixon regards me as a sort of memory bank with contacts,' Patrick went on.

'Contacts he couldn't even begin to dream of?' I said with a smile.

'Possibly, but in the case of Brinkley the answer's no. We were never on the kind of terms that means I know of people he associated with, or his friends, who I can now go and ask about him. That's why I'm floundering.'

'And the criminals he's associated with, the ones we know about like the Hiershal brothers, can't know where he is either.'

Patrick considered. 'Probably not. I think I'm desperate enough, now you mention them, to go to Barking and look out Zeti Hiershal.'

His phone bleeped a text. These are usually from one of the children.

'Katie?' I asked.

'No, it was Greenway. He says that if I drop in tonight I might learn something to my advantage.'

'Not black tie then?'

Patrick smiled. 'No, he suggested after ten.'

'That's a bit late. How about a small raid earlier to stir him up a bit?'

Sometimes, when in receipt of an idea or suggestion that is alluring but generally of a *verboten* nature, Patrick's eyes sort of glow. I've noticed it with James Carrick too so perhaps it's a man thing. A certain type of man though – the go-getters.

'His place must be bristling with security devices,' Patrick murmured.

'I wasn't necessarily suggesting anything too intrusive.'

'Ingrid, raids are intrusive.'

'I was thinking along the lines of the surprise of him finding us sitting at the dining-room table.'

'He's not living there on his own.'

'Erin? You think she might freak out and have a heart attack? Hardly, she used to be in the Met. Besides, she knows us. So does their teenage son, Benedict.'

'Why do you want to do this?'

Perceptive of him. 'Because he's being an utter coward. He was ordered to give you back the Glock and certain instructions and then washed his hands of it. I'm furious with him.'

'Also on orders, according to Dixon.'

'I really wish someone would explain to me what the hell this has to do with Dixon – whatever he says. He's turning into what my father would have called the Smell on the Landing. According to him Brinkley handled cases that also involved MI5 and that's the reason for his interest. That must apply to quite a few senior cops who worked, and still are working, at Scotland Yard as an awful lot of it's about terrorism these days.'

'Time will tell,' Patrick muttered.

The Greenways live in North Ascot, which meant more driving, and we know exactly where the house is as we take Matthew there when he stays with them as a companion for Benedict during the school holidays. I hadn't really been serious with regard to a 'raid', and was sure that we would arrive and politely ring the front doorbell despite the fact that on Patrick's suggestion we were wearing our dark-blue surveillance clothing, a kit bag of which is always kept in the car.

Er . . . no.

Being April, it was dark when we arrived at just after eight, a slight glimmer of light still in the west in an otherwise overcast sky. The property could well bristle with security systems but the large wooden gates were wide open, tasteful lights lining the drive illuminating flowering spring bulbs and the trees above. We drove towards the house, all sneaky plans presumably having just been abandoned. As we got closer we could see that vehicles were parked outside a double garage, the lights on in the porch at the front door illuminating Greenway's Audi, another more expensive saloon and a Range Rover Evoque, glittery enough to look brand new. We parked ours next to it and, the available space now being limited, I disembarked into a holly bush. Prickly.

'They already have visitors so two more won't hurt,' Patrick said under his breath.

The front door wasn't secured and there were no squeaks

or rattles when it was opened. The hall within was warm, bright and roomy, big enough for a Georgian side table and the almost life-sized figure of an Arabian horse made out of driftwood that Erin had bought in the West Country. The murmur of voices and the tell-tale muted clatter of cutlery on plates came from the dining room towards the rear. Someone, a woman, laughed loudly. She sounded as though she'd had several drinks.

The thick pile of the sky-blue carpet ensured that our feet made no sound as we approached. The door ahead of us was half open but concealed us from those within as the dining table was around to the right. Only visible was the Greenways' very elderly Golden Retriever, Rory, who was lying on the floor and now lumbered to his feet and plodded slowly towards us, tail wagging. He knows us and there were the obligatory pats.

Patrick pushed the door very gently and it swung back. We went in and there was dead silence for a few seconds before a woman uttered a muted shriek, her hands to her mouth.

'Lousy security,' Patrick remarked.

'Who the hell's this?' the man sitting opposite her demanded to know, glaring at us.

'Patrick and Ingrid, two of my employees,' the commander answered, recovering. 'I asked him to come along and run a dummy raid to see how safe Erin and I are.' He smiled brightly and slightly desperately at us and I could almost hear the cogs in his brain whirring. 'It's rubbish then?'

'You might have warned us, Mike,' scolded the woman who had shrieked.

'Rubbish,' Patrick agreed. 'But please don't let us spoil your meal.' He seated himself on a small sofa. I followed suit and there was a short silence.

There were four couples at the rectangular table, Greenway and his wife Erin seated at either end, the latter calm but looking a bit puzzled. Facing each other across the length of the table – those with their backs to us had turned to stare – were an elderly couple who I guessed might be neighbours, and to their left a younger pair. The remaining two were another man and woman, the one who had shrieked, her companion only of interest because he was bald, perhaps shaven-headed, and appeared to be quite tall – we would know that when he stood up – and whose face, which I recognized, had gone from really pale to red in as many moments as it would take me to write it down if this were one of my novels.

I was beginning to wish that it was.

Greenway appeared to gather his wits and said, 'Allow me to introduce you. Retired RN captain Paul Wells and his wife Noreen live next door. Jason and Francesca Le Blond are old friends and have a son at Benedict's school, and Kevin Freeman is a recently retired company director from Wemdale. He's here with his partner who's an author and writes under the name of Alice Woodlake. Someone to chat to, eh, Ingrid?' he finished by saying in jolly fashion.

Mike is never jolly.

Ms Woodlake, gaunt, wearing big beads and dangly earrings, a sort of getting-on-rather hippy, looked at me as though she would rather chat to a bad case of shingles. I'd never heard of her.

'Would you like to join us and have something to eat?' Erin asked, probably frantically trying to remember what she had in the way of edibles left in the kitchen. The last time we had seen her she had just been rescued from being shut in a hotel room by various 'suspects'. Greenway had released her and that was the beginning of a romance.

We told her thank you but we'd eaten.

Without moving my head much I knew that Patrick was regarding the bald and possibly tall man with interest that would probably soon turn into the kind of savage stare that has made strong men blench. Suddenly he can seem too damned dangerous to be in the same room with.

True enough, after a few moments had elapsed Freeman said to him, 'I resent the way you're looking at me.'

'Just trying to remember where I've seen you before,' Patrick said quietly. 'Yes, I know. It was in photos taken at a London hotel where you appeared to be big chums with a convicted criminal.'

If air could turn to glue . . .

'I think we're talking about mistaken identity here,' the man said coldly. 'And, by the way, are you quite sober?'

'Quite,' Patrick replied.

'You're lying. It has to be drink or drugs.'

'I'm stone cold sober. And as far as the other matter goes, there are photographs.'

Freeman turned to Greenway. 'You obviously knew about this intrusion.'

'No,' said the commander. 'I didn't.'

'But you've just told us that you asked him to check your security here.'

'Yes, but I didn't say when – and neither did he. There's no point in security checks being *arranged*, is there?'

'Sorry, Mike, but I really resent some erk bursting in on us like this and I hope that you intend to reprimand him accordingly.'

Greenway merely smiled at the impertinence.

All this was quite fascinating and it was obvious that Patrick would have to steer a very careful course. Why was this man here? And, dreadfully, was Greenway in some kind of scheme with him? But no, he couldn't be, or he wouldn't have sent the text asking us to come here tonight. The mention of Wemdale had rung a warning bell as James Carrick had been involved with police corruption in that town and almost died as a result of his investigations.

Noreen Wells cleared her throat and tentatively said, 'Well, Mike, perhaps if you and your employees go somewhere for a few minutes to enable a discussion about the security to take place it will save any further awkwardness.'

'That's a very good idea, thank you,' Greenway said, jumping to his feet. 'Erin, perhaps you'd serve the dessert.'

The three of us left the room and the commander led the way to his study. When we arrived he shut the door rather forcefully and said, 'Did you *really* have to do it like that?'

'It was Ingrid's idea,' Patrick told him with a big grin and a wink in my direction.

'Sit down,' the commander said wearily after a little silence. 'Look—'

Patrick interrupted him: 'You know that man. I sent you the photos as I'm aware you still keep in contact with HQ even when you're on leave. I resent that you said not a word and really do need to be told if you were part of that scam at the London hotel when Ingrid was assaulted by Denny Whitman.'

The commander looked shocked. 'I can assure you that I wasn't.'

'How did the fact that we were going to be there get out then?'

'Well, as you said yourself at the time, Patrick, it really was priceless that you were made Colleague of the Month at your new insurance job after crossing swords with a guy who happened to have escaped from a prison van. I admit to sharing that around among a few workmates – who wouldn't?'

'Would that have included one-time workmates in the Met?'

'Yes. Are you positive it was him?'

'I am. He has what appears to be a birthmark on his left temple near the hairline and Ms Blakeney had an extremely good camera.'

The commander appeared to come to a decision. 'OK, it was why I got you along, the fact that Freeman would be here tonight. The business of that woman taking photos was a real bonus.' He took a deep breath. 'This project has been my idea alone but I do have the backing of the director. My interest hinges on the unproven information that at one time Freeman and Wallingford served in the same CID team together in Dalesland Police, the force that covers Wemdale. Wallingford definitely did. You'd be quite correct if you now pointed out to me that Dalesland has bugger all to do with the Met, Brinkley and the low life he's been accused of associating with.'

'Quite, but I'm all agog,' Patrick said sarcastically.

Unperturbed, Greenway continued, 'Brinkley was some kind of Met liaison officer with MI5, wasn't he?'

'Yes, but only for D12, where Ingrid and I worked.'

'Right, and when the department folded he went back to the Met and was given a small outfit of his own, possibly to neatly tidy him away until he retired. But before that and in the course of his job with your lot he'd run into Charles Dixon, the MI5 man you've also come across.'

'Who has just asked me to hand Brinkley over to him.'

'Which is understandable, because basically he's on

Brinkley's side and the last thing he wants is for Wallingford to get his hands on him as he doesn't trust him.'

'Please explain how you know where Dixon stands on this.'

'I do have contacts as well, you know,' Greenway answered, perhaps a little offended.

'So you do. I don't trust Wallingford either.'

'Rightly as it happens. Wallingford – and there's some doubt now as to whether it's his real name – appears to have fingers in quite a few small criminal empires in what I'll call out-of-the-way places in the West Country and the north-east of England, including Wemdale. I said "appears" because although there's some evidence against him it's not a lot and mostly from snouts and other informers. The info that does exist comes from Freeman's side of things as he still has family and friends connections up there.' The commander paused for a few moments and then went on. 'You'll be wondering where the evidence comes from with regard to Freeman being suspected of involvement. Some of it was literally on someone's dying breath.'

'Another informer?' I asked.

'No, his brother-in-law, Craig Hamilton, who incidentally wasn't on the illegal side of anything. He was actually a solicitor in Wemdale and did some digging, no doubt angry that his sister had married a man who incidentally he detested and suspected of being a crook. He was diagnosed with lung cancer but before he died told a trusted friend where the information that he'd accrued could be found. This was in his garden shed in a fireproof metal chest of drawers and just consists of a paper file. The friend, who knows nothing about it, was instructed – begged really – to take it personally to the National Crime Agency HQ in London and that's how it ended up on my desk. It's pretty explosive stuff and one of the main points made is that he knew – and this was garnered from what he actually overheard Freeman saying to someone in a phone conversation at his own house – that Wallingford and Freeman had decided to set themselves up in business. They'd collected a wealth of evidence against various individuals, criminals, and the plan was to make money out of them through blackmail and extortion. It was the kind of evidence that might not stand up in a court of law but they themselves thought it might have a lot of truth in it. They planned to head to the south-east, quite a long way from where their dealings were taking place, control it from afar and outwardly appear to be perfectly respectable people. But there's a large hole in this, the iffy bit – there's no trace of anyone called Freeman serving in Dalesland Police.'

'A very large hole,' I said. 'But he could have changed his name.'

'Yes. And by the way, Ingrid, Erin tells me that the so-called – and, I have to admit, fairly insufferable author – in there, who isn't Craig Hamilton's sister as she divorced him, is reputed to write rhymes for greetings cards.'

I'm afraid I sniggered. Even in grim times there has to be a couple of these or one would go right off one's noddle.

Patrick leaned forward and spoke quietly. 'Mike, why didn't you tell me all this before?'

'Because I wasn't sure how I stood with you as you'd left the NCA and thought you'd probably washed your hands of us, especially after my stupid behaviour at that nightclub – although I realize it happened a while back. I really regret it now.'

'All is forgiven,' Patrick said with a grin. 'Even big cheeses make mistakes.'

'Thank you. As far as this affair goes, the director said I was mad if I believed things found in garden sheds – that info only surfaced a few days ago – that incriminated a well-regarded serving commander when all she really wanted to know was the whereabouts of Brinkley. Sorry, I should have got in touch when it turned up but still thought you'd tell me where to get off.'

'Wallingford has some one-time cronies looking for Brinkley too, who I understand from Dixon has got himself a gun.'

'That *is* worrying,' Greenway said slowly. 'It makes it all the more imperative that we find him.'

'Why is Freeman here tonight?' I asked.

'He lives not far away and he and Alice Woodlake are involving themselves with local good works, no doubt to bolster his image. He and I are on the parish council. I need to find out more about the man, and if possible his continuing association with Wallingford. But the priority is still to find Brinkley.'

How did he propose to do that without asking the man outright? I wondered. Not that Freeman would tell him. I still wasn't convinced that everything was out in the open and said, 'You seemed quite nervous when you came to see us about Brinkley's disappearance.'

'Was I?' Greenway responded blandly.

'Any threats?'

'Cops, the NCA, the Met, small-town nicks, whatever, often get anonymous threats.'

Patrick uttered a long-suffering sigh.

'Threats that might come from a workmate who happens to be an old chum of Wallingford's or has access to a grapevine that he, Wallingford, also keeps an eye on?' I persevered. 'Someone to whom you might have mentioned our trip to London?'

The commander got up from his chair and went for a little walk to the other side of the room. Then he turned and said, 'OK, that *is* possible, but God knows who. I found a note on my desk, handwritten in caps, the gist of which was to leave everything alone or life might get awkward for me and my family.'

'When was this?' Patrick asked.

'The day after the director gave me her blessing to look into Brinkley's disappearance as certain people were muttering about it. I reported the note to her and that was when she told me to get you involved and give you back the Glock. Obviously, receiving the stuff found in the shed happened afterwards – but she's still dubious about that.'

'And despite the note you found, there didn't appear to be any kind of security in operation here tonight. The place was wide open with the front door unlocked.'

'Yeah, I got a bit involved with asking people what they'd like to drink.'

And worried, overworked and with the director breathing down his neck? Was that the reason he had taken leave? I wondered.

There was silence for a few moments, loaded with censure on the one hand and slight sheepishness on the other which Patrick broke by saying, 'What do you want me to do about Freeman?'

Greenway thought about it and then said, 'Well, he turned up at your hotel, didn't he? Someone took photos of him there. I can't tell him that you made a mistake when he was there as large as life. I'll make no comment about it but if he says anything I'll make light of it and tell him that, checking our security apart, what you do is your business and it's your problem and not his if he just happened to be around when something unpleasant was going on. I'll let him know that I reckon you're bloody bad-mannered for gatecrashing like this and bawled you out. Who knows – it might make something happen.'

'Get yourself some official protection,' Patrick said grimly.

After urging us to treat the search with the utmost urgency, the commander showed us out.

'I take back everything I said about Greenway,' I admitted when we had returned to the car. 'That note he received really rattled him – more than he's admitting. He's probably already regretting asking us to the house tonight. I'm also wondering how he was going to explain away our presence if we'd turned up at the time he wanted us to.'

'Good point. And Freeman might have had no idea what the people targeted at the hotel *looked like* if he was on a mission from Wallingford and would have had to get Whitman to ask the hotel to point out the insurance company people. Thought about from that angle, I screwed up by confronting him.'

'But if Greenway had been a bit more forthcoming in the first place . . .' I left the rest unsaid.

'Yes, but I intend to make full use of the opportunity he's given me.'

'I still don't understand why our room booking was cancelled.'

'Confusion and ineptitude on the part of various villains?'

He drove a short distance along the road and then pulled

up and reversed into a rough track that led into a patch of woodland. Very rough, judging by the way the vehicle bounced along over fallen branches and heaven alone knew what else. Then, still just in sight of the Greenways' entrance gates, he stopped and killed the lights.

'Glad we bought a dark-blue car,' he murmured.

'Freeman's not going to forget that he was spotted at the hotel,' I pointed out. 'When he goes home he might lie low for a while.'

'On the other hand, Greenway might do a good job of convincing him that I really am the erk who checks security systems and changes the light bulbs. Which car was his, d'you reckon?'

'Well, I expect the neighbours walked and the car that isn't the Audi probably belongs to the pair whose son's at Benedict's school. So the Evoque?'

'My thought exactly. We'll follow that one then.'

We sat there for just over half an hour and then Patrick's mobile rang. It was Greenway, speaking in a very quiet voice, to tell us, if we were still in the vicinity, that Freeman and Alice Woodlake were just leaving, the former very cool in his manner. Their car was the Evoque, he confirmed. Patrick thanked him, not mentioning that we were less than a hundred yards down the road.

I had opened my side window for fresh air and as it was a windless night heard the vehicle's doors slam and the engine start up. There was the sound of spurting gravel as the wheels slipped.

'Whoever's driving is angry,' I said.

'Good,' Patrick murmured with a chuckle. 'Angry people do stupid things.'

Which manifested itself in the brakes being slammed on at the entrance when the presence of an approaching vehicle was only noticed at the last moment. It then drove away at, well, stupid speed. We pulled out and followed at a sensible distance. No one has to tell Patrick anything about surveillance tactics.

'I'm sure he's at the wheel,' he said suddenly. 'And well over the limit judging by the way he took that last bend. Shall I report him, just to liven things up a little?'

'Only if he does something that endangers someone else,' I advised.

We drove for a few more miles in the direction of Bagshot and then turned on to a minor road to Camberley. A short distance farther on we entered the village of Blackbrook. Our quarry didn't slow down at the thirty-mile-an-hour speed limit sign and at one point the nearside wheels ran over a neat grass verge planted with narcissi outside a cottage making quite deep ruts. Then, a short distance further on, the Evoque swung into a drive on the opposite side of the road. We went past for a short distance, parked in the comparative gloom between two streetlights and sat in silence for a few moments.

'A little snooping?' Patrick queried, but he wasn't speaking to me, just thinking aloud, so I didn't respond.

'If Brinkley really is investigating Wallingford and Freeman I wonder how far he got before they realized he was on to them,' I said. 'I'm guessing that sundry yobs working for the Hiershal brothers in Glastonbury and London are responsible for the placing of headless rats in various places and possibly other intimidation that we don't yet know about.'

'Yes, a little snooping,' Patrick decided. 'Please sit in the driver's seat and be prepared to drive off and leave me if circumstances get a bit hairy.'

'Be really careful,' I urged.

'I'm not too sure that Brinkley's wife isn't involved as well,' Patrick said, opening the driver's door. 'Bit of a toad, wasn't she?'

'That's slandering toads,' I told him.

'It's important to get Carrick involved too,' Patrick continued. 'He's the one with the first-class honours degree in Wemdale. *Don't* follow me, all right?'

'All right,' I acknowledged.

I wasn't anticipating that he'd do anything really risky so I was quite content to stay put. Nevertheless, the next half hour went by very, very slowly. There was a little light traffic and, once, a man on foot came out of the drive nearest to me and stared in hostile fashion for a few seconds before turning and going back. Some people really do think they own the public highway outside their homes.

Did I ever envisage when I fell in love with Patrick at the age of fifteen that I would be doing things like this? No, perhaps not, but instinct had told me that life wouldn't be boring. My mother had been appalled. 'He's turned your head with his good looks and is downright dangerous!' she had shouted at me. 'You only have to look at him to know that. A pound to a penny he'll end up behind bars.' My father, more intelligent, more level-headed and not prone to raising his voice, had also raised concerns. 'Charismatic, likely to be promoted to major soon and the son of a churchman?' he had mused. 'It's a heady mix, Ingrid. You'll have to be strong and tame him.' I'm not too sure that I've 'tamed' Patrick, but he's certainly mellowed over the years, very much so.

My mellowed man reappeared a few minutes later smelling of crushed leaves, earth and – horrors – foxes and I resolved to file everything he had been wearing in the garden until it could be washed.

'They had a blazing row as soon as they got in – carried on with it probably – and I could hear every word from just outside their living-room window,' he reported with relish, combing bits of vegetation from his hair with his fingers. 'Shall I drive?'

I had driven most of the way to Berkshire so was glad to take up the offer.

Settled behind the wheel, Patrick continued, 'It's not exactly evidence but Woodlake raged at him about his boorish behaviour, drinking too much and being downright rude to people she wasn't sure were Greenway's employees. In fact, she was damned if they were. He took her up on that, demanded to know what she meant and she said OK if they *were* employees, did he realize that meant they were cops? Behaving in insulting fashion towards them, she yelled on, hadn't exactly improved their image with the Greenways and their friends and might even make them suspicious. As I'd already thought, she'd had a drop too much to drink too, was slurring her words a bit, but I think it gave her inspiration. I've left out all the swearing as I know you're a lady at heart.'

I stuck my tongue out at him and said, 'Anything else of note?'

'Only that she finally slammed out of the room saying that he was on his own from now on. That could mean anything and there's no way of knowing whether she lives there or not. I waited around for a bit but she didn't leave the house and drive off in the small Fiat that was parked outside. It all went very quiet so I came away.'

We set off and, like the night before, we got home at around midnight.

The following day would be taken up with the family but Patrick had to cut the grass in the churchyard this afternoon as there was a flower festival over the weekend in aid of a local hospice. He had taken over the responsibility of it after the death of his father but hasn't been able to find anyone who cuts it to his satisfaction. Matthew was recruited to go with him to snip off any untidy bits of the hedges that might catch on people's clothing. All morning ladies had been arriving at the church with fragrant carloads and I had a couple knock at the door sent over by Elspeth for foliage as this is always on offer in what I still regard as her garden. The cold weather of late had knocked things back so all that was available was a limited amount of osmanthus and small branches from a wildly overgrown bay tree.

This 'normality' was all very well but I was haunted by the knowledge that John Brinkley was quite likely to be in a difficult position, if not actual danger, and we seemed to be doing nothing to help him.

'Couldn't find the blue woolly-pully I had on last night,' Patrick said, putting his head round the kitchen door.

I pointed to the washing machine and disclosed that, together with everything else he'd been wearing, it had stunk like a skunk.

'Can you machine wash it though?'

'No, I just wanted to see what it looked like several sizes smaller,' I retorted.

He laughed, went away and then came back. 'I'm thinking of dropping in on Carrick this afternoon. Coming?'

As so often happens when you call on people without prior warning, we were told the DCI was out on a job. We asked the young constable manning the reception desk where he was and the information was only forthcoming when Patrick had shown his warrant card. That should have been produced in the first place, 'sir' was told. We left, my partner muttering something about 'uppity little sod'.

Carrick wasn't far away, casting his gaze over the aftermath of a stolen van having been driven through the front of a Chinese restaurant in the London Road during the previous night. No one had been on the premises at the time and, according to a uniformed constable who had asked us for our identities, the crime had all the makings of a Triad feud. An added complication was the dead body in the driving seat of the vehicle, the man having apparently been killed by a thin metal pipe of some kind that had been part of the shopfront, a broken end of which had come through the windscreen. No, not 'apparently': the corpse was still in situ and the pipe had impaled him in the neck to the extent of skewering him to the head rest behind. One quick glance was more than enough for me.

'I've heard of being hoist by your own petard, but this takes it to a new level,' Patrick murmured, taking a closer look.

Carrick, standing a short distance away, looked round on hearing his voice. 'Have you turned up thinking it might be Brinkley?' he called.

'No, and this man wasn't Chinese either,' Patrick replied.

'I *had* noticed that.'

'Can we make an appointment to talk to you about Wemdale?'

Carrick paused and then said, 'Seven thirty at the Ring o' Bells tonight?'

'You're on. Bring the boss.'

'I can't, she's on duty. You do realize that I shall require paying in the shape of a couple of tots.'

'Isn't that police corruption?'

EIGHT

There was no snow on our journey across the village green this time, just torrential rain. Not only that, one of the two streetlights in the lane on the north side of the green had failed. We had brought a torch, which suddenly went out.

'Our guardian angel appears to be stoned in the pub tonight,' Patrick muttered.

I said nothing, partly because my teeth were chattering with cold. I was wearing a waterproof but had quite thin clothes on underneath, mainly because I was sick of wearing winter woollies. When would it ever warm up?

It seemed as though the entire village was in the pub, open fires blazing, windows steamed up, the public bar deafening with chatter and almost impassable due to dogs underfoot. Unable to spot Carrick in the crush, we headed towards the other bar, which is mostly a restaurant these days, and spotted James in a small space between a fruit machine and the door to the kitchen. We joined him and were immediately in the way.

'Have you eaten?' Patrick asked him.

'No, I thought I'd chuck something in the microwave later on.'

Patrick went off and quickly returned. 'There's a small table in a corner free but we'll have to grab it now.'

'How's the Chinese Triad case going?' I asked when we had seated ourselves somewhat snugly.

'The van was stolen but the rest of it wasn't a crime.'

'How's that?'

'The bloke behind the wheel is suspected of either having had a heart attack or losing control of the vehicle and swerving to avoid some idiotic youth on a bike who'd been riding on the pavement on the opposite side of the road and suddenly veered across it right in front of him. Two good witness statements. Obviously, the PM will tell the full story – not that it will do him much good.'

Drinks were bought and, because Patrick and I had just had a snack with the younger children at their mealtime, the older two eating with their grandmother, we ordered a sharing platter we could mostly eat with our fingers, there not being sufficient room for three dinner plates on the table.

'Wemdale?' Carrick said thoughtfully. 'Why that hell-hole?'

'Dalesland Police are back in the news,' Patrick told him. 'Look, we don't want to resurrect bad memories and we'll understand if you don't want to talk about it. You could have died.'

Working on a murder case a few years ago that involved Dalesland Police's DCI Derek Rogers, who had had connections with criminals, Carrick had found his 'suspects' but had been outnumbered and imprisoned inside an old boiler in a derelict factory. The only clue as to his predicament had been a phone call he'd made, interrupted, to our home saying that he was in trouble, under siege in Wemdale. I had taken the call, Patrick being in Scotland and, after I had contacted him, he had immediately driven to the north-east to try to find him. Working on the theory that the DCI wouldn't have gone down without a fight, Patrick had gone into the most disreputable pub he could find and watched for the arrival of what my father would have referred to as 'gallows fodder' who looked as though they had come off worst in a fracas. Sure enough, this inspired thinking paid off: three individuals had turned up who had fitted the description perfectly and he had taken a risk and put some money on their table. After being led to where Carrick was, he had then been forced to further impede their recovery when they decided they wanted his Rolex watch as well.

'It wasn't all bad,' Carrick said quietly. 'When you forced open the door of that boiler it was the best moment of my life.' He smiled, a little emotional. '*Then* you took the three of them apart using the filthiest fighting tactics I've ever witnessed in my life.'

'And removed my money from their pockets when I saw

the state you were in,' Patrick said reflectively. 'What's the British equivalent of trailer trash?'

'Ingrid's here so I won't say it.'

'Can you give us the background to the case?' I asked. Like Patrick, who must know all there was to know about it, I had only been involved right at the end.

Carrick finished his whisky and Patrick rose to fetch him another, but the DCI said he'd have one later when he got home as he was driving.

'It all started with the body of a film producer being found on the River Avon weir in Bath,' he began. 'Martin Gilcrist had latterly specialized in controversial subjects and had produced a film about police corruption. It was a very compli-cated story and I won't bore you with all the details but it revolved around a retired DS by the name of Alan Terrington and his boss DCI Derek Rogers, who was still in the job. Rogers was all cosy with a career criminal known as Smiler, aka Frank Norris. He gave Norris the times of drug raids planned to hit him personally, and also the identities of other drug dealers so Norris could make them disappear. He didn't seem to have had much in return – that is, nothing that could be traced in the way of money – but Complaints discovered that Norris had given him the nod about the whereabouts of wanted persons. And, in a nutshell, Terrington murdered Gilcrist, perhaps on Roger's behest, although nothing could be proved and Terrington died before he could be brought to trial. Rogers was chucked out of the police, as again, no concrete evidence, only the word of either snouts or already implicated police personnel. He's probably on a yacht some-where in the Med. I never thought he was quite right in the head, frankly.'

Patrick said, 'On Greenway's instigation we've come across a recently retired company director from Wemdale by the name of Kevin Freeman. There's no info on what the company was. Freeman, and there is good photographic evidence, was the man at the hotel in London who we *think* paid Denny Whitman to mess up our weekend. It was definitely him at the hotel.'

'What's his angle though?'

'Pass. Another thing that's emerged is that AC Luke

Wallingford was also from Wemdale although not at that rank in the police then, obviously. Freeman and Wallingford are reputed to be best pals, connection not known unless they're both Masons. Freeman's brother-in-law, a solicitor, gathered quite a lot of evidence against him before he died, which is in the shape of a paper file. Greenway now has it. This *might* be the evidence that Brinkley was trying to get hold of, as well as digging into Freeman's and Wallingford's alleged involvement in small-time crime in off-the-beaten-track parts of the UK – the West Country and the north-east, including Wemdale.'

'But what on earth was the point of the assault on Ingrid and messing up your weekend in London?'

'I'm not sure,' Patrick replied.

I said, 'It might have been to try to make Patrick lose his temper and do Whitman real harm – so he could have been arrested and seriously discredited.'

'The name Kevin Freeman doesn't mean anything to me,' Carrick said. 'And, as you know, I'd never heard of Wallingford either.'

Patrick was relating what had happened during and after our 'raid' on the Greenways when our food arrived, a huge plateful of sticky ribs, chips and all that went with them. Not much else was said while we demolished it. OK, the bones, a bit of limp parsley and a burnt chip were all that remained when we'd finished.

'What now?' Carrick asked, wiping his fingers on his napkin. 'You say that the man from MI5, Dixon, told you that Brinkley's in London. He's had plenty of time to go somewhere else.'

'Perhaps he keeps watch on Wallingford,' I said. An idea presented itself. 'Suppose . . .'

'What?'

To James, I said, 'How old was Rogers when you were involved with this case?'

'Mid-forties, I suppose.'

'What did he look like?'

'Tall, slightly overweight, jowls, moved like a bulldog.'

'Hair?'

'Grey, well cut.'

Thinking aloud, I continued, 'Greenway said there's doubt that Wallingford is the AC's real name. He's tallish too, but slim and quite athletic-looking.'

'Not him then.'

'What about Freeman?'

'You think he might have changed his name from Rogers?'

'But if he'd changed his appearance a bit as well, had his head shaved, assumed a butter-wouldn't-melt-in-his-mouth manner, got himself a respectable job having faked a few qualifications . . .'

'To what end though?'

'Money, social standing, a sort of up-yours to his former employers.'

'Freeman has what looks like a birthmark on his left temple,' Patrick reminded me. 'Did Rogers?' he asked Carrick.

'I can't remember,' the DCI replied. 'It could have been hidden by his hair.'

'It wasn't very obvious though,' I countered.

Carrick pondered. 'Your only possible lead then is that the two blokes were in Wemdale at the same time and there's unsupported evidence against them. That's flimsy.'

'Working fairly closely in Wemdale,' Patrick added.

'And Brinkley might be trying to make the connection between his old boss Wallingford, and dodgy doings in that force and other areas. Folks, all I can suggest is that you go and find Brinkley and ask him instead of farting about trying to discover what he's up to.'

Patrick chuckled. 'Old son, we were hoping that one might lead to the other.'

I said, 'As James has just pointed out, Brinkley's had plenty of time to go somewhere else. If he follows Wallingford he could even be in Wemdale.'

'Or even dead,' Patrick observed soberly.

'Is he an official missing person?' Carrick asked.

'Not that we know of,' Patrick answered. 'His wife hadn't done anything about it when we spoke to her. She despises him and doesn't want him found.'

'You know, I feel really sorry for this man. Everyone hates him. Does he deserve it?'

'No,' Patrick and I said together.

We desperately needed a breakthrough.

It was not the breakthrough we wanted, but the next morning Patrick got a call from Commander Greenway to tell him that even though it was the weekend, he'd been contacted by AC Wallingford to complain about Patrick's 'grilling' of him. Greenway had replied that he himself was also under orders and would deploy his staff how and where he thought best. He had gone on to say that Wallingford had made serious allegations about a retired commander so it was natural that he would be questioned. Angered, Wallingford had then gone on to demand to know if that meant also harassing his friends, which of course Greenway had found interesting to say the least. How did Wallingford know unless Freeman had told him what had happened? The AC had ended the call – 'must have slammed down the phone', Greenway had said – after saying that he hoped future investigations would concentrate on the job in hand.

'And I hope he's rattled,' Patrick said. 'OK, James is right in a way. As I've said before, instead of investigating sundry low life that may or may not be controlled by Freeman and Wallingford, and who if we're honest won't tell us anything useful unless I put pressure on them in a fashion that'll get me arrested, let's concentrate on Brinkley. The nearest point of contact we have, in fact the only one, is his wife. Let's go and call on her again.'

We were too late. Someone had already called on Sarah Brinkley and cut her throat. As soon as I had seen the police vehicles and incident tape across the driveway entrance, I had a horrible feeling of despair. Having found somewhere to park further up the lane and Patrick had shown his warrant card we'd asked no further questions of the female constable on the gate. After convincing her with a combination of authority and charm that I was his assistant, we went up the drive.

'Oh, it's you,' said DCI Sue Manning. She appeared to be

taking the air outside the front door. 'If you want to go in you'll have to put on all the kit.'

'Are you all right?' I asked this very pale woman.

'I'll be all right in a minute – not very good with bloodbaths, that's all. Poor woman obviously didn't stand a chance.'

'Is Lazno Hiershal still in custody?' Patrick asked. 'He might be connected with all this.'

'Yes, thank God.'

'Who found the body?'

'Her cleaner, a young woman living locally who's saving up to return to the Czech Republic. Understandably, she's highly upset and we're looking after her while an interpreter's found as her English isn't good enough for her to be able to tell us what she wants to.'

'Have you been able to tentatively piece together what happened yet?'

'It's obviously early in the investigation, but easy to see that a window's been forced open in a utility room next to the kitchen. Although the kitchen itself is modern with double glazing, the utility still has an old-fashioned wooden sash window which, as you probably know, are reasonably simple to open from the outside if you know how. There's mud that must have come off his shoes – and I'm assuming until I know otherwise that the intruder was male – on the window ledge and on the top of the tumble dryer directly below it. The garden's a mess so nothing strange about that. There's mud in the hall and on the stair carpet as well. The attack took place in Mrs Brinkley's bedroom and I'm guessing that she was either asleep when it happened or heard a noise and got out of bed. Her body's on the floor between the bed and the door but there's a lot of blood on the bed and up one wall. As I've just said, she didn't stand a chance.'

'Do you think the killer exited the same way he came in?'

'He might not have done as there are the marks of blood-stained fingers on the inside of the front door.'

'Any other signs of disturbance, things obviously missing?'

The woman didn't seem to mind being questioned like this. 'It looks as though a search has been made, but whether that was her killer remains to be seen. We'll know once forensics have made a report.'

'Is there anything you'd like me to do?' Patrick asked her.

She appraised him. 'I'd really be most grateful if you'd give me your opinion of the crime scene. That's if you don't mind, of course. I take it you've had training in the correct procedures.'

Patrick nodded. 'Yes, and also played a major role in my own bloodbath.' After she'd directed him to where he could obtain protective clothing he went off, wending his way through various personnel and vehicles.

'Was he badly hurt then?' the DCI asked me in a whisper.

'He was blown up in a hand grenade accident during service with Special Forces,' I replied.

'A soldier then.'

I nodded.

'That's horribly ironic.' She took a deep breath. 'Violent murder isn't something that I've come across before here in Glastonbury. Other than having to cope with the usual anti-social behaviour, shoplifting and people like Lazno Hiershal – it's usually reasonably quiet. Not forgetting the festival and people looking for King Arthur and/or high on everything you can think of.'

'Ma'am?' someone called from the front door.

'Duty calls,' she murmured and went in.

I stayed outside. It was also horribly ironic that this woman had been killed just when spring seemed to have finally arrived, the sun warm on my face. It made me angry, but I didn't think anything could be gained by immersing myself in the bloodbath indoors and I would only be in the way. Always prone to be self-critical, neither could I accuse us of anything we could have done that might have averted this. It was nonetheless a huge shock. Surely no one looking for her husband had done this. I then went on to wonder if those searching for him on the behest of Luke Wallingford were retired police or – and this with a stab of alarm – people he had once arrested. Violent criminals? From Wemdale?

The investigation went on all around me and I moved so as not to be in the way here too. People came and went – a photographer, a woman who was perhaps a pathologist, another squad car. After around ten minutes Patrick reappeared and stripped off his protective clothing, putting it in a plastic sack that someone held out to him. He spotted me and came over.

'Bad,' he said, taking a deep breath. 'It looks as though she was knifed several times before her killer finished her off. It's possible it was an aggravated burglary. We might even be talking about a psychopath.' He took another deep breath. 'I've no mandate to go poking around here so I suggest we leave. I've spoken to the DCI and she said she'd keep me up to date with any findings.'

'You don't think Brinkley might have really lost it with her after she put his flat and this house on the market?'

'With a knife? The man's rumoured to have acquired a handgun of some kind. God knows though, Ingrid. Perhaps he's had some kind of mental breakdown.'

There was the chance that Brinkley had had nothing to do with her murder and didn't even know she was dead. With this in mind, and admittedly by now getting a bit desperate, we decided to stay in Glastonbury overnight and, quietly, go 'sightseeing'. We checked into a small hotel and then set off into the town.

This place is said to have a powerful atmosphere, not only because it is the cradle of Christianity in England and, before that, the site of pagan worship, but it is also reputed to be the burial site of King Arthur. Hence the remark by Sue Manning. I wasn't sure that I had detected any 'vibes' yet but the thought that religious activity had been going on here for thousands of years was sobering.

'There's a museum of pagan heritage here,' I said as we wandered down the High Street. 'That might have appealed to Lazno Hiershal.'

'I really don't think that yob has any bearing on this,' Patrick said, gazing down a gloomy alleyway as we went by. Always alert.

'I'm only trying to be helpful,' I murmured. 'There are plenty of tea shops too, as you obviously need refuelling.'

He stopped walking, stared into space, and said, 'You know,

the killer must have been covered in blood. Manning said there were bloody fingermarks on the inside of the front door. Then where did he go? No one said anything about traces of it in the drive although that evidence might have been obliterated when the cops arrived. Did he make his escape round the back or go across the field?'

'I caught sight of a couple of crime scene people heading down the side of the house towards the back garden.'

'And if he went across the field he would have had to get over the boundary fence. That wouldn't have been much of a problem. I wonder if they'll bring in a dog.'

Still trying to be helpful, I reminded him that there was what had looked like a small wood below the field.

He hooked an arm through mine. 'This is where I put on my best tracking hat.'

We hurried back to the hotel where the Range Rover had been left in their car park.

There was a five-barred gate that led into the field that we had passed on the way to the Brinkleys' house. Patrick parked the car on the verge opposite, got out and spent a couple of minutes examining the gate and the ground nearby without touching anything. I was superfluous so stayed where I was. Then he came back, drove a little further along until he found somewhere to turn and then took us back the way we had come, taking the next road on the left, actually a narrow lane. This cut through the woodland at the bottom of the field and the trees appeared to come to an end about fifty yards off to the right.

'I'll stay here,' I said as he prepared to go off again when we had parked a short distance up a little track on the left-hand side of the road.

Patrick flashed a smile at me. 'I'll give you a full report when I return, ma'am.'

Definitely a Watson to his Holmes, it was pointless for me to accompany him as I might inadvertently destroy evidence. I settled down for quite a long wait and gazed around me. You sit quite high up in Land Rovers of all kinds, which is a real bonus when driving in country lanes as you can usually see the approach of other vehicles over the hedges. Women feel safe in them too, although I have secreted a large spanner in a compartment in the dash to wallop any yob who tries to get aboard while I'm out in it on my own. It's also a good vehicle for spotting in the car park at crowded supermarkets, as long as you can remember roughly where you left it, that is.

The trees here, mostly mature beeches and sheltered on this south side of a small valley, were in almost full leaf, the hazy sunlight shining through them imbuing everything with a magical greenish hue. I could imagine this place in autumn having a golden glow, a little bit of heaven on earth. Perhaps Glastonbury's powerful atmosphere had reached me. I suppose I daydreamed for most of the time that Patrick was away: to switch on the radio seemed almost sacrilegious; the clamour of the modern world would drive away something here that was timeless, perhaps even sacred.

Eventually, I glimpsed the man in my life, and he was coming towards me from the last direction I would have expected him to – from across the other side of the road. He was looking grave. As he signalled to me that his hands were muddy, I opened the driver's door and gave him a wet wipe to clean them with.

'I've found the murder weapon,' he told me. 'Quite a large cook's knife of some kind. I've left it where it is and I'll stay here while you go and tell the DCI or whoever's been left in charge. It's easy to see where the killer got through a gap in the hedge from the field, blundered through the trees – there's even a smear of blood on one of the tree trunks – crossed this road and then carried on blundering until he – yes, a bloke, you can tell from the size of footprints – reached the place where he dropped the knife. It looks as though it was dropped rather than thrown. Then whoever it was seems to have collapsed nearby and slept or was unconscious for a while. That suggests a drug addict, someone stoned on something anyway. After he woke up, perhaps quite a long while afterwards when it was just getting light, he got to his feet and climbed over a gate that gives access to another field. That slopes into the valley and it's not far from the lower boundary of that to the edge of the town. We need a dog now.'

Sue Manning was still at the scene of the crime. 'He's

what?' she demanded to know. Then, when I had repeated the news, she said, 'Well, I hope to God he hasn't destroyed any of the evidence.'

'You're talking about someone who used to be an under-cover soldier,' I said, stung on Patrick's behalf. 'I suggest you go and talk to him yourself and he'll give you a full account of the killer's route after he'd gone down the field and entered the trees. I'll take you myself if you like as I'll have to pick him up anyway.'

'Oh,' she said. 'All right.' She promptly gave orders for some of her team to follow us.

'A dog might help,' I suggested.

Irritated – perhaps because the murder scene had really upset her and the NCA was ahead of the game and therefore being irritating – she issued more orders.

'You seem to know quite a lot about the man you work for,' she said when we were in the car.

'I don't work for him in the sense you mean. He's my husband.'

She said 'Oh' again and fell silent.

Not one to display glee in such circumstances unless he just happened to detest the particular police officer he was talking to, Patrick took Manning off to show her the evidence. He would be pointing out every footprint, each bruised bit of vegetation, broken twig and the place where the man had slept or collapsed. The knife was placed in an evidence bag, scenes of crime people arrived, incident tape was put in place, photographs were taken and, around twenty minutes later, a dog handler turned up with his canine assistant. From the spot where the weapon had been found the dog set off with enormous enthusiasm in the direction of the gate that led into the lower field.

At last, Patrick appeared. 'Lunch,' he said. 'I'm famished.'

'It's getting on for dinnertime,' I pointed out.

He glanced at his watch. 'So it is. A pub then.'

'Too early.'

He had to settle for tea and what my grandmother would have called a couple of 'stickies'.

It seemed pointless but during the evening and after a meal

in a Chinese restaurant we walked round the town, from Main Street into West End where we turned right into High Street. There, a couple of pubs, the Becket Inn and the George and Pilgrim were subjected to some interior surveillance, chosen mostly on the grounds, I teased Patrick, that they served real ale. I was endeavouring to create a lighthearted mood as it wasn't difficult to realize that the sheer ghastliness of the killing had had an effect on this battle-hardened one-time soldier as well. I also felt it important not to mention the day's events unless he did.

On his second pint of Butcombe, he said, 'I can understand a junkie off his head breaking into a house in the town to try to find money or something he could sell to get more drugs. But the Brinkleys' place is a ten-to-fifteen-minute walk away, say half a mile along a road with no pavements. Manning said no cars have been found abandoned nearby so it doesn't make sense. And whoever was in that wood was completely out of it, which suggests he'd had a fix, even an overdose, before or after the killing. Was he in a fit state to wield a knife?'

'People on drugs are monsters with the strength of monsters,' I said. 'There might even have been drugs *in* the house.'

Patrick pulled a face. 'I hadn't thought of that, but it has to be factored in. The woman was a bit squiffy when we went round to see her, wasn't she?'

'I did get the impression she'd been drinking rather than taking anything else though.'

'So did I.'

I went back to the hotel, Patrick saying that he'd wander back streets and alleyways for a while. I gathered later that he'd met a couple of PCSOs doing exactly the same thing in connection with the same case so he called it a day.

There seemed to be nothing we could achieve by staying in Glastonbury, so the next morning we packed up and prepared to leave after breakfast. This one-off job of Patrick's gave every indication of turning into an ignominious failure – not something with which he could easily cope. Over breakfast, which as far as his full English was concerned, was also disappointing, his mobile rang. There was no one else in the dining room so he stayed where he was to answer it. From hearing a one-sided conversation I guessed it was DCI Manning.

'Apparently the dog lost the scent but they've arrested someone,' Patrick said at the end of the call. 'A down-and-out whose clothing was covered in blood and can't remember who he is. He was found on a bridge over the River Brue by cyclists at around eight this morning and giving every impression of being about to chuck himself in. Apparently he's in a very confused state. He's been checked over by a doctor who said there doesn't seem to be anything physically wrong with him other than the effects of whatever it was he took. Blood tests have been done but we won't know the results of those for a bit.'

'One of the vulnerable and desperate people employed by the Hiershal empire?' I wondered.

'Looks like it, doesn't it?'

'She said we can go and cast our gaze over him if we want to.'

'I can't see what good it'll do. If he's in such a bad mental state he won't be able to tell anyone anything.'

'Which of course would be all part of their plan. But from the point of view that I've been hired to look into this and might be expected to write a report, I suppose I ought to. You don't have to come if you don't want to.'

But I did, thinking that we could call in at the police station on our way home.

The arrested man had been put in a cell while it was decided what to do with him and was slumped on the narrow bed with his back to the wall, arms hugging his knees. I guessed that after his clothing had been removed for forensic testing he had been given a shower before being dressed in what looked like old tracksuit bottoms and T-shirt as his dark hair was still damp. As he looked up at our entry I thought the doctor's conclusions hasty to say the least. Haggard, with at least a week's growth of beard, his eyes red, skin grey, this man looked ill.

Most definitely, it was John Brinkley.

NINE

'John,' Patrick said softly. 'What the hell have you been up to?'

There was a blaze of recognition in the brown eyes. 'Patrick?' he croaked. 'For God's sake . . . please . . . please, you've got to help me.'

He then started to shake violently and I turned to the constable who had accompanied us. 'Tea, hot, sweet and quickly please.'

'I shall have to lock the door. He's been violent,' the man said.

'Lock it then. We know him. And tell the DCI.'

Amazingly, Sue Manning arrived with the tea. 'Is this your man then?' she enquired. 'Brinkley, was it?'

Patrick told her it was, adding, 'I do have to question your doctor's findings. He's seriously malnourished and still under the influence of drugs of some kind judging by his enlarged pupils. He ought to be admitted to hospital to enable a few checks to be done.'

'No!' Brinkley shouted, jumping to his feet. 'They'll find me there!'

Gently, but in a manner not to be argued with, Patrick sat him down again. 'You're safe,' he assured him.

'Not if you let me out of your sight.'

Whether by this he meant Patrick personally or the police in general was hard to tell but nobody asked and he was given his tea. It was quite shocking to see the way he cradled the hot drink, gazing down into it as though needing the warmth and security of holding such a homely thing.

Patrick sat beside him on the bunk. 'Who's "they", John?'

'Dunno. Blokes with their faces covered. What did you say my name was?'

'John Brinkley. You'll remember more when whatever

someone gave you wears off. Please don't worry about it.' He smiled. 'I'm really chuffed that you remembered mine.'

'You told me I smelled like a knocking shop.'

'You did.'

The man actually chuckled. Then he said, 'My brain seems to be in a fog but I have an idea some cop wants to arrest me – but not here, nothing to do with you. Why are you here anyway?'

'I was asked to look for you. You went off and no one knew where you were.'

'Does it matter? Can't a man go where he likes when he's retired? Yes, that's right, I'm retired. I think I used to work in London.'

Patrick patted his arm. 'I need to talk to the DCI here. Rest.'

Brinkley looked up as Patrick rose and spotted me. 'Ingrid! How lovely to see you. Still writing?'

I nodded and smiled.

We left the cell and went to Manning's office.

'Feed him and he'll recover more quickly,' Patrick said when the door had been closed.

'This is getting a bit complicated,' Manning said, having opened the door again to accede to his suggestion and ask for the prisoner to be given a meal.

I thought this a serious understatement but I kept quiet. When I get involved in what I shall call an inter-cop situation away from home ground, I tend to keep a low profile.

We seated ourselves and the DCI went on, 'From what you've already told me I think I've built up an accurate picture. He's wanted in connection with an investigation into police corruption in the Met that was instigated by his previous boss, AC Luke Wallingford. Also, he's thought to be in danger on account of connections with gangland bosses and information he may or may not have about them. Is that anything to do with the reasons his one-time boss wants him arrested?'

'Quite likely,' Patrick replied. 'Brinkley's being accused of supplying useful information to those mobsters.'

'Is there any evidence?'

'Wallingford's created a paper file that we've seen – I've no idea if anything's been done digitally – that contains a photo of Brinkley with a couple of dodgy characters who operate in the West Country and London standing at a bar in a club or pub. Their names are Lazno Hiershal and his brother Zeti. There's more stuff in the file, details of payments into a bank account said to be Brinkley's and other uncorroborated info – not convincing either.'

The DCI shook her head, perhaps in puzzlement.

Patrick continued. 'Ann Shipton, the woman Brinkley went out with and might have lived with for a while and who is a previous girlfriend of Lazno's, told Ingrid and I that a man called Luke Wallingford was part of the Hiershals' group or words to that effect. I'm not sure why Brinkley would touch this woman with a barge pole if he wasn't actually checking up on Wallingford.'

'Also,' Sue Manning said, 'I understand MI5 wants this man found, presumably to ensure that, if and when it comes to court, nothing sensitive is made public as he worked on sensitive cases for them. I'm not at all sure how they could prevent that. Not only that, you've been brought out of what I'll refer to as retirement from the NCA – although frankly I don't think you're retired at all – to look for him. This situation, I have to say, is unprecedented. It's like something in a . . . a crime novel.'

I could relate to that and, intent on using at least some of this incredible story, was relying on my partner with the excellent memory to note down the nuts and bolts of it in case I'd forgotten anything.

'Mr Gillard,' Manning went on, 'what do you suggest I do if senior personnel from the Met roll up here and demand I hand him over to them?'

'Well, for one thing I don't suppose anyone on these premises has yet announced his arrest on the appropriate websites. And for another, he won't be here because you'll have already handed him over to me.' This with a little smile.

'No, sorry, that won't do. Brinkley appears to have murdered his wife. As well as the circumstantial evidence that exists already, we need to know whether he was actually under the influence of the drugs that he'd taken when it happened or had them administered to him afterwards.'

'Medically that might be very difficult or nigh-on impossible,' Patrick said. 'And going on from what I've said just now, if anyone from the Met does arrive you'll have to ask yourself how they know he's in custody. Another thing is that Wallingford makes it plain in the file that he has one-time colleagues looking for Brinkley, who mentioned, if you remember, that he was being pursued by men who had their faces covered. Mobsters? Wallingford's lot? If the latter I'm not sure that's legal.'

The DCI rearranged herself in her chair in irritable fashion. 'You're probably right but Avon and Somerset will still have to handle the case and I shall fight my corner on this.'

'Ma'am, I really admire your courage. Would you for one moment consider giving your suspect to a DCI in Bath?'

James will kill him, I thought.

She stared at him in amazement, but before she could respond, Patrick continued, 'I'm confident I can arrange to get this case brought under the aegis of the National Crime Agency. Commander Greenway, my boss when I was working full-time, was ordered by the director herself to get me involved. They even gave me back my Glock 17 for rather unconvincing reasons. Serious crime is involved in this and now we have the murder of Mrs Brinkley. By the way, I don't think he did it.'

'There's plenty of evidence,' Manning observed dryly.

'He could well have been present.'

'Whatever happens, I insist on him being interviewed this afternoon.'

'That's your privilege.'

'But I still can't see what taking him away from here achieves other than you yourself fulfilling at least two of your assignments.'

Doggedly Patrick went on. 'It would remove your suspect for his own safety from the area while investigations continue and throw anyone off the scent who wants to get hold of him for the wrong reasons.'

'He can be kept on remand. He would be quite safe there.'

'I have an idea that he wouldn't be accepted at a remand centre as, right now, he's too mentally disturbed. And in case you were worrying that your staff would have extra work having to liaise with Bath CID, that's my job.'

One had to applaud the logic but this lady was no pushover.

'I'd have to consult on this,' she hesitantly said after a short silence. 'And I'd want you to confirm that the NCA is prepared to take over the case.' She eyed Patrick sternly. 'Preferably in a phone call from your Commander Greenway. Not only that, I'd want to know that the DCI in Bath is completely happy with the arrangement.' She got to her feet. 'Sorry, but I'm overdue to give a briefing on another case. We can discuss this later when I've had a chance to think about it.'

When she had gone Patrick and I glanced at one another.

'I'll start with the most difficult one,' he said.

Yes, Carrick.

Fortunately, the Scotsman was in his office and in a reasonably happy mood – for him, that is. This was because people in his team had nabbed, virtually red-handed, a gang of youths who had broken into houses on an estate in the south of the city several times. They had been stealing what they could find to sell in order to buy drink. If pickings were too thin they had taken their revenge on the hapless residents by stealing cars and joy-riding in them before torching the vehicles on a recreation ground. Luckily, the night before, someone had spotted them and called the police.

I was sitting close to Patrick – with Manning's permission we had remained in her office – so I could hear both sides of the conversation.

'You've got him!' Carrick exclaimed after the subject had been broached. 'And you want to bring him *here*? What the hell for? You reckon my budget'll stand it?'

Patrick said, 'I think the NCA will take responsibility for it so it'll only be temporary. But he can't be kept in a police cell for much longer and in my opinion it's important to get him to a safe house in an area where he's under both our noses. OK, I know it's not your case, but I'm concerned that as soon as the news gets out Wallingford will demand that he's handed over.'

'I've just got it up on my screen. It's out – as of two hours ago.'

My husband swore under his breath.

'But yon AC won't be able to get him out of the NCA's hands, will he?'

OK, James didn't like ACs. This had been hinted at before and I wondered if it went back to his time in the Met when he had worked for the Vice Squad, as that department had then been called.

'Probably not,' Patrick agreed but sounding a little doubtful.

'I'll want confirmation that Greenway's up for it.'

'I'll get on to him right now.'

'And I'll have to trot it past the super at HQ.'

Patrick groaned.

I went to find us coffee while Patrick tried to contact the commander. When I returned I found that he had hit a snag: he couldn't get hold of him.

'Can you contact the director?' I asked. 'She's the instigator of getting you on board.'

'I tried that too. She's in Harrogate for a conference. Her secretary said she'd call her personal mobile and give her the news.' His own mobile was back on a corner of Manning's desk and as soon as he had finished speaking it rang. He grabbed it, looked surprised when the caller spoke and then became very grave.

'Where are they now?' he asked. Then, 'I'll be right there.'

Patrick jumped to his feet and headed for the door. Over his shoulder, he said, 'That was Manning. She's just been told that a security van's arrived with three men. They've produced a piece of paper that they've said is a warrant for Brinkley's arrest.' As we headed down the corridor at some speed, Patrick continued, 'A DI is talking to them but she's had a quick look at the bit of paper and thinks it's iffy. As it looks as though he might be my prisoner do I want to have a look at it? Too right I do!'

The trio and their van, a white one with no markings, were in a yard at the rear which otherwise had space for a few cars, those presumably of senior personnel. It was surrounded by a very old and historic-looking stone wall some ten feet in height with more razor wire than might be deemed necessary on the top of it. As we got there Manning arrived, emerging through another doorway. Not being very tall she was dwarfed by the three in their uniforms which were also adorned with more bits of intimidating kit than might be deemed necessary.

'Look, these are my orders!' one of the new arrivals literally shouted at her, waving a piece of paper in her face.

'That's as may be, and I've already seen it,' said Manning calmly, 'but I don't have to obey your orders. And I'd like to point out that I'm in charge here.'

The man's lip actually curled and he gave his companions a look that mirrored his contempt. 'This is from London, lady, important, not your Tesco shopping list.'

'May I see that?' Patrick said, moving to Manning's side. Her DI, who was young and red in the face with anger at the insults aimed at his boss, also moved closer to her. He appeared to be on the verge of doing something he might regret afterwards.

The paper was thrust at Patrick with a belligerent question: 'Who are you then?'

'National Crime Agency,' Patrick replied calmly, gazing at it. 'I want to see your IDs.'

'We're a private security agency. We don't have IDs.'

'Then you can't have him. Not only that, if you don't sod off by the time I've counted to ten, I shall arrest you.' And with that he tore the warrant to shreds and let them trickle through his hands to the ground.

The three advanced on Manning, who backed off a little.

'Or,' Patrick continued quietly, drawing his Glock, 'I might just blow your bloody heads off instead.'

They gawped at it, frozen. Then, as if the ice encasing them had dropped off, they ran, leapt into the van and roared away.

'We *should* have arrested them,' the DCI protested.

You should have arrested them, I thought. And if you were already suspicious you should have mustered a few more of your colleagues.

'They're hirelings,' Patrick said. 'And you'd have learned nothing useful. Are warrants normally delivered by civilians?'

'No,' she replied.

Patrick picked up the bits of paper. 'What's wrong with it? It looked all right to me.'

'That style of warrant went out of use at least five years ago and we were told to shred any we had left as it was a security risk to just put them in the bin. Who were they acting for, do you think?'

'You tell me, ma'am, but all my fingers are pointing at Wallingford.'

The DCI shrugged in a resigned manner. 'I handled that badly. I have to confess that they frightened me rather. Thank you for your back-up.'

'Lock the outside rear doors?'

'Yes, I'll get it done. I suggest we interview Brinkley as soon as it's practical. It might help if you're both present as observers.'

'I know what you're thinking,' Patrick said to me as we went back inside. 'That Manning was right – we should have arrested them. But I foresaw an ugly situation instantly developing when she might have been injured if they'd tried to rush in. Not only that, *if* that trio were indeed at one time members of Wallingford's team then now they've failed he might do something to give himself away.'

'He could have done all this in the correct manner and sent an official car for him,' I pointed out. 'He has the authority and the means.'

'Which rather points to his accusations against Brinkley being a load of crap after all, doesn't it?'

At two thirty that afternoon, John Brinkley was taken to an interview room. After a meal and a short sleep he definitely looked better, more his old self, but nevertheless still seemed confused. There had been a discussion as to whether he should be told that his wife was dead. DCI Manning thought not yet. I wasn't sure, but Patrick said he should be told on the grounds that we couldn't discount that he might be acting and had always in the past refused to take the blame for anything.

Unusually, the DCI had decided to conduct the interview

herself. This seemed sensible as there was the possibility that national security matters were involved. I had wondered, briefly, if Charles Dixon, the MI5 man, had had anything to do with the forestalled attempt to get hold of Brinkley, but dismissed the idea out of hand. Those ruffians hadn't been his handiwork.

Sue Manning completed the opening formalities. She had brought with her the young DI she'd had with her earlier whose name we had discovered was Mark. With her permission, I would take notes on behalf of the NCA.

'Mr Brinkley,' she began, 'please tell us what you can recollect from yesterday morning up until the time you were found on a bridge over the River Brue this morning.'

'I seem to remember that I got away from something dreadful,' he answered. 'And I would like to point out that I'm a victim of some kind of crime and not the perpetrator of it. But you're making me feel like a criminal.'

'Your clothing was covered in blood and because you're uninjured it obviously isn't yours. Can you explain that?'

The man shook his head. 'No.'

'Could it have been as a result of the something dreadful? Please try to remember.'

'They had masks over their faces. That was bad enough.'

'What kind of masks?'

'Those balaclava things. You know, like those things Special Ops cops wear.'

'Navy blue or black?'

'Navy blue.'

'Were they cops, d'you think?'

'Could've been, I suppose. But why? What were they doing in my house?'

'So you remember being in your house.'

'Yes, it's just come to me. But there was something wrong with it.'

'Such as?'

'It was all blurry and the walls sloped. Then they went off at right angles. Not sure why but it made me feel really nauseous.'

'That doesn't make much sense.'

'Could you have been lying on the floor?' Patrick asked softly.

'Trust you to hit the nail on the head,' Brinkley said with a big smile in his direction. 'Yes, that's exactly right. I must have been on the floor.'

'And before that?' Manning queried.

'Nothing, just blackness. Oh, yes, before we went to the house, quite a long time ago actually and I can't remember much of what happened in between, they'd made me tell them the security codes for my entrance gates and the car. They hit me.'

'And after you were on the floor?'

'Nothing. More blackness.'

She produced an evidence bag containing the knife Patrick had found in the wood. 'Have you seen this before?'

Brinkley visibly shuddered. 'Yes. I know now. You've reminded me. It was lying on the floor with me. Lots of blood on it.'

'A woman was murdered in your house.'

Sitting in one corner of the room and slightly to one side of him, I saw the shock hit home. And with the shock came returning memories. It was all there on his face. He remembered. I think we all stopped breathing. Then his face crumpled and he wept like a child.

Manning moved to stop the recording and pause the interview but stayed her hand when Brinkley waved to her as he struggled to restore his composure and then resumed speaking.

'They took me up there.' He gulped. 'To our bedroom. And there she was, dead. Murdered. Poor, poor woman. And what had she done to deserve that? She lied, but no one deserves to be killed for that.'

'Lied?' I echoed.

'Well, of course, Ingrid. She lied. Then they smeared blood on me, even wiped the blade of the knife on my clothing and forced me to hold it.'

'Hadn't you killed her then?' Manning asked innocently.

'No, of course not. Why would I? I didn't even know the woman.'

I think my hair stood on end.

'It was your wife,' the DCI said.

'Who, Sarah? How could it have been Sarah? Don't you think I know what my own wife looks like? She's in Italy. I arranged for her to go there for safety when all this wretched business started.'

'You care for her then.'

'Of course I do.'

'But it looks as though you lived with another woman, Ann Shipton, in Glastonbury for a while.'

'Yes, I feel really bad about that now. I'm praying that Sarah will forgive me. It was the only way I could get information on the Hiershal brothers.'

'So some other woman had been living in your house pretending to be your wife?' Clearly, the DCI didn't believe him.

Out of the corner of my eye I saw Patrick shake his head. She had abandoned a very useful train of questioning.

'I remember now,' Brinkley said. 'They told me she'd put the house on the market. And my apartment in London.'

'Why?' Patrick asked bluntly.

'To force me to stop investigating corruption at the Met – in particular the smart-arse I used to work for. To ruin me.'

'Name?'

'Luke Wallingford, the bastard.' Brinkley took a deep breath. 'May I have a hot drink? I feel quite weak. I have an idea I was shut up somewhere dark for a bit . . . you know . . . nothing to eat or drink . . . It was horrible . . .'

Manning did pause the interview then and Brinkley was taken back to the custody suite where, we were told, he immediately lay down, virtually collapsed, on to the bunk.

Back in Manning's office and after speaking to her, Patrick immediately contacted James Carrick. 'James, I can't get hold of anyone and there's already been one attempt to grab Brinkley. Initially, he needs to be in hospital under guard and we've learned enough from him to know that there's more going on than we realized. I desperately need you to send an ambulance to collect him. Sorry, but I don't have the authority to do that and the DCI here has just told me that she can't get hold of anyone to sanction it *either*.'

Not one necessarily to bother with permissions, Carrick did as he was asked, pulled strings in the shape of the local doctor who attended suspects and victims when necessary and the ambulance was soon on its way. I'm sure the others felt the same but it was a huge relief to me when Brinkley was put into the care of medics for the journey. He went quite calmly.

'We ride shotgun,' Patrick announced, having told the DCI that he would take full responsibility for removing her suspect and promised to closely liaise. 'And I've asked them to go like hell.' He added, with a grin in my direction, 'What have I got to lose except a couple of jobs?'

At the last minute, just as we were starting off, Manning provided us with a police escort. That went at the front, the ambulance in the middle, while we brought up the rear. She had called to us as we left to say that preliminary tests on the blood on the suspect's clothing had revealed it was the same group as the murder victim's and DNA results would follow. That was hardly a surprise.

With blue lights and sirens, we hit the A39. At the most, the journey would take half an hour unless there was a hold-up. The weather was good – dry, warm and sunny with a promise of it being hot later – and I was feeling happy that the job was over. There was a lot more to do, of course, but Patrick's part of it had ended. At least, that was what I was trying to tell myself but my cat's whiskers were off the scale.

We had been going for some fifteen minutes in light traffic, the speedometer registering a steady seventy, when I noticed Patrick frowning and frequently glancing in the rear mirror.

'There's a white van behind us and gaining,' he said. 'I'm not saying that it's the same one we've come across already today, but . . .'

The 'but' manifested itself very shortly afterwards when, on a straight section of highway, the van pulled out, forcing a car coming the other way to swerve, and overtook our little convoy. Around thirty yards ahead of the police car it suddenly slewed across the road and despite the police driver braking hard his vehicle slammed into the side of it. The ambulance also braked but couldn't avoid hitting the escort car. It had taken seconds, just seconds, and we were heading straight for the collision.

In the next instant I felt that my seat belt was slicing me in half, there was a bang and then the airbag exploded in my face, knocking me back into the seat. For a moment I was stupidly dazed – and simply didn't know where I was or what was happening. I think I shut my eyes. The Range Rover reversed at speed amid shots and shouting. Then the driver's door slammed. My first instinct was to get out of the car but I forgot my seat belt. I undid it. I noticed the deflated airbag at around the same time that a shot hit the vehicle, rocking it slightly. Patrick wasn't in the car, a fact that was also slow to sink in, so I flattened myself as best I could across the cubby box in the middle and the driver's seat. More shots cracked out and then there was an eerie silence.

A harsh voice shouted, 'Make a move and he gets it!'

I risked raising myself so I could see out of the driver's window. Outside, Patrick was standing with his back to me, a hooded man holding a gun to the head of the paramedic ambulance driver, one arm around the man's throat. Moving my head slightly and very slowly I saw that another two men wearing hoods had forced open the door of the ambulance, which was slightly damaged where we had hit it, and as I watched, one of them ran up the ramp and clubbed the female paramedic to one side. Then, John Brinkley was unstrapped from the stretcher and hauled out. Nothing seemed to have moved in the escort car.

By this time a few vehicles following us had stopped and a woman driving the first, a van, got out, perhaps thinking that it was an accident and with a view to offering assistance. She came to a halt, rigid with shock, when the masked man holding the ambulance driver turned on her and yelled, 'Forget it! We're 'aving that van and we don't need *you*! Sod off!'

'Bastard!' she shrieked and then unwisely moved to get back in the van but leapt out of the way when he fired a shot at her. Amazingly, considering she was standing so close to him, it missed and, terrified, she bolted all the way across the hard shoulder, jumped over the barrier and dived into the trees and shrubs on a bank at the side of the road. Therefore she wasn't a witness to the hooded man, fatally distracted, falling to the tarmac, the one who had fired at him immediately ducking behind our car saying to me, 'Get down. Stay put,' as he went by on the near side.

More shots, a man screamed, followed again by a weird silence. Hearing a heavy vehicle of some kind I disobeyed my instructions and saw an articulated lorry stop on the other carriageway. In the road another hooded man was lying inert, the one with him seated holding his leg and rocking backwards and forwards, perhaps with pain. John Brinkley was standing gazing down at them both, looking baffled. I couldn't see Patrick for a moment and then noticed that he was up by the escort car.

I got out of the Range Rover and ran to Brinkley. By this time the lorry driver had left his cab and was approaching.

'Please look after this man for a little while,' I begged him. 'Don't let him out of your sight.'

'Is this on the level?' he wanted to know.

'Yes. Police. And he's very vulnerable right now.'

Patrick called to me. 'I've reported this. These guys are slightly stunned. Please see to the injured paramedic.'

'No, it's all right, love,' said the driver, coming up behind me, looking pale. 'I'm OK. I'll see to her.'

She was unconscious and we ended up lifting her on to the stretcher.

A woman, presumably a driver in the growing queue behind us, ran up and furiously said to me, 'When the hell are you going to shove this lot out of the way so I can get home?'

I followed her back to her car and took the registration number of it as I had a good idea she'd been drinking.

Whether it was because we were now on the outskirts of Midsomer Norton, not very far from Bath, I don't know, but it's sufficient to record that James Carrick arrived some fifteen minutes later. It was a long fifteen minutes, the road hot and dusty. By this time John Brinkley had been transferred from the cab of the lorry – where the driver had been regaling him with stories of his time in the Navy and given him a takeaway coffee he had bought at a recent stop – to another police vehicle. Out of the corner of my eye I could see that the injured attacker was being attended to by the crew of an ambulance that had been travelling in the other direction, returning from a call. The first thing they had done was to yank off the bala-clava he was wearing – 'Have to see if you're suffering from shock, mate,' I'd heard one of them say – for which they received a mouthful of abuse.

Aware that Patrick was giving an account of what had happened to other police who had turned up, I first checked on the condition of the paramedic who had been knocked out. She had recovered consciousness but despite her protestations her colleague wouldn't allow her to move from the stretcher. Then, very belatedly, I remembered the female driver of the van. Why hadn't she reappeared? Perhaps she had and I hadn't noticed.

'It's OK for you to come out now,' I called into the thick vegetation, cupping my hands so my voice carried.

There was no response.

Had she been so terrified that she had kept on running? Or perhaps tried to get a signal on her phone to report what had happened, failed and gone higher up to try again? Or had she been hit by a stray bullet?

I climbed over the barrier and headed up into the greenery. It was steeper than had appeared from below. Immediately, virtually all sound from the road was muffled and, the further up I went, the quieter it became. A bird twittered a little tune. Ahead somewhere, a dog barked. Then I saw a foot wearing a trainer wedged against the base of a small tree.

'You're quite safe,' I said. 'They're either dead, injured or have been arrested.'

The foot moved quickly as though she had got to her feet so I went closer.

'Are you hurt?' I asked, still unable to see her.

'On your own then?' the woman asked.

I didn't like the question or the tone in which it had been uttered. 'Not really,' I replied.

'But, like, right now?'

This was creepy. I voiced my thoughts. 'I have an idea you're the driver of the getaway car and he ratted on you.'

'Come any closer and I'll kill you,' she whispered.

I didn't answer, just changed course and moved around with a view to arriving from another direction. In this I succeeded as I suddenly saw her standing with her back to me. On hearing my approach, she spun round and my ears rang with shock at the look on her face, a kind of frozen snarl. This woman *was* hoping to kill me.

Ignoring a small bush, she threw herself at me like an attacking dog, hands like claws. We both fell, knocked off balance by the force of her attack on the slope. Hitting things, twigs and leaves whipping my face, we rolled down the slope and crashed into the barrier. I was first up – she was overweight and ungainly – and swerved to one side as she struggled to her feet and came at me again, panting.

As noted in the past, I don't fight women. I don't go in for biting, nail raking, hair pulling and screaming on account of having been shown a far better course of action. So I merely sidestepped again and clipped her on the jaw when she was roughly at right angles to me.

TEN

'I'm sure I know that woman,' James Carrick said after a slightly groggy van driver was arrested and led away, mouthing hatred at me. 'I have an idea she's got form and is one of the Huggins clan.'

'From Southdown St Peter?' I queried, still able to smell the none-too-clean woman on myself.

That village, quite close to Bath, has a history of providing a rich haul of customers for various 'houses of correction', as they used to be called. Back in Victorian days an advertisement for a housemaid in a local newspaper contained the sentence: 'Ladies from Southdown St Peter need not apply'.

The DCI nodded. He had brought Lynn Outhwaite with him – she had just been promoted to DI – and put her in charge of the investigation.

The aftermath of the attack was going on all around us when blue lights and sirens could be heard approaching and, having weaved their way through the stationary traffic, two further police cars arrived. Five officers leapt out of them as though attending a major incident, some of them appearing to be armed.

'What the hell . . .?' Carrick muttered.

A uniformed woman got out of the front passenger seat of the first car and came over. I'm not an expert on police ranks but guessed from her badges that she was a superintendent. 'Who's the senior officer here?' she imperiously demanded to know.

'I am,' Carrick said and introduced himself. Then he said, 'I like to know who I'm talking to.'

She ignored that and said, 'I have a Metropolitan Police warrant for the arrest of a man by the name of John Brinkley. I understand that he's in your custody.'

'He's in my protective custody,' the DCI replied. 'And a suspect in a case of murder that took place within the area that's the responsibility of this force.'

'He has other charges to answer in London.'

'More serious than murder?'

'That's not your concern.'

'I suggest, ma'am, that it is as the NCA's involved.' He cast about for Patrick, and, having spotted him talking to Lynn, tried to attract his attention through the mêlée but failed.

'I'll get him,' I said and ran across.

'Is it the Met?' Patrick asked.

'Too right.'

'Thought as much.' To Lynn, he quickly said, 'What are the protocols when one force demands another one hand over their suspect?'

'Well, you've already done it once today,' she retorted, hot, bothered and obviously stressed by the present situation. 'What happened then?'

'No, I merely asked for him to be transferred to another DCI within the same force's area,' he reminded her gently.

'Oh, yes, sorry – of course. Well, I should imagine rather a lot of tact's involved.'

'Thank you.' And he went off towards the new arrivals, muttering, 'Tact, Gillard, tact.'

I followed and arrived just behind him. Truly, right now this author was feeling as though she was her husband's unlucky mascot.

'NCA,' Patrick said, producing his ID. 'You can't have him.'

OK, to hell with tact.

The woman, probably in her early forties and with the kind of Nordic looks that might have been admired by Hitler, whipped a folded piece of paper from her top pocket and shoved it under his nose.

'This is the third attempt today to remove Brinkley from my custody,' he said, taking and unfolding it. 'The first lot said they were from a security company and had an invalid arrest warrant, the second has just tried violence – God knows who they are – and now you've come along with another invalid arrest warrant.'

'Invalid?' she queried.

'Out of date form.'

'That's quite irrelevant.'

'Not as far as I'm concerned, it isn't. It didn't take you long to drive down from London, did it?'

'We set off very early.'

'Brinkley wasn't found until eight this morning. Are you resorting to crystal balls for your investigations?'

'Don't be ridiculous!'

'You can't have him.'

'Look, I can arrest *you* – for obstruction.'

'Carry on. I take it Luke Wallingford's behind this.'

'He's my ultimate boss.'

'I'll let you into a little secret – he's bent.'

She ignored that too and said, 'The personnel with me are armed, so I suggest you cooperate.'

Patrick turned to James Carrick. 'Is she making history here?'

'Aye,' said the Scot heavily.

'You can't have him,' Patrick said for the third time.

By way of an answer she turned and marched back to her group. Whispered orders were issued and the five spread out. Two went off to where Brinkley had been taken into another ambulance, two came over to the three of us and the fifth just stood around looking threatening.

Lynn noticed what was happening and also approached. 'What's going on, guv?'

'We've been hijacked,' Carrick said.

'And we can't start shooting other cops,' Patrick added, pitching his voice so the super could hear.

Moments later, one squad car containing her, Brinkley and one member of her retinue left at speed along the clear road in front, the other car bringing up the rear. Unconcerned, they had left behind them two dead bodies, one injured 'suspect', one unhurt getaway van driver, probably, and two slightly injured constables, not to mention personnel from the Avon and Somerset force who had arrived to deal with what had occurred.

In the heat and dust of the road Carrick and Lynn went off to sort everything out.

Patrick swore and then said, 'No, she's not having him.'

'Not for the first time, your oracle urges caution,' I said.

'I'll see that bloody woman in hell before she hands him over to Wallingford,' he said, appearing not to have heard me. And with that he hurried over to the Range Rover, got in it and drove off before I could tell him that it had stopped a bullet but I didn't know where.

'I'm volunteering,' I went to tell Carrick. 'Patrick's gone off in the car with my handbag in it. If I work like crazy here does that pay for a lift home when you've finished?'

He gave me a fleeting smile which I took to mean yes.

But first I had to get hold of Commander Greenway, my mobile thankfully in my pocket. Following the trend of it being a lousy day so far he didn't answer his phone, forcing me to leave a message.

As I had expected, James Carrick had to stay for a couple more hours and by now, of course, we were presiding over a traffic tail back probably several miles long. I helped as best I could, taking notes for Lynn Outhwaite – in shorthand for ease but knowing I would end up having to type it up later as I had a good idea no one at the nick would be able to read it – as she interviewed, among others, the driver of the original ambulance, his colleague having been taken to hospital for a check-up. A few drivers and passengers of following cars were spoken to. Scenes of crime personnel worked, seemingly oblivious to everything going on around them.

'I'm a mite worried about your Brinkley,' Carrick said when permission to remove the dead had been given. By this time, and from the other direction, Highways people had arrived to cope with the wrecked vehicles – they would have to wait – together with traffic police to try to sort out the jam.

'So am I, but I don't see what Patrick can do,' I replied. 'And I've no idea if the NCA in the shape of Greenway can do anything either.'

Finally I got home. By this time it was the late afternoon and, after drinking a glass of water and two mugs of tea I headed for a shower. The Range Rover wasn't outside the rectory and I hadn't expected it to be, but nevertheless I was concerned about Patrick as well now. Then I had to push that to the back of my mind and get on with making something for the family's dinner. Fortunately Carrie had shopped – she's paid a high salary including living arrangements and the use of a car for being an Ingrid substitute when we're away – so after a big hello with the children I set to and made a family-sized chicken curry.

'Mum, you could have a tracker fitted to the car so you know where Dad is,' Matthew said when I was serving up.

'In the past he's had to remove ones that other people have put there,' I told him. 'And it's not always a good idea for others to know where you are.'

'He ought to have a car like James Bond's,' Justin piped up, following this with roaring car engine sound effects while wildly waving his arms around.

'Dad's not like that,' Matthew said scornfully. 'OK, he's great and been a soldier and a policeman but that doesn't mean he carries a gun, chucks big crooks around and throws knives. Don't be silly.'

'I bet he does!' Justin yelled back. 'He fired the shotgun in the air when some horrible boys banged on Grandma's windows.'

Horrible boys? No, late-teen fledgling criminals actually.

'Mum, tell him he's silly,' Matthew pleaded. 'He'll only start bragging at school.'

'He's not wrong,' Katie said quietly. 'You've forgotten things that have happened and never notice anything anyway.'

Before this could develop into a full-scale argument, which it does sometimes, I got in quickly: 'You're all a bit right – now please eat your dinner.'

At eight that evening I finally managed to contact Greenway. Predictably, he was furious. Less predictably, he was furious with Patrick.

'Well, as he said himself, he could hardly start shooting cops,' I countered – yes, furiously.

'I can't believe that some kind of measured discussion couldn't have taken place,' he fumed. 'For God's sake, your husband's one of the most articulate blokes I've ever met. And where was Carrick while all this was going on?'

'Being a DCI faced with a super,' I replied. 'If we'd had a commander present things might have been a bit different.'

Silence.

I went on, 'Right from the beginning of this you've been nigh-on impossible to get hold of. Frankly, Mike, you've gone to ground. Patrick may well have been in a position of command when he was in the army, but a Met superintendent wouldn't have taken any notice if he'd tried to reason with her *or* told her to sod off.'

After a little more silence from the other end of the line, he said, 'Do you know where Patrick is?'

I said I didn't and that I deliberately hadn't tried ringing him, hoping he would contact me when he had something to tell me.

'I'll see what I can do,' he said and ended the call.

By the next morning I hadn't heard anything from anyone and was on the verge of phoning Patrick when Carrick contacted me.

'That man injured in the attack isn't seriously hurt and can be interviewed today,' he said without preamble. 'He's in the Royal United. Do you want to be present?'

'Absolutely,' I replied, thinking that it might be a good thing if my husband's shooting skills were getting a little rusty if we were left with people to question.

'If you come to the nick we can go together. You know what parking's like at the hospital. Oh, and that female van driver isn't a member of the Huggins clan.'

'It was just the lank greasy hair and BO that made you think she was then,' I said.

'No doubt,' he acknowledged dryly, pronouncing it 'Nay doot'.

'I know who *he* is though,' I said as we approached the man in the hospital bed. 'His name's Eddard Crake. He does odd jobs for Lazno Hiershal, who is a bigger crook than he likes to make out.'

'They usually tend to try to give the opposite impression,' Carrick observed.

'He lurks in Glastonbury possibly because he thinks the cops won't find him there. But they have and he should still be on remand for seriously beating up his one-time girlfriend, who incidentally, Brinkley appears to have lived with for a while.'

'I like the Glastonbury connection after what happened yesterday.'

I resolved to bring him up to date with what Greenway had told me about the alleged Freeman/Wallingford partnership.

Crake, whose strange complexion and hair colour obviously weren't due to cement dust after all, had pretended to be asleep as soon as he had spotted us. That he wasn't seriously injured manifested itself in that he was on only one drip attachment and otherwise untrammelled.

We seated ourselves one on each side of the bed and I prepared to take notes, again in shorthand.

'Hi Ed,' I said before Carrick could speak, thus earning a look of great disapproval from him for at least two reasons.

Crake's eyes opened and he glared at me. 'You were the one with that cop what put the screws on me when I was at work,' he said accusingly.

'He asked you a few questions,' I corrected. 'And this latest job was promotion, wasn't it? Instead of fixing dripping taps in houses belonging to a dodgy landlord you're now involved in armed kidnap. As you yourself said, Lazno always evades the police because he's so clever. Only he isn't any more, so you won't get paid.'

'Lazno's out of it now,' he agreed. 'He should've left that stupid bitch alone. I don't work for him no more.'

'So Zeti's king now, is he?'

'You talk too much,' he muttered and closed his eyes again.

Odd how some people think you can't easily guess the truth when they're trying to be evasive.

Belatedly, I introduced Carrick and Crake stayed like something dead.

'Where had you been ordered to take Brinkley?' the DCI asked.

'I don't know what you're talking about.'

Well, at least he was talking.

'You were in a van that deliberately caused a crash with a police car and an ambulance.'

'Nah, it was an accident. The front near tyre blew.'

'It didn't.'

'Go away.'

'It will help your case if you cooperate.'

I bent a little closer and said quietly, 'Brinkley's hot. He was a top cop before he retired. That was why the Hiershals wanted to get their hands on him, because he knows enough about them to get them put in the slammer for a very long time.'

Did he? Hopefully, he did.

'Which suggests,' I continued, 'that you were told to do something to him that would have stopped it happening. That would have made you an accessory to murder.'

'So I ain't now then,' Crake muttered. 'Good.'

'But . . .' I whispered grimly.

'But?'

'When you get out of prison for attempted kidnap and all the other bits and pieces the cops'll think up especially for you, Zeti Hiershal is going to be very annoyed that you screwed up. He's going to make sure that what's left of you is finally found rotting in a ditch somewhere on the Somerset Levels.'

'Nah.' He hadn't said this with much conviction.

'But if you cooperate he'll be in prison together with Lazno so you'll be safe.'

I think I held my breath. But he could be described as industrial-strength stupid, couldn't he?

Hospital equipment bleeped, a phone rang and, in the distance, a woman laughed.

After staying silent for what seemed a long time, Crake said, 'Yeah, OK. We was to have dumped him in a quiet road somewhere and then run him over a couple of times. To make it look natural like.'

Somewhat inured to the workings of the criminal mind after writing about it and first-hand experience over several years, my skin nevertheless crawled.

'The other two with you,' Carrick said. 'Who were they?'

'All I know is that they were illegals. From some godforsaken hole or other.'

'Do you know their names?'

'I'd only met them yesterday morning.'

'Come on, think. It's important.'

Crake sighed. 'They didn't seem to speak much English. One was Stuey, or something like that. He was the black guy. The other one didn't say nothing other than yes and no.'

'Which one was given the gun?'

'Stuey. He seemed to know what to do with it.'

'Did you get the impression that they'd worked for the Hiershals before?'

'I didn't think about it. Are you going to leave me alone soon? My leg hurts like hell.'

'I'll fetch a nurse for you. Are there quite a few people working for them like that?'

'Yeah, on and off and they pay them in drink and drugs and sometimes money, otherwise they have to get it themselves. There are women too. I think they keep one or two for themselves – you know, for housework, cooking and sex. The rest get sold on.'

'That's slavery!' I was unable to prevent myself from exclaiming.

'Yeah, well, the pair of them *are* right bastards.'

'Please tell us where Zeti can be found,' I said.

He shook his head. 'No idea. He's normally in London but turned up when Lazno was nabbed.'

'Where was the van kept?' Carrick asked.

'It wasn't. It was stolen.'

He called over a nurse.

'I'll get on to the DCI in Glastonbury,' Carrick said when we were back in his car. 'What Crake's told us is actually more to do with her than me although, obviously, we'll have to liaise. And Ingrid, you really can't question suspects like that. Some of the things you said probably aren't true.'

'I have it on good authority that all forces have their *Life on Mars* moments,' I countered.

He smiled thinly and then said, 'Would you email Sue Manning with what was said just now?'

'Yes, but I can't do it *instantly*,' I told him. 'Plus, I don't have a laptop with me.'

'I do.'

This meant that we ended up in a café with Wi-Fi where,

in exchange for my tapping out the interview and sending it off, he bought me an early lunch.

Patrick rang an hour or so later to apologize for not getting in touch and to report that he'd followed the convoy to the outskirts of the capital and then the dash warning lights had lit up 'like a bloody Christmas tree' and he'd been forced to stop. The Range Rover was now in a main dealer courtesy of the RAC and he'd caught a train into central London where he'd stayed the night at his club. When he got there he discovered that the battery of his phone was flat and he'd been unable to borrow a charger until ten minutes ago. Yes, he had my handbag. He sounded very fed up, asked me why I hadn't told him the damned car had a bullet in its guts and finished by saying that he would check on it and let me know what his next move would be.

I was trying not to think about what might be happening to Brinkley.

This didn't remain entirely in doubt for long. I listened to the news at lunchtime to hear that during the previous evening two police cars in Hammersmith had been forced to stop and masked men had seized a suspect at gunpoint and made off with him. The Met had only just released the news for what were described as 'security reasons'. There were no further details except that it was understood a superintendent had been in one of the cars.

I discovered that I was staring into space, unable to believe it. This news was utterly staggering. I toyed with the idea that it might have involved someone else entirely and in the next moment my mobile rang. It was Greenway.

'Heard the latest?' he asked.

I said that I had, just, and added, 'You could have told me last night.'

'I only heard about it a few minutes ago myself. I'd really like to know why they've been keeping it so close to their chests in house. I'm not happy about that, especially as I have someone working on the case.'

I brought him up to date with that someone's call and the questioning of Crake and he promised to put out an arrest warrant for Zeti Hiershal whether DCI Manning had already done so or not. Meanwhile, he added grimly, it was to be hoped that a full operation was in progress to find Brinkley.

Patrick got home in the early evening having travelled by train and got a taxi from Bath station. He had also had a conversation with Greenway and could hardly believe what had happened either. Concentrating for a moment on immediate practical matters, he went on to say that the car would take a while to repair, and given the damage to certain bits and pieces he was amazed it had got so far.

'I take it we're insured for things like that,' I said.

'Not now I'm a temporary cop, it appears. It's a dangerous occupation and I'm not covered.'

'Did you really have to tell them that?'

'Yes, as I had to explain how the bloody thing got shot up, didn't I?'

'Rats!' I exploded. 'It's criminal damage pure and simple.'

'You phone them then.' He went off to have a shower.

I found the paperwork and did just that. Patrick might be highly articulate but writers have a way with words that is more . . . creative.

OK, an insurance wonk said finally. Criminal damage and please send invoices and full details.

'Who?' Patrick said loudly, rocketing into the kitchen and making me jump. 'Who were they? I can only think it was Zeti Hiershal's London mob.' He commenced to pace around like something seriously deranged in an X-rated movie and I was glad the family appeared to be at someone else's house.

'Then calm down and really think,' I urged, basting a roasting chicken.

He paused. 'Eh?'

The bird back in the oven, I said, 'Whoever it was would have been under orders as it smacks of someone a bit better organized and intelligent than that would-be crime lord. Hiershal can't have been directly responsible for the trio with the invalid arrest warrant who arrived at Glastonbury nick either. It was odd that the super from the Met had one too. Were they identical?'

'No, the second one was OK.'

I stared at him. 'But you said . . .'

'She told us that Wallingford was her ultimate boss and I'm convinced he's bent. *That* makes the warrant invalid.'

'She seemed to believe you though, but if she'd issued it she'd know it was OK.'

'So she hadn't. Fascinating, isn't it?'

'Patrick, has it occurred to you that Brinkley might have been lying about this all along and Wallingford really has been trying to pin him down for ages?'

'Are you being the Devil's advocate?'

I gave him a saucepan containing drained potatoes to mash. 'If you like.'

He grabbed the masher, milk and butter and then said, 'I've thought about it at length but recent events have changed everything. As you've just said, those three with the genuine but out of date warrant can't have been under orders from a mobster. *But* it could have been obtained from a dodgy cop. That theory's thrown into disarray when we remind ourselves that Wallingford has easy access to current and perfectly legitimate warrants. *But again* – and I'm not sure about this – I should imagine that records have to be kept and the things are numbered anyway. Which again does suggest covert behaviour on a cop's part.'

'And the fourth and successful attempt to get Brinkley?' I queried. 'Ostensibly, that was the work of some kind of criminal gang – as you suggested, Zeti Hiershal. If Wallingford was behind sending the super to stop us, was he also behind the London hold-up to divert the blame away from himself?'

'That's a good theory. Well, all these characters seem to know what everyone on Brinkley's side's doing.' He paused, found a fork and proceeded to thrash in rather too much butter followed by a slosh of milk. As I had hoped, working off some of his wrath.

'Seasoning,' I said, passing over the salt and pepper mills. 'And I shouldn't ask, but what the hell can you do?'

'First, I intend to phone Dixon.'

'I still don't understand his interest, even if Brinkley was working on sensitive stuff. It was quite a long time ago.'

Patrick shrugged. 'Who knows, he might merely hate Wallingford.'

I hated it that people were playing with not only a man's freedom but possibly his life.

The saga continued in the same vein in that Charles Dixon was unavailable. Then, and I wasn't around at the time, Greenway rang Patrick and I was soon to learn that the conversation was short and to the point.

'I'm to talk to the super who took Brinkley off us – no, I'm to grill her,' Patrick said, finding me in the nursery where Carrie was having trouble getting Mark to settle for he was screaming blue murder, most unusual. 'Teeth?' he asked, having to raise his voice over the yells.

'Could be,' Carrie said. 'I'll give him some Calpol, but I'll have to do it when he's calmed down a bit or he might choke.'

'And we can't expect your mother to keep helping with the children,' I pointed out, keen for him not to dump the child on Elspeth and about to pick up the baby myself.

'Walkies then,' said Patrick before I could do anything. He scooped up the crimson-faced Mark together with a blanket and went off with him. The wails faded into the distance.

I told Carrie that we would do everything necessary and she could relax. I went downstairs. Neither Patrick nor Mark were anywhere obvious, and I knew that the two elder children were at friends' houses, Justin playing with racing cars in his bedroom, so I got on with clearing away the dinner things. Fifteen minutes later there was still no sign of father and son so I went through the conservatory and out into the garden. It was getting dark but quite a warm evening.

I strolled, enjoying the scents of spring, a light breeze in my hair, the last twitterings of birds going to roost. My wanderings took me down the drive, the scent of spring flowers borne on a light breeze, then across the village road and on to the green. A couple walking a dog wished me goodnight and when I glanced skywards a little bat flew over my head. Then I saw that two figures were sitting on one of the seats, the one nearest to the church entrance that had recently been put there in memory of Patrick's father, John, who had died some months previously. One of them appeared to be holding a baby, a wonderfully silent one.

'I have to say that I didn't expect anything like this at all,' Charles Dixon was saying in his hushed voice when I reached them, gesturing to the sleeping infant. 'Good evening, Mrs Gillard.'

I greeted him and sat next to Patrick. His presence here was nothing short of weird.

'A word of explanation,' Dixon continued, obviously having just got there. 'Your call, Patrick, arrived when I was at Bath station hurrying for a taxi. I've arranged to meet someone at a hotel in the city tomorrow morning. Nothing, incidentally, to do with the John Brinkley case. And I hope you don't feel you've failed as far as he's concerned – I don't expect you to take up arms against the Metropolitan Police. As I was staying fairly locally I thought I'd come and tell you personally. And there you were on the village green with your little boy!'

He might have gone into the pub first for a drink then rather than been dropped off at the rectory gates.

I invited him to come home but he shook his head and said, 'Thank you, but no. I've had a very long day already and my taxi's waiting for me.'

'And Brinkley?' I prompted.

'I'm not at all optimistic about him. I don't know who has him now but it might be a London gang. Frankly, I can't think what they'd do with him other than kill him.'

I was dismayed: the idea didn't seem to bother him a lot. But then again, this man never gave away any hint of what was going through his mind.

'But how did they *know*?' Patrick said. 'How could it have been a London gang unless a cop who was involved with all this told them?'

'I have to admit, the ramifications are baffling,' Dixon murmured.

'Would you like to hear about the other attempts to grab him yesterday before the Met super came along?' Patrick asked him.

'Other attempts?' the man echoed, clearly shocked.

'I wasn't about to go into details over the phone but there

were two.' He then gave him the full account and when he had finished the man was silent.

'Greenway wants me to question that super,' Patrick added. 'But I can't see what that would achieve as she'd only stonewall me. I'm not even convinced she's a big player in this.'

'I don't think she stuck to protocols, you know. You could challenge her with that.'

'She refused to give us her name. D'you know who she is?'

'Regrettably, I don't.'

'To hell with protocols!' I burst out, really angry with him now. 'Is anyone looking for Brinkley? Is he just going to be abandoned?'

'Indeed no,' Dixon answered. 'The Met have instigated a comprehensive search and are raiding the homes of known associates of the Hiershals. With no luck so far, I'm afraid.'

'He won't be anywhere like that,' Patrick said thoughtfully. 'If he's still alive, that is.'

I was wondering what had happened to the firearm that Brinkley was reputed to have.

Suddenly remembering that he hadn't sent James Carrick the photographs of the man at the hotel who we were certain was Kevin Freeman Patrick did so. Even though it was just after ten pm he received a reply almost straight away. Yes, Carrick said, this man was indeed the DCI Derek Rogers he had fallen foul of in Wemdale.

We rejoiced, that is high-fived, and temporarily filed the information.

ELEVEN

Later that same evening DCI Sue Manning contacted Patrick to give him the blood test results for John Brinkley which had just been emailed to her. He had apparently been given a cocktail of drugs, the nature of some being indeterminate as they had already mostly been eliminated from his system. Opioids had been detected though, including Fentanyl. Also Psilocbin, a psychedelic drug, sometimes referred to as magic mushrooms. She asked Patrick if he knew of any drug problem Brinkley might have had in the past, the answer to which was an emphatic no. The general feeling was that the man had had them administered to him as there had been no established needle marks on his arms and he hadn't appeared to be desperate for another fix – if anything the reverse had been true. So no, he wasn't an addict.

'If Brinkley's telling the truth it's rather a clumsy way to frame a man for murder,' I commented when Patrick returned to the living room and related the conversation to me. He had offered to check that the children were asleep. 'But who was the murder victim – that woman we met who was pretending to be his wife?'

'Sue doesn't know. They're checking. The PM showed what everyone knew already – that the woman had died from multiple knife wounds.'

'I have a horrible feeling that she'd been hired for the impersonation job and they'd intended to kill her all along.'

'So whatever's driving those behind this, it has to be what I can only describe as life-changing for them if it all goes wrong – the end of a police career, no pension, plus a long prison term.'

'We know where Kevin Freeman lives,' I said.

The mesmerizing grey eyes that had been the wow factor when we first met fixed on me now. 'Is that the oracle in full production mode?'

'Umm.'

'I take it then that you want to search his place from top to bottom.'

'You said yourself that Brinkley wouldn't be where people were looking for him.'

Patrick pondered for a moment or two and then said, 'Greenway wouldn't countenance an official search with a warrant as there's no evidence, even though he pointed him in our direction in the first place.' Glancing at his watch, he added, 'It's a bit late to do anything now.'

'And North Ascot isn't exactly a five-minute drive down the road, so I wasn't suggesting that we went there right now – even if we had the car.'

He fixed himself a small tot and subsided tiredly into an armchair. 'Which we don't. I'd forgotten for a moment. God, I've failed with just about everything so far, haven't I? I should have really retired – told Greenway to find someone else to do the job. I'm thinking of doing that anyway, but men are bad at accepting they're over the hill, aren't they?'

'There are two questions there,' I said quietly, shaken to see how upset and depressed he was. 'The answer to the first is no and to the second you aren't. Also, I still love you to bits.'

Tossing down the rest of his drink, Patrick got to his feet, gave me a smile and a little wave and went to bed.

A truly hardworking woman, Sue Manning called Patrick's mobile again at eight thirty the next morning. I spoke to her as he was shaving.

'The murdered woman has been identified,' she said. 'We had to resort to scouring local dentists for records as her killer, or killers, appear to have removed everything from the house that would have told us her identity. She was a local woman by the name of Tracy Adams and her dentist happened to know that she's Ann Shipton's sister – or rather was – and also knew that she was divorced but had kept her married name. I gather that the dentist had become quite friendly with her which might explain how she knew so much about her client. Did Miss Shipton mention a sister to you?'

I told her that she hadn't.

The DCI continued, 'Naturally, and although I'm aware that she said she was leaving the country for a while, I'm now putting every effort into checking the truth of that as there's a chance she might be in danger. It seems that anyone who might have been associated with the Hiershal brothers isn't safe.'

'Have you gleaned any more evidence from the Brinkleys' house?' I asked.

'The place was quite dirty so there were a lot of fingerprints and potential DNA samples, which were taken and sent off to the lab. But work so far hasn't thrown up anything useful other than Brinkley's fingerprints being on the murder weapon and in other places. But it's his house so the latter's to be expected. Oh, the bloody marks on the front door were mostly smeared but there was one good print. That was Brinkley's too.'

'And he said they put the knife in his hand.'

'I know, but that's not an unusual ploy in knife crime. He would be aware of that.'

'Do you have access to Zeti Hiershal's records?' I asked on an afterthought.

'I've requested them from the Met but that was only yesterday.'

I thanked her and brought her up to date with the rest of the news in case she wasn't aware what had happened the previous evening in the capital. I got the impression she was quite glad that Brinkley was no longer in Somerset even though they still had him as number-one suspect for the murder. After the call I wondered if she'd thought, as had I, of the possibility that if he wasn't guilty, drugged or no, the woman had been merely there to be murdered in an effort to get Brinkley sent to prison for a very long time, whether she was his wife or not. And would they have murdered the real Sarah Brinkley if she'd stayed at home?

'Which rather ties in with what John told us,' I said out loud after the call. 'That he sent his wife away for safety when it all started.'

'You don't usually talk to yourself,' Patrick observed, appearing in the doorway.

'I do actually,' I replied, and then went on to tell him what Sue Manning had said.

'It rather destroys their case,' Patrick mused. 'Those behind the murder, I mean. How is anyone going to explain away the fact that the woman was living in a house that didn't belong to her? Brinkley would hardly have installed her there. Unless the story is going to be that he was having it away with her after getting rid of his wife to Italy and sent Ann Shipton packing. And although he said he was confined in some way, no one seems to have investigated how he got into the appalling state he was in. This has gone on for far too long. I shall confront Freeman with the fact that he appears to have a new identity.'

I said, 'Before you do that it might be a good idea to ask Dalesland Police if they have a file photo of DCI Derek Rogers and send it to James – just to make sure his memory isn't at fault.'

'Good thinking.'

He sent off an email quoting his warrant card number. There was nothing we could do now but wait, not that we sat around of course. I went food shopping – you can never have too much in the fridge when you have five children – Patrick got on the phone to try to get the Range Rover brought to where it could be repaired locally, having discovered that the dealership hadn't even started work.

Just after lunch, some three hours later, the photo arrived and after taking a look at it – there was no doubt that it was the man calling himself Kevin Freeman even though his head was now shaven – we borrowed Elspeth's car and drove to North Ascot. On the way Patrick contacted James Carrick, sending him the photo. He confirmed the identification and went on to say that he wanted to be involved, immediately, today, in view of what had happened to him in Wemdale. I think Patrick succeeded in putting him off but we were both surprised by his reaction.

We should have known better.

It was pouring with rain in Berkshire, large and quite deep puddles at the sides of minor roads forcing me to slow down as I had no wish to drown the engine, this little vehicle not being what I was used to driving. My partner in tackling crime was in pensive mood, quite likely still brooding about being 'over the hill' and having 'failed with everything so far'. But what else could I say to him that might help?

There were three cars parked on the block paving drive in front of the house, Freeman's Evoque not being one of them, so perhaps he was out or it was in one of the three garages. I hadn't noticed any security devices like cameras but as soon as we stepped out of the car the front door opened and there stood the greetings card writer. She wasn't smiling.

'You're not welcome,' she called. 'Leave.'

'The world seems to be full of people who don't want us to call on them,' Patrick said. 'Be so good as to tell Freeman that I'd like a word.'

'He's not here.'

'Look, it would be really embarrassing if I barged you out of the way and went in because I'm actually quite a polite sort of guy. Or I could suggest to Ingrid that she does it as she thinks you're a complete phoney for calling yourself an author.'

I remained perfectly serene. The business of helping me with my physics homework all those years ago obviously had to have some kind of payback.

The woman went back inside, leaving the door ajar. Nothing happened for a couple of minutes, during which time we moved a little closer. Then, Kevin Freeman emerged.

'This is all beginning to tie in rather neatly,' Patrick said as the man approached. 'I understand that at one time you called yourself Derek Rogers, chum of Alan Terrington, another bent cop, and also big friends with Frank Norris, a mobster in the north-east known as Smiler.'

'Rubbish!' Freeman said. 'You're still drunk or under the influence of drugs.'

'I've an official photograph of you sent to me today by Dalesland Police that dates back to the days when you were a DCI in Wemdale,' Patrick continued. 'You were subsequently chucked out of the police as, at the time, there wasn't enough evidence to connect you to Norris.'

'I'm warning you,' Freeman said quietly. 'Get off my back.'

'Luke Wallingford warned me off too but *your* activities are history in that it happened,' Patrick went on. 'And now, here you are with a new identity messing about with the likes of Denny Whitman in an effort to prevent me from doing my job. But I'm not interested in you at all for the very good reason that you'll soon be behind bars. What I really want to know is the whereabouts of John Brinkley.'

Smirking, Freeman crowed, 'That idiot retired Met commander who lost his mind to drugs and murdered his girlfriend? He's in custody, isn't he? I should get your facts right if I were you. Meanwhile, get out!'

He turned on his heel and strode back to the house.

Patrick and I exchanged amazed glances. Nothing had been made public so how did he have such insider knowledge?

'Wallingford must have told him,' I said as I was driving a subdued husband away.

'And if Brinkley really is in police custody, I can't get to him,' Patrick muttered, finding his phone. 'Not only that, and if it's true, since when have the police been removing a suspect from other police by utilizing masked men? They've beaten me. This is a criminal cartel and I don't see that I can do any more.'

He reported to Greenway, who right then was non-committal, and we went home.

Mike Greenway didn't see what else Patrick could do either, promised to confer with the director for further instructions, thanked him and told him to abandon the assignment. This was dreadful of course, but I resolved to concentrate on home matters as sitting around wringing our hands would achieve nothing. The pair of us have always been fairly pragmatic people, but the situation hurt as we had been outgunned, literally, by those regarded to be on the side of the law. We had failed and although John Brinkley was ostensibly in custody, I had a horrible feeling about it.

Failure was a word I intended to banish though and I reverted, not for the first time, to trying to make everything as normal as possible, for everybody's sake. The following

Monday Patrick went back to work and we slipped into our daily routine. I discovered that this was a relief to me personally as it meant I could get on with writing. All previous notions of plots involving a retired police commander getting himself into trouble due to his knowledge of criminal gangs and bent cops were tossed into the mental wastepaper basket.

We didn't hear from Commander Greenway.

'The pub. For a meal. With the Carricks. Seven thirty,' Patrick announced laconically when he got home at the end of the working week. He paused in his journey upstairs to have a shower. 'That's if you're not doing anything else.'

'I'm not, but dinner's already in the oven,' I told him. 'We can have it tomorrow if I stretch it somewhat.' Stretch the chicken casserole rather a lot actually as the whole family tends to eat in on Saturdays and Sundays unless the older children are at friends' homes. I would have to make another one.

'That's all right. I'll do one of my prawn things so there's a choice.'

I rather hoped he would go and shop for the ingredients for this himself – it's actually a glorious fish pie containing not only prawns but haddock, monkfish and fresh salmon – and then he'd realize how wildly expensive it is.

Unusually, the Ring o' Bells was quiet for a Friday and we had the choice of several tables so opted for one in a corner. The Carricks arrived a few minutes later and as they seated themselves Patrick's mobile rang. He groaned, moved to switch it off and then saw who was calling. He excused himself and went back outside as not only is the reception poor in Hinton Littlemoor but we both hate it when people take calls in restaurants and other public places.

'It's bad,' he said when he returned.

'Greenway?' I guessed.

For a moment it seemed that Patrick was struggling to speak. Then he cleared his throat and said, 'Brinkley's been found – or his body has. In the Thames at Tower Bridge – yesterday. He'd been shot twice in the head and was only identified with difficulty.'

Utterly shocked, no one said anything for a few long moments.

'Is it a definite identification though?' asked Carrick, ever the practical Scot.

'Apparently so. The body was still wearing the tracksuit he'd been issued with by Avon and Somerset police – it had their logo on it. Dental records are being checked but it seems certain, although there are no more details at the moment.'

There was another quite protracted silence.

'They've won,' Patrick said grimly.

'No,' Joanna said. 'They haven't. Someone, one of their henchmen, will eventually talk.'

Without saying anything both men rose to go to the bar to fetch drinks and Joanna and I didn't break the silence while they were absent. Words couldn't convey how appalling the news was.

After our meal during which, again, hardly anything had been said, Carrick seemed to come to a decision. He said, 'I wasn't going to mention it to you tonight, but in view of what's happened I'm going to. I've done something that might catch this Rogers/Freeman bastard.'

'What's that?' Patrick enquired, stirring his coffee.

'Well, obviously, I knew nothing about what Greenway's just told you, but I've let it be known on certain restricted Met websites that it's just come to my attention that the past illegal activities of disgraced ex-DCI Derek Rogers will soon come back to haunt him. This kind of cryptic remark is quite usual on the websites and, as we know, everyone in the job hates bent cops.'

'That's *dangerous*,' Patrick told him. 'Bloody dangerous. He probably won't have access to that but Wallingford will.'

'Precisely.'

'James, are you going to invest in a bulletproof vest?'

'Well, I already have a stab vest,' the DCI answered with a jaunty smile.

Predictably, Joanna didn't look at all happy, and I got the impression it was the first she'd heard of it. It occurred to me then that I was being downright naive in not realizing that Patrick's name must be just about top of Freeman's list of those who represented a threat to him. And now Carrick, who had more personal reasons to want him behind bars, would be on it if he had been unwise enough to put his name on what he had written. Perhaps he hadn't. His anger was understandable though, for not only had Rogers been responsible for shutting him up in an old boiler but before that had had him savagely beaten up, poured vodka down his throat and later arrested him for being drunk and disorderly. Carrick, whose constitution is that of a horse, had managed to throw up the alcohol that had been forced into him – I understand all over the reception area of Wemdale nick – and had subsequently tested as virtually sober.

'What are you going to do?' Patrick asked him.

'Set up some kind of sting.'

'It'll have to be a damned good one.'

'I'm working on it.'

'You and who else?'

'There's this guy I know who used to work for MI5 and happens to carry a shooter.'

'Have you asked him?'

'I'm waiting for the right moment – when he's had a couple of tots back at my place.'

'I think you'd better come and have a couple at mine, it's nearer.'

Joanna and I just looked at one another.

'We *have* to pitch it right to get the two of them,' Patrick said, well into his second tot. He turned to me. 'Ingrid, you're really good at plots. Any suggestions?'

'No, I'm not going to write my own husband's suicide note,' I replied. '*You're* the trained strategist.'

This remark seemed to press the button marked DEFAULT POSITION and he went quiet, pensively staring at nothing. The others might have thought I had insulted him in a way they didn't know about and he was sulking but all that was happening was . . . well . . . strategy. Then his mobile, on the coffee table before him, rang again and I snatched it up as there was every indication that its owner, jerked out of his thoughts, was about to throw it into the farthest corner of the room.

'A postscript to my last,' Greenway's voice said. 'I'm at home but I'd asked to be kept in the loop and have just been told that the armed group that grabbed Brinkley from the police car are part of a gang. That bit's obviously no surprise but they've been identified courtesy of CCTV, partly to do with their vanity of committing crimes on motorbikes adorned with certain logos, skulls and other stuff, the same kind of thing on their helmets. Apparently there's a motorbike nerd on the team who knows about that. Suspicion has fallen heavily on Zeti Hiershal and co, who the Met have been trying to get hold of for ages in connection with any number of offences. I told them what you pair had found out about him and his brother.'

I imparted the news to those present and we all brooded about it for half a minute or so until Carrick said, 'D'you reckon the super who managed to avoid giving us her name was in on the third attempt?'

'She said Wallingford was her ultimate boss,' I reminded them. 'Do we have a scenario where, having failed to get him at Glastonbury and again on the road to Bath due to the incompetence of those doing it, the super's armed intervention was the fallback and she'd been shadowing us all along? She may be perfectly on the line of course, under orders and been fed a load of lies, although in my view removing a suspect from other cops using an element of threat on a public highway is downright weird.'

'I don't see how you can concoct a sting when they both know what the pair of you look like,' Joanna said. 'Unless you're going to phone him up, disguise your voice and say you know all about his dark deeds and what's he going to do about it along the lines of giving you rather a lot of money.'

The tone in which this had been uttered could be described as boiling point scorn. In other words, she thought her husband's idea was crap.

He carefully cleared his throat. 'Well – er – no.' And to Patrick: 'Well? Do we do it?'

'Of course,' said Patrick. 'For a start, I suggest we get Zeti Hiershal.'

The Scot looked dubious. 'I couldn't be in on that. It's already the Met's case.'

Well, quite, I thought. The problems were obvious already.

'No, the NCA would have to action that,' Patrick told him. 'I shall have to wait to see what Greenway has to say tomorrow.'

'That wasn't the sort of thing I had in mind at all,' Carrick said irritably.

'OK, tell us what you had in mind then,' Patrick said.

'Just you and me, nothing official and not involving other cops.'

It was Patrick's turn to look doubtful.

The DCI got to his feet. 'OK, forget it. Goodnight and thanks for the tot.' To Joanna, he snapped, 'Are you coming with me or walking home?'

Joanna rose, gave her hosts a brilliant wide smile, a wink and followed her husband who had already disappeared in the direction of the front door.

'Bloody hell,' Patrick whispered. 'I reckon he was planning on me killing him.'

'I'm sure that what happened to James in Wemdale has been festering on his mind for ages,' I said the following morning. Neither of us had slept very well. 'And you know yourself how wound up he gets. Like you really.'

'Yes, but I usually get constructive results,' Patrick replied. 'I'm hoping that it was mostly the whisky talking.'

I couldn't find it in me to agree with any of that but there's no point in having an argument first thing in the morning over a perfectly good pot of Earl Grey. Then, as had happened before, his mobile, which I had requisitioned and put within *my* reach, rang.

'God, I'm going mad!' Patrick yelled. 'Just having to sit around while other people keep phoning me!'

I answered the call – it was DCI Manning at Glastonbury. She apologized profusely for contacting us so early but went on to say that the body of the woman at the Brinkleys' house having been identified as Ann Shipton's sister, they had gone to her address to tell her, mainly because they wanted someone to formally identify the body and were hoping she had returned from wherever she had gone. She was at home and had obviously been highly upset, had blurted out that she had known her sister was involved with the Hiershal brothers 'somehow' and had then ranted and raved that she wanted to really drop them in it and tell all. But then, terrified, had changed her mind and said they'd kill her too. She had been told that there was no solid evidence to point a finger at them but had replied 'who else?'. Finally, when the DCI had herself become personally involved with what might turn out to be an important witness, she had offered her police protection, which, after due thought, had been accepted. Sue had finished by saying, 'She's taken her house off the market – if that's relevant to anything.'

Before I could tell Patrick about this Katie came into the kitchen and dropped some school stuff on a chair. Her expression was asking a question she didn't like to ask.

'Everything's fine,' I said. 'Dad's just fed up with people phoning him but not being able to do anything himself.'

Patrick reached out and drew her towards him for a cuddle. 'People who shout at the breakfast table are the pits,' he said. 'Sorry.'

She brightened. 'Oh, and Mum, Justin's saying he doesn't want to go to school ever again. He's hiding under the quilt.'

'D'you know why?' I asked her.

'There's a new girl in his class. She kissed him yesterday.'

'Please go and pull the quilt off him, tell him it's something he'll have to get used to and remind him that it's Saturday. He won't be given any breakfast if he doesn't get a move on as I can't stand the kitchen being cluttered for half the morning.'

She skipped off.

Patrick chuckled and said, 'I'm not sure where that lies in the parenting skills handbook.'

'People who lay down rules about parenting are the pits too,' I retorted.

A little later, he rang DCI Manning and it was arranged that we would interview Miss Shipton, or be present when someone in her team did.

We arrived and here I was, again, in Glastonbury, in the same interview room to witness the questioning by DS Stephen

Newton of the same woman, the only difference this time being that Patrick was present and also the DCI.

Ann Shipton looked a lot better than when I had last seen her, when she had been assaulted by Lazno Hiershal. But she was still worried and looking from one to another of us as though wondering what we could do to help her. The DCI had told us beforehand that she had been thinking of charging her with assisting a criminal but had then realized that in view of her sister's death she might learn more about the Hiershals with a sympathetic approach.

After the formalities had been completed, emphasis being placed on Miss Shipton being present voluntarily, Sue Manning indicated to DS Newton that he should start the interview. He began by offering condolences on behalf of all of us and then asked Miss Shipton if she had known that her sister, Tracy, had been living in John Brinkley's house impersonating his wife.

Miss Shipton shook her head. 'No, I knew nothing about it. I had an idea she was up to something though as she hadn't been in touch. She always goes quiet then. But I stopped worrying about her ages ago – I mean, she's older than me and ought to know better.'

'To your knowledge,' Newton said carefully, 'did she get involved with the Hiershals in other ways – illegal ways, I mean?'

'Well, she went out with Lazno before I did. That was when she was still married to an old chum, Darren Adams, but he's gone off with a girl who worked in the chippy. God knows what went on. What a mess, eh?' she finished by saying almost triumphantly.

Sue Manning cleared her throat. 'Have you any idea why she was in that house pretending to be Mrs Brinkley?'

Despite ongoing enquiries the woman was yet to be traced.

'No, I've just said, haven't I? She said nothing to me about it and I know nothing. But those bastards killed her. I know they did. Who else could have done it?'

'There's a theory that someone might have tried to make it look as though John Brinkley had murdered her.'

'Well, I suppose he could have done.'

'But why on earth would he want to kill your sister?'

'Perhaps he got drunk and thought Tracy was his wife.'

'Yet according to him he'd sent his wife away to Italy for safety. Miss Shipton, I feel I have to tell you that John Brinkley's dead. His body was found in the Thames.'

'John . . . dead?' After a little pause, she added, 'As I said, perhaps he did kill her by mistake when he was drunk or something like that, and then committed suicide when he realized what he'd done.'

I felt we had had more than enough of this stupidity and, true enough, Patrick muttered something under his breath. 'Tell me,' he then said quietly. 'Where did you get the money to buy your house in the town here?'

'Are you allowed to ask questions like that?' she shot back at him.

'Yes, he is,' the DCI answered.

'Well . . . I – I saved up, didn't I?'

'From your wages in a betting shop?'

'You've been snooping around in my private affairs!'

'It's what cops do,' Patrick told her in a bored voice.

She glowered at him mulishly and then discovered that you can't outstare Sauron.

'OK, Lazno put some money into it. It was a business. We were going to build on the parties idea and have people for weekends or a bit longer – and charge them, of course. He had to have a better kitchen put in.'

'And you were hoping to sell it on the quiet but have taken it off the market because you hadn't told him and he was very angry when he found out. Which was why when we came round he had assaulted you.'

'Yeah. And he did put the rats in the place, whatever he's saying. I know he did. He wanted me out.'

'Whose name is on the deeds?'

'Mine.'

'But he put up some, or most of, the funds?'

'Yes, but that's not illegal, is it?' she shouted.

'It's called money laundering. How long have you lot been knocking around together, perhaps including Darren Adams who your sister married?'

'Not all that long.'

'And when did Luke Wallingford come on the scene?'

'I don't want to talk about him.'

'Is he the boss? The one behind all this?'

'I'm not saying anything about him.'

'I thought you wanted to help us find out who killed your sister.'

'Yes, but I don't want to go the same way as she did.'

'You're actually implying then that he's deeply involved and you're too scared to say so.'

'Bloody clever clogs, aren't you? I'm not saying any more about him.'

'Have you heard of a man by the name of Kevin Freeman?'

'I think he came to a party once. Lazno said he was a chum of Luke's. I didn't like him – a bit of a thug if you ask me.'

The DCI said, 'Miss Shipton, do you have any real evidence against any of these people? If we're to find Tracy's killer we need some.'

'No, not really. I said that because I was scared and wanted police protection.'

I had a sudden ghastly picture in my mind of John Brinkley standing in the road in the heat and the dust looking down blankly at the two armed men Patrick had shot after they had tried to abduct him. And the state of him when he was found, malnourished, filthy, drugged, not knowing his own name. He had told us that he'd been shut up somewhere . . .

To Miss Shipton, I said, 'Are there any cellars in your house?'

She started as though having not expected me to speak. 'Er – yes, I think so.'

'Don't you know for sure?'

'Well, I think Lazno knows. He might keep stuff down there. But I hate underground places.'

I looked at the DCI. 'A search warrant?' I suggested.

'But you can't!' Shipton cried. 'I haven't been arrested or anything and I came here of my own free will. Don't you dare go poking around in my house!'

I gave her one of Patrick's *Jaws* smiles.

TWELVE

I t would haunt me that we ought to have thought of it before and it was no use trying to console myself by saying that we weren't the only investigators involved in the case. Any question mark over the matter was soon removed when a warrant was issued and a cellar discovered in Ann Shipton's house. The door to it was concealed behind a tall fridge-freezer in the kitchen which, judging by the scratch marks on the floor, had been moved quite a few times. Below, down a flight of worn stone steps, were two rooms separated by a wall with an archway in it. In the farthest one was an old iron bedstead with a filthy mattress on it, a bucket obviously used as a toilet, and piles of ages-old rubbish. What dim light there was came through a low window level with the ground outside, the thick glass green with mould on the inside, the exterior mostly obscured by weeds. It wasn't designed to open and needless to say the whole of this dank, gloomy and airless underground nightmare stank to high heaven.

Miss Shipton was promptly arrested. She had left the police station after her 'voluntary attendance' and of course had been perfectly free to do so, but had made the mistake of going straight home to pack her bags. When confronted with the search team which rolled up on her doorstep quite soon afterwards, armed with the warrant, she had tried to escape through the back door but had run straight into an enterprising soul who had stationed herself there and had been gently escorted back indoors while the search was made. The suspect was duly transported to the nick and left to cool off in a cell where she could also run out of obscenities to describe her captors. Not to mention spit.

'John begged me to help him but I couldn't,' Patrick muttered while we waited for our lunchtime sandwiches in a café. 'God, I know it's not been proved yet but I can't bear the thought of him down in that filthy hole.'

'His DNA will be all over it if he was incarcerated down there though,' I said.

'And it's Wallingford, isn't it? The Shipton woman wouldn't talk about him, which can only mean one thing – she's scared. Wallingford and Freeman, or Rogers as he used to be, are behind all this. I want to know *exactly* what it is that those two are doing to warrant killing Brinkley and Tracy Adams. At least Ann Shipton's going to be remanded in custody for her own safety.'

And shortly to be questioned under caution, of course.

This time only the DCI and Patrick and I were present, the former giving every impression that she was sick of the sight of the woman in front of her. She wasn't alone in this.

'So,' Sue Manning began. 'It's time for you to stop pretending that you don't know anything about what went on in your own home. How long was John Brinkley kept prisoner down there?'

The woman, who had refused to have legal representation, shrugged. 'No idea. That was Lazno's doing. Anyway, right now it's three against one. I call that intimidation.'

'OK,' said the lady. 'I'll leave it up to the National Crime Agency. Strictly speaking, it's their case.' She got up and left the room. To me, on the way out, she had added, 'Please make notes if it assists with your own investigation.'

Patrick immediately seated himself in the chair she had vacated and for the benefit of the recording related what the DCI had done. Then he made himself more comfortable, gave the suspect a sunny smile and said, 'Right, end of lies. You'll be quite safe if you're remanded in custody so I want to know every last detail of your relationship with the Hiershal brothers, Wallingford and Freeman.'

'Relationship?' Shipton protested in her rather twangy voice. 'You're making it sound as though I was being screwed by all of them.'

OK, just by some of them perhaps, I mentally amended. The question had just popped into my mind – now poor Brinkley was dead, were we actually supposed to carry on with this? Patrick's brief had been only to find him.

'Then explain exactly what went on,' Patrick encouraged.

'And then you might not find yourself being charged with being an accessory to murder.'

With downcast eyes and a look on her face of the deepest loathing – of her situation, Patrick and whole world in general – Miss Shipton thought about it. For rather a long time. If she imagined that her inquisitor would lose patience and give up she was mistaken for, if necessary, he can have the calm perseverance of a cat waiting at a mouse hole.

'It's been a disaster right from the start,' she mumbled at last. 'Lazno and Zeti came from the north somewhere – they used different names then. They ran some kind of gang and got arrested and spent time inside. But that didn't put them off and when they came out they got involved straight away with a bloke called Norris – Frank, I'm fairly sure his first name was. He liked to think of himself as some kind of crime lord. I suppose he was really as Lazno said he virtually controlled the place he lived in. I think it began with W but—'

'Wemdale?' Patrick interrupted.

'Yeah, that's right, Wemdale. Well, the next thing that happened – by the way, this all came out one night when Lazno had had too much to drink and was practically in tears feeling sorry for himself – was that the cop who had nailed him by the name of Rogers disappeared from the scene and word went round that he'd been chucked off the job. The grapevine had it that he was bent and had been friendly with Norris and, not only that, had almost killed a cop from the south who had been out to expose him. Anyway, when Norris's gang was broken up Lazno and Zeti ran for it and came down here thinking of setting up something in this area. Thought they'd be out of reach of the cops here. Some time later, after me and Lazno met, Lazno told me he'd met Rogers again, only he was now calling himself Freeman. Did Lazno and his brother want to work for him, he'd asked them, as he'd decided to go into business, as he called it. That's all I know really.'

'Really it isn't,' she was crisply told. 'What happened after that?'

'Well, they did go and work for him! That's all.'

'But not just in Glastonbury.'

'Oh . . . no. I'd forgotten that bit. The pair of them made

contact with chums in Wemdale and arranged to help them in some way. God knows how.'

'To sell on stolen property well away from where the crime had been committed? Launder money by buying houses to use as a base for further criminal activities or to sell on later at a profit? Like Lazno put up the money for yours?'

'Perhaps. But Luke and Freeman didn't hang around. They cleared out. Lazno bragged that he was now their right-hand man.'

'At what stage was John Brinkley brought to your house and shut in the cellar?'

'About a week after he left me. I didn't care, he'd said I disgusted him so I reckoned it served him right.'

'So was he down there when we came round and prevented Lazno from half-killing you?'

'Yes, he was.'

My skin crawled. The bitch had said *nothing*.

'So you let him starve in that filthy cellar.'

'He didn't want to eat – they doped him up so he'd stay quiet.'

'What reason did Lazno give for his treatment of him?'

'It was orders from the other two. He had some kind of evidence against them.'

'But you did know Brinkley was a retired cop.'

'No, I didn't. John told me he was in banking so I thought it was about money.'

'It's always about money. Did Lazno tell you that your sister was at Brinkley's house impersonating his wife?'

'No. I expect he thought I'd be furious. I am.'

Had they really thought that they would get away with selling property in joint ownership, without the presence of one of those owners? But why had they killed Tracy Adams? A possible explanation came to me immediately. Perhaps she had refused to get further involved or was going to go to the police. Plan B then: kill her, implicate Brinkley and then kill *him*. Sorted.

As if reading my mind, Miss Shipton said, 'I really am upset about Tracy . . . terribly. So I'll tell you something else. After Lazno was picked up by you lot I got a phone call from Zeti telling me to keep my trap shut, or else. He said he'd told those he called "the bosses" that Lazno had been nicked and they were going ballistic saying it was my fault. Well, as you can imagine, that frightened me rigid. Then – and I think this was to frighten me even more – he said they were planning on doing something about it personally. That's when I decided to talk to the police.'

'You could have told me about Brinkley when we rescued you from Lazno,' Patrick said furiously.

'Then I *would* have been a dead woman.'

'If you'd told me about him he'd still be alive, would have imparted the evidence he'd collected so far and all this lot would probably be behind bars on remand!'

'I didn't think of that,' she mumbled.

Patrick got his temper back under control. 'Where in London does Zeti live? We know that his manor's in Barking.'

'I've told you before, I don't know. But he's mentioned in the past that he goes to a good pub – the Barking Mad Bar.'

'Any idea if it's near where he lives?'

'No, not a clue.'

'Have we learned one bloody thing?' Patrick asked bitterly a while later when we were in Sue Manning's office. 'Not only that, I'm convinced she knows more than she's admitting.'

'I'm not too sure about that,' I replied. 'She's never been the brightest button in the box and even if things had been discussed in her presence most of it would have gone over her head.'

The DCI had been elsewhere but now entered. 'I've just listened to the recording,' she said. 'The woman will have to be remanded in custody for her own safety. Meanwhile my team will carry on concentrating on the investigation into the murder of Tracy Adams. Have you seen the PM reports on John Brinkley?'

Patrick shook his head. 'No, I shall have to get that from Greenway. But he'd already said it was pretty obvious that the cause of death had been two shots to the head.'

Sue seated herself. 'I sympathize; it must be a real blow to you. Does this mean that the commander will recall you?'

Patrick grimaced. 'It was by way of a one-off job as officially

I'm retired. But whatever he says I shall go and get Wallingford and Freeman. But first it's important to find Zeti Hiershal.'

'I take it you're telling me this in confidence,' she said with a thin smile.

'If you like,' Patrick replied, giving her a tired smile back. 'And I'd like to thank you for your help and support in this.'

'To save you unnecessary work, I could contact the Met and ask them about the pub Miss Shipton mentioned. It's involved with a case I'm working on after all.'

Patrick's work phone rang. He apologized and answered it. He said, 'Hello, Joanna,' and then went quiet, listening. Finally he told her he'd contact her again very shortly and rang off.

'I hope it's not bad news,' I said.

'I don't know what it is really,' he replied. And to the DCI, 'This *is* in confidence. That call was from Joanna Carrick, who by the way is a WPC in Frome, the wife of DCI James Carrick who you already know about. To cut a long story short it was Carrick who tried, a few years ago, to expose Freeman – DCI Rogers in those days. Rogers almost succeeded in killing him and this has been burning a hole in James ever since. Joanna has just told me that he's "gone off somewhere" to quote her words, and refused to tell her where. Just as Ingrid and I have a few working rules about this kind of thing, what he's done has broken quite a lot of theirs. She's very worried, and so am I now that he's gone after Freeman and to hell with the consequences.'

'Did you expect that he might do something like this?'

'I got the impression when we last met that he wanted me to shoot the man. He knows the NCA's given me my Glock 17 back.'

Sue's eyebrows rose. 'What did you say?'

'It wasn't actually discussed but he did want the pair of us to do something covert.'

I think at this point the DCI whispered a few swear words. Then she said, 'I really hope you intend to try to stop him.'

'Yes, ma'am, I do. Even if it means shooting the bastard after all.'

She started to smile, thinking him joking and then realized that he wasn't.

*   *   *

'The worse thing,' Joanna said when we caught up with her later, 'is that he didn't give me the first idea of what he intended to do.'

'When did he go?' I asked her.

'Early this morning. I knew he wasn't going to work as he usually wears a suit and tie for that, but was just in jeans and a sweatshirt. I should have expected something like this – he's been brooding for days.'

'D'you reckon he's gone to confront Freeman?'

'He might have done. But James isn't a fool; he'd make sure he had some kind of legal grounds so he could arrest him.'

I felt she had said that more in hope than conviction.

'And he doesn't know where he lives,' Joanna added.

'Ingrid and I do,' Patrick said. 'We met him at Greenway's place.'

'You haven't told him, have you?' she asked in something approaching anguish.

'No, but James is a very good cop and it wouldn't take him long to find out.'

My impression that we were still going round in endless circles was further driven home when Patrick's mobile rang yet again. He went out into the Carricks' garden to answer it.

'Time to move,' he reported when he returned. 'That was Greenway. He's been asked to hand over the information that was found in Freeman's brother-in-law's garden shed and doesn't want to as he doesn't trust the one doing the asking.'

'Who? Wallingford?' I enquired.

'No. A female Met super who may or may not be the woman who removed Brinkley from us. He didn't name her and was very cagey about it.'

'He doesn't have to do as a super asks, surely,' Joanna said.

'No, but it's being dressed up as an official request, everything on the line and very polite. Obviously, he's worried.' He then told Joanna that the commander had received vague personal threats.

'What action does he expect you to take?' she asked. 'Surely all he has to do is tell this woman it's out of his hands and give it to the director.'

'If only things were that simple.' Patrick sighed.

'What's he going to do with this file then? Meekly hand it over?'

'He said he'd told her that since it was the weekend he was at home and the file's in a safe at work where it's going to stay until Monday morning. It isn't – it's at his place as he's planning to go through it properly as he'd only read it quickly before.'

We both looked at him, driving him to ask, 'Do you have any suggestions to sort out this pig's breakfast?'

We didn't.

'Please don't let James do anything stupid,' Joanna begged when we were on our way out.

By way of an answer Patrick lightly put his hands on her shoulders and kissed her cheek.

'Enough,' he said when we were back in the car. He wouldn't be further drawn.

This time we did politely ring the doorbell at the Greenways' home and Mike himself answered it.

'I thought you might turn up,' he said. He looked as though he hadn't slept for a week.

'I want the file,' Patrick told him grimly when the commander, instead of inviting us in, walked out into the front garden for a short distance forcing us to follow him.

'I've got to the stage where I think the house might be bugged,' he said, coming to a stop. 'It might not be true of course but—'

Patrick cut him short. 'But you have every expert at your fingertips who would run their gizmos over the place and tell you for sure. Mike, what the *hell* is going on?'

He didn't appear to hear the question. 'Erin's gone to stay with her mother in Cambridge but I can't take Benedict out of school as he's in the middle of exams. You don't want this file; you have a family of your own. I have no choice but to hand the damned thing over.'

I asked him if he'd received more vague threats.

Greenway muttered, 'The man's dead though, isn't he? Is it really worth it to carry on messing around with this?'

'Give me the file,' Patrick said softly, perhaps thinking the same as I was, that the man appeared to be on the edge of some kind of breakdown.

Greenway just looked at him. 'No, my conscience won't let me do that.'

'OK, Plan B then. Do your security cameras cover this part of the garden?'

Surprised, Greenway gazed about and then said, 'Er – no, just the drive itself and by the front parking area. Why?'

'Could there be others that you didn't install?'

'No, I did actually check that.'

'Is the file still a paper one?'

'Yes, it is.'

'Go indoors, get it, plus your car keys, and hurry out as though you're going to drive away. I'll get to your car first and draw my Glock on you. I'll grab you by your shirt to show that I mean business. Hand over the file. I'll give you a bit of a push and Ingrid and I will make a run for it. You act too shocked to follow. I suggest you then contact the director, tell her what's happened, but obviously not that we planned it – you'll have the video evidence as proof – and that previously you'd received more threats.'

'She'll think you've taken leave of your senses – or worse, acting for whoever's behind Brinkley's murder.'

'I don't think she will. I'm the maverick, the loose cannon, aren't I? This whole business has got completely out of hand and, frankly, you should have sent the file, or given it personally, to the director as soon as you received it.'

'What are you going to do with it?'

'Offer to sell it to the highest bidder.'

Amazingly he went along with this and after the little piece of theatre had taken place we left, Patrick pointedly holding the file, a slim red and rather battered one, in full view and giving it to me as we got back in the car.

'I hope you're not going to take this home,' I said.

'Only for a very short time, but first I'm going to stop somewhere not far away and make sure it's what it's supposed to be.'

'The threats he's received must be quite serious,' I mused aloud. 'Probably aimed at Erin and Benedict.'

'Not only that, he's been overworking for years and probably not even taken his full quota of annual leave. But I still can't understand why he hasn't got himself official protection.'

A couple of miles along the road we pulled up in a lay-by. I opened my window and it became very quiet as late Saturday afternoons in semi-rural areas of England tend to be. There was hardly any traffic, with just a few cyclists and several people jogging. I wondered what Patrick would do with the file. There were so many unanswered questions I simply couldn't see an end to it.

'Um,' Patrick said after a little while, looking up and staring thoughtfully through the windscreen. 'You remember Greenway told us that Craig Hamilton, the solicitor who wrote this, had overheard Freeman talking to someone over the phone at his own house. To recap, the gist of it was that Freeman and Wallingford intended to set themselves up to extort money from criminals they'd dealt with in their careers. Well, that someone was a person he'd asked for by name at the beginning of the call: Herman Grünberg.'

'Grünberg!' I exclaimed. 'He was one of Simon Graves' mob. He's dead.'

'Yes, but he wasn't around eight months ago if the dates on this paperwork are correct, which solicitors usually are. It appeared from the way he was talking that Freeman knew Grünberg and was asking him if he wanted to join them – he named Wallingford – in what he called their "business venture". He then went into a few details, chuckling after saying that the police would never put two and two together and catch them. Hamilton, who of course had no idea who Grünberg was, didn't catch the rest of the conversation as he went away, worried that Freeman would discover that he was eavesdropping.'

'It's a bit strange he had that kind of conversation in somebody else's house.'

'I call it arrogance.'

'Is there any other information?'

'There is. On another occasion Freeman was again at his house – it was his sister's birthday and after she'd married the man – when she came into the garden where he was pruning the roses and asked for his advice. He'd already told her that he was worried about her choice of partner and she'd hit the roof at the time and accused him of living in the past and she didn't need his permission to get married. Now though she was concerned about the company he was keeping, as she put it, "yobs who looked as though they would knife you to avoid saying hello". She said her husband made a lot of whispered phone calls and slammed the door of the room he was in if he caught sight of her. He went away for days at a time without telling her where he was going. His secrecy, together with inviting people to the house who she was sure were criminals and flying into a rage if she asked him about them, was the reason she eventually divorced him, and how to go about that was the advice she needed from her brother. He didn't specialize in family matters but put her in touch with someone who did. Later, Hamilton found out – he doesn't say how – that Freeman used to be DCI Derek Rogers. I haven't read it all yet but he makes it pretty clear that he loathed the man.'

'But why Grünberg though?'

'I don't know. But his crony Graves was another bent cop, wasn't he? Perhaps there's some kind of old boys' network.'

I hadn't wanted to be reminded of the Simon Graves/ Herman Grünberg episode and the aftermath of the one-man raid Patrick had carried out at the gang's HQ in London, Saint Edwina's, a so-called mission. I had visited the scene with Greenway. Graves' body had been down in a basement reached through a concealed hatch in the kitchen floor. He had been shot in the throat, a wild shot for Patrick, after Graves had fired at him when he was halfway down the wooden steps that led to it.

'Does it say where the ex-Mrs Freeman is now?' I asked.

Patrick turned a page. 'Yes, in a postscript he says that she's a botanist and working in the Cape doing research for Kew Gardens. Hamilton notes that he's relieved she's out of the way while Freeman's a free man. He's added an exclamation mark.'

'It's a real shame Hamilton's dead.'

We were silent for a few moments and then I said, 'What about James?'

'I'm not his guardian angel.'

'Greenway might be thinking that you're his.'

Another silence.

'This still isn't real evidence,' I said. 'Nothing concrete that will put the pair of them behind bars.'

'No, a good brief will tear it apart as the ravings of a sick man detesting his sister's husband. Whispered phone calls and yobbish callers don't make a case for prosecution. Greenway might just as well have handed it over instead of us having a pantomime.'

Perhaps we needed to go trekking somewhere remote after all. Looking for Yetis.

'I simply don't know what to do about James,' Patrick continued. 'I can't camp in the trees in Freeman's garden in case he turns up waving an AK-47.' He rested his head on the side window for a few moments. 'God. I'm still screwing everything up.'

I wanted to weep for him.

We arrived back home, both very tired and depressed. Officially, of course, Patrick had no need to do anything else with regard to his assignment. Brinkley was dead and as far as the file went I wouldn't blame him if he burnt it. But there was still the question mark over what the director of the NCA would do when she discovered that Patrick had 'forced' Greenway to hand it over. She might demand that he give it to her, in which case he probably would, gladly. It was next to useless anyway.

I had forgotten all about Charles Dixon.

The following morning, Sunday, Patrick, who I thought was in a more positive state of mind, had volunteered to sing in the choir as they were short of male voices. Since the death of his father the services have been taken by a series of visiting or retired clergy since there was a drastic shortage of priests. As he occasionally does, he had taken the two elder boys along to sit with him in the choir stalls as Matthew is quite interested in music and Justin was going to get another lesson in being quiet and still for an hour. He protests a bit but actually likes the ladies of the congregation making a fuss of him after the service, one of whom occasionally brings him sweets: strange, and huge, brightly coloured jelly spaceships and monsters that she gets from heaven knows where.

I was busy in the kitchen preparing lunch while keeping an eye on Vicky and Mark, who were playing a game in the living room with the large blue teddy bear that Matthew had won at the village fête. It involved a lot of loud shrieks and laughter, and not for the first time I was thankful that we had no near neighbours. I bit back a very non-Sunday exclamation when I heard a car on the gravel outside followed shortly afterwards by the doorbell ringing.

'I'm so terribly sorry for arriving out of the blue like this,' said a well-dressed, fair-haired woman. 'But I simply didn't know where else to go.'

I must have looked at her a bit blankly because she said, 'Oh sorry, I don't think we've met. I'm Sarah Brinkley.'

I invited her in, took her to my writing room and called Katie, who was upstairs in the room she shares with Vicky. When she came down I begged her to oversee the little ones for a while as it was Carrie's day off and I had a visitor. She pulled a face as, right now, she prefers ponies to siblings, the youngest of whom, in mitigation, I sometimes have to remind myself, are actually her cousins, and takes every opportunity to try to make Justin behave himself as he irritates her. Lots.

I returned to the study with an apology but Sarah Brinkley waved it away with a laugh and said, 'John and I couldn't have children.' A little shrug. 'And now it's too late of course.'

I went tingly with horror when I realized that she might have been referring to their ages and didn't know he was dead.

'You are Ingrid, aren't you? Patrick's wife?'

I said that I was and that he would soon be back.

'Before I went to Italy, John said on no account should I just turn up at home when I came back. He gave me this address and said to contact you when I returned and give you something if I couldn't get hold of him. I can't and he didn't give me a phone number to call you. I'm afraid I found that all a bit baffling. I still do and again, many apologies for turning up like this.'

I told her that when Patrick arrived I'd make coffee. Ye gods, what *did* one say to her?

'John always spoke highly of him.' She took a deep breath. 'I don't know if you've spoken to him but things did get very difficult at home. I knew he was investigating someone in the Met whom he suspected of corruption, something that I gathered he'd been doing for years, even before he retired, and he'd become completely obsessed about it. It drove a wedge between us actually as he thought of little else. That this entailed living with some woman to get information about criminals she was consorting with I'm afraid was the last straw, and I told him I needed to get away, for a while or even permanently. He seemed quite understanding about that and said I'd be safer away from home, which *I* didn't really understand. But I'm wondering now if the memory stick he entrusted me with and said to give to you had something to do with it. He just said it was "back-up", whatever that means. Sorry, I don't understand computers – sewing machines and machine embroidery are more my thing. I make costumes for theatres and TV companies and the ones for period dramas are complicated and a lot of work.'

A counter-tenor was coming in from the rear of the house, through the conservatory, singing the chorus from 'Thine be the Glory, Risen Conquering Son'. Patrick usually sings tenor but his natural pitch is higher, something he's a bit coy about. And yes, when I left the room and directed him into the study he did go a bit pink.

Deliberately taking a little longer than I normally do I made coffee then, having stood down Katie and replaced her with Matthew, who is content to play with the little ones for a while as long as he hasn't anything he regards as more important to do, I carried it in. Sarah was in tears, Patrick with a consoling arm around her shoulders. I hoped he hadn't given her any of the details of how her husband had been treated.

She said, 'I feel so awful about this. Poor John. But he wouldn't share with me what he was doing – perhaps he thought it too dangerous to tell me about. And I feel dreadfully guilty because I'm now worrying about myself. Where am I to go if I can't go home? How can I arrange his funeral? And you say that those ghastly people have put John's London flat *and* our house on the market. Can I take them off? How on earth did they do that without proof of identity?' She wept afresh, looking for another tissue in her bag.

'Yes, you can,' Patrick told her. 'But I don't know the answer to how they did it. As far as his funeral goes, you can only arrange that when the police have released the body. Can you stay at a hotel for a while?'

'Well, yes, I suppose I could. I've got all my travel things with me and I should imagine I can return my hired car wherever I am as I got it from a national company.'

'D'you mind telling me where the memory stick is now?'

'Oh, yes, silly of me.' She rummaged in her bag again. 'I had every intention of giving it to you this morning. Here. I'm glad to be rid of it.' She handed it over. 'Although it beats me that much information can be on something so small.'

'What happened to his computer?'

'Well, unless those people stole it, it's at the house.'

'Did John say anything about it when he gave you this?'

'Yes, come to think of it, he said he'd erased the file. At the time I thought he meant he'd rubbed it out, but that's wrong, isn't it?'

'Do you know anything at all about what John was investigating?'

'Nothing. But he'd had it in for Luke Wallingford – I hadn't mentioned his name, had I? – for years. Oh dear, you don't think he had anything to do with John's death, do you?'

'It's not impossible,' Patrick answered. 'Have you ever met him?'

'No. And John would never have socialized with the man.'

'Do you have any idea where he lives?'

She frowned and was silent for a few moments. Then she said, 'John did once remark, rather cuttingly actually, that he hoped somewhere or other was ready for Wallingford as he'd found out he was moving house. It might have been Maidenhead but I can't really be sure now.'

'One more question. Did John have a hand gun of any kind?'

She frowned. 'Well, I know there was one in the house at some stage but he never spoke about it. As I've just said, he was obsessed about Wallingford and became convinced that the man was out to get him. He once said to me that he'd have to do something to protect himself and knew just the person who would help. I went into the room we called an office one day and his computer was showing a website advertising guns for sale.'

'He could well have been researching weapons in the course of his job,' Patrick pointed out. 'Ingrid does it as she writes crime novels.'

'That's what I first thought. But then, shortly afterwards, I found a rather battered and not very big cardboard box in the recycling. There was a leaflet in it, stuck, accidentally possibly, to the inside of the lid. It was the details of a pistol of some kind.'

'Can you remember what it was?'

'No, sorry, I can't. John came along just then so I closed the lid of the wheelie bin. I was a little worried about him already and was beginning to think he was getting a bit deluded, but that might be too strong a word for it. The more senior he became in the police the more I'd noticed it. He posed rather, wore clothes that made him stand out, the kind of thing that used to be described as natty. I'm sure it would have put his colleagues' backs up, including Wallingford's. Heaven knows what's on the memory stick – perhaps just a lot of imagined nonsense.'

I was desperate to discover what was on it, but right now we had to make sure that this woman was safe and inform certain people of her arrival. We booked her into a hotel in Bath, a small one in a side street that we knew was good, and Patrick escorted her there – she would never have found it otherwise as satnavs tended to deposit one in a cul-de-sac – with me following in Elspeth's car to bring him home.

The file that we had obtained from Greenway was in the church safe in my writing room. Neither that nor the memory stick could remain with us for very long.

THIRTEEN

Computer science isn't my thing either, but I knew there was every chance that the memory stick was encrypted in some way or protected by a password. But, then again, if Brinkley had wanted other people eventually to have access to it the information might be easily available. Unless, and this was depressingly more likely, he'd had every confidence of presenting the evidence himself.

All this and other conflicting theories had been going through my mind ever since we returned from Bath. I served lunch, long overdue and thankfully only soup and sandwiches. Patrick, with apologies, had asked for his soup in a mug, the same way it's given to the youngest, and a few sandwiches on a plate and had disappeared into the study with them and his laptop. Mother presided over the anarchy that only a meal with little children can produce. Matthew and Katie escaped as soon as they could so I was left with the clearing up rather wishing that I was somewhere else. Out on George, Patrick's horse, perhaps, the wind in my face as we cantered along the Monks' Way . . .

'It's what we've been after!' Patrick said, appearing at speed a while later. 'He instigated real investigations. It seems he hired informers, people he'd come across in his career, to infiltrate gangs in the East End. One of them, a one-time Royal Marine who was living rough and struggling to overcome PTSD and a drink problem and had done a stint of training with the SAS, got into an outfit run by Zeti Hiershal. This man's role in the gang was just that of hired thug – he'd played stupid – and he succeeded in taking photographs with some kind of spy camera Brinkley gave him. They're all on the memory stick. Among others, there's Wallingford, large as life in a pub with sundry low life, some of whom Brinkley must have looked at mugshots in order to name, and another shot, taken at the same location from a different angle a few minutes later, showing Freeman. He's sharing a joke with Lazno.

'There's more, including one photo that I find hard to believe but Brinkley obviously did. In his arrogance Freeman must have decided to get his hands dirty. Again among others, there's a shot of him, with no face covering, helping in a raid on a jeweller's shop that they'd just smashed into using a stolen digger. In broad daylight too. Guess who's driving the JCB? Brinkley's undercover man went to ground after this, Brinkley said he paid him off and told him to get out of the capital. Another informer, an old lag who'd been a snout for years, was a regular at the Barking Mad Bar, in Barking, and had followed with interest what he called the gang's fairly regular "board meetings". As the drink flowed they got louder and louder. To a contact in the Met, not Brinkley, he'd passed on quite a bit of information he'd overheard. None of that has photographic evidence but his contact is still a serving officer, who again, Brinkley has named.'

'But presumably the contact didn't do much about what he'd been told,' I commented.

'Apparently a couple of raids were forestalled but the snout didn't mention Wallingford and Freeman by name, probably didn't even know who they were. All he did know was that it was Zeti Hiershal's mob. He did mention that Lazno sometimes turned up there, adding that the brothers didn't get on and there were always arguments. Finally, Zeti told him he didn't want to see his face again. That must have been comparatively recently.'

'Is there anything else?'

'Just a couple of minor details.'

'Is it enough to get them arrested?'

'No, it needs a thundering great postscript. Any ideas?'

'You've asked me that before.'

'That was before.'

I had, in fact, already had a tentative one and said, 'You said something to Greenway about offering to sell the evidence to the highest bidder. Were you serious?'

'I'm always serious about things like that.'

'Then go for it. James mentioned in the pub that he'd made it known on what he called certain restricted Met websites that Rogers' past activities were about to catch up with him. You could find out what these websites are and—'

'I know what they are but the passwords will have been changed and no one's given me the latest ones,' Patrick interrupted. 'I shall have to find out.'

'You could leave an anonymous message, tweet, whatever the hell goes on, that evidence against him from another quarter has now surfaced. That will be picked up, hopefully, by Wallingford because he's still a cop. Will he tell Freeman? Whatever he does he'll want to get his hands on the information in case it implicates him as well. My guess is that if he thinks he's safe and nothing points to him he'll be happy to betray Freeman. Do we know if they're close buddies?'

'I can't imagine either of them being close buddies with anyone.'

'No, nor me. You'll need Greenway on board for the next bit. He could contact Freeman on some excuse or other and then mention casually that he's discovered that what you said that evening at his place was correct – that he, Freeman, had been recognized at that hotel consorting with a criminal. Not only that, evidence in the form of a paper file and a memory stick had been found and you now have them.'

'But why on earth would Greenway tell the man all this? He'd be compromising his own position.'

'A friendly warning, perhaps? They're both on the parish council so the avoidance of scandal is paramount?'

'I still don't like it.'

'Bear with me. It's possible – and you'll have to be very careful here – that he'll contact you with a view to getting hold of the evidence as, despite what the Woodlake woman said to him later, he might still think that you're an erk who does menial jobs.'

Patrick grimaced. 'He might send along a hit squad instead.'

'That would be extremely risky for him because right now he's pulling out all the stops to create a front that he's squeaky clean. To call in any of Zeti Hiershal's mob would be disastrous for him if it went wrong, which it could do so easily. Not only that, he'd have to rely on people he'd normally regard as stupid.'

'I'm warming to it,' Patrick conceded. 'I'll trot it past Mike.'

But, as had happened too often before, Greenway was unavailable.

'Imitate his voice and make the call,' I suggested, in receipt of this news.

'I did actually think of that. But Freeman's ex-directory – I can't get his number.'

'Phone the parish clerk – those details will be on the council website – and charm the number out of whoever it is.'

The charm worked, although I've no idea what Patrick said. But he didn't then go on to contact Freeman pretending to be Greenway as he thought, rightly on reflection, that such a deception was unethical and unnecessary. But he did call Freeman, speaking as himself. I wasn't present when he did so, but when he found me in my writing room with Mark and Vicky he had a thoughtful smile on his face.

'After ranting and raving for a bit he said we'd have to meet in order to discuss it,' he reported, seating himself in a tub chair and taking Mark on his lap. 'A place of his choosing. So I said the venue would be of *my* choosing and I'd contact him. Let him stew for a bit.'

'This might turn out to be a very bad idea of mine,' I cautioned.

'If it goes wrong, it goes wrong . . .'

I could think of any number of ghastly scenarios if it went wrong. For one thing Freeman and Wallingford could well be close buddies, confer and smell a sting. I said, 'Who are you going to ask about the passwords?'

'It'll have to be Carrick but he's not answering his phone either. God alone knows where the man is and what he's doing.'

'Try Sue Manning.'

'I really must buy you some chocolates,' Patrick said, plunging off again having put his rather bemused son back on the floor.

'A nice big box, please,' I called after him. 'Belgian preferably.'

I discovered later that the DCI had been a bit cagey about it, but when Patrick explained what he intended to do she had become a little more enthusiastic. She had provided him with the information he wanted and for half an hour or so he undertook a little study of the content. Then, having soaked up the general style he composed a suitably cryptic entry and signed it 'An Interested Colleague'.

As far as that went we could only wait. Meanwhile, Patrick had to continue with what he called his 'day job'. This entailed borrowing his mother's car, rather restricting my activities unless I borrowed Carrie's, something I don't like to do. Then, on a morning towards the end of that week when he had to visit an address in Wells he made a short detour to come home for coffee.

'Greenway,' he announced as he came through the door. 'He rang me. First of all he apologized for being an idiot when we went round there but said the situation was getting to him and he hadn't been very well. He went on to say that Freeman had called him and said that I was blackmailing him. Greenway told him I'd forced him to hand over an evidence file and he'd given me the boot from his department for incompetence and insubordination. I reported that Mrs Brinkley had turned up with a memory stick compiled by her husband with rather a lot more evidence on it and he got rather excited and wanted to know what it was. I gave him the gist but said he'd have to come here in order to get full details as it was in the church safe and I was damned if I was going to let it out of my possession. He's coming, this evening, and I'm going to try to arrange a meeting between him and Mrs Brinkley, again tonight.'

'We'd better invite him to dinner.'

'We can't really as he's keen to question her and go back tonight.'

In my view this had worked out rather well as it still appeared to Freeman that Greenway was a 'friendly'.

But the damned file and memory stick were still in our house. This was preying on my mind rather – the writer's imagination picturing that Götterdämmerung Rhinemaiden turning up on the doorstep with her cohort of armed groupies – so I broached the subject.

'Don't worry,' Patrick said soothingly. 'I'm going away for around twenty-four hours and taking them with me. If anyone asks, you don't know where I've gone and you don't know the safe combination anyway and neither does Elspeth.'

'But she must—' I began.

'Yes, she did know it when Dad was alive, but I had it changed quite recently as that's never a bad thing to do occasionally.'

'The church silver will be needed,' I pointed out.

'That's in a fairly new safe in the vestry and has been for a while. The one here holds the parish records, which are arguably more valuable.'

'Your mother ought to be told what it is,' I persisted.

'I agree. I'll give it to her when this business is over and then no one can bully her.'

The next morning Patrick left quite early, at a little after seven a.m. Greenway had turned up roughly twelve hours previously having got a taxi from Bath station, and the pair of them had disappeared into the study for half an hour. He had only wanted coffee and when they had finished Patrick gave him a lift into the city where he was meeting Sarah Brinkley at eight. When he returned Patrick hadn't had a lot to tell me as I knew nearly all of what was going on already and he hadn't yet had any feedback from the commander. The only new piece of information was that Freeman had rung Greenway again saying he wanted Patrick arrested. He had been told that the matter was an in-house problem which would be dealt with.

The 'around twenty-four hours' stretched to thirty-six. Then, at just after eight the next evening he returned and, other than looking tired, gave no indication of having been involved in any brushes with either what I must still regard as the law or sundry mobsters. Giving me a quick kiss, he told me he was starving and went upstairs for a shower. Nerves still clanging – I still have this horror of him going out of the door and that I'll never see him alive again – I found him some supper.

What seemed a long time elapsed but was probably only half an hour before he reappeared with an apology and saying that he had been helping Matthew with his homework. And no, very much like his real father, our adopted son does not spend Saturday evenings skateboarding around the village with other teenagers as it simply doesn't interest him. Katie was spending the weekend with a school friend whose parents breed Exmoor ponies.

I asked the question at the top of my mind. 'What have you done with the evidence?'

As I had expected, Patrick poured himself a tot before he replied. 'I gave them to Dixon.'

'Did he really want them?'

'Indeed, yes. It appears that Wallingford, like Brinkley before him at one time, works on cases involving national security. So, practically *no one* outside MI5 can get their hands on it now.'

'I get the impression then that Dixon was really more interested in that than Brinkley's fate.'

'Is he that hard-boiled?'

I shrugged. I didn't know. I had always thought the man too enigmatic by half.

'I've arranged to meet Freeman,' Patrick continued. 'Thursday evening at six. I told him that I'd been chucked off Greenway's team but as evidence had turned up I was minded, if he himself didn't want it, to give it to Wallingford to do with as he pleased as I was sick to death of the whole damned business.'

'Did he believe you?'

'Well, he got the same story from Greenway.'

'Where are you meeting him?'

'D'you remember that Russian criminal who changed his name to Anthony Thomas?'

'Of course.'

'There, where we met him and he was arrested with a few of his henchmen.'

A few of his seriously crumpled-by-the-time-Patrick-had-finished-with-them henchmen, that is. 'The ruins at Virginia Water.'

'I've forgotten what they're called.'

'It's not what they're called, it's what they are – a fraction of the temple of Leptis Magna in Libya. They were given to George the Fourth by a local dignitary.'

'Yes. He liked follies and ruins, didn't he?'

'Why there?'

Patrick cast himself into an armchair. 'I was quite taken with the place. Plus, it's a really good venue for a showdown. Is there anything to eat?'

'I've fixed you cold meat and salad. By the way, do you still have a job?'

'Where d'you think I've been all day? I went straight to the office when I got back this morning.'

'A phone call would have stopped me thinking that you were in the Thames with half your head missing,' I snapped.

'Ingrid, you're grumpy,' he said in a silly voice.

Which made me laugh, of course, but I was still annoyed with him.

Patrick continued, 'He's insisting I arrive on my own and we meet in the car park where, in his words, we'll "negotiate". I gave him my work mobile number and told him to phone me if I'm late as the traffic can be terrible at that time of the evening. I intend not to arrive at the car park at all but when he calls me – he'll have to – I'll say there's been an accident and I've had to leave the car in a road near another entrance and walk so we can meet at the ruins. So I'll set him off walking along by the lake and, as you know, it's not close by. I'll be watching him and if he brings anybody with him they won't be able to remain hidden all the way. He won't come alone, of course, he'll have back-up.'

'I hope you'll have back-up too.'

'I'm working on that.'

'This sounds horribly to me like you're offering yourself as bait.'

'Yes, in a way, but he hasn't had the training I have. And if he recruits any of Zeti Hiershal's lot they'll be right out of their comfort zone as they're streetwise urban rats, not rural ones.'

I could see the logic behind this but it didn't help allay my concerns much.

'I'm hoping,' he went on, 'that they'll confer and both turn up. Then it'll get really interesting.'

Ye gods.

*   *   *

Having somehow crammed a day's work into a morning – I didn't ask how – and succeeding in getting the Range Rover fixed by the Wednesday evening, Patrick planned to set off just after lunch on Thursday. I was going as well – I wanted to – although my role, if any, had not as yet been discussed. Nothing had been discussed. I was trying not to bother myself with the thought that although Virginia Water might be perfect for a showdown, it was also a public place with any number of people wandering around with buggies, other children and dogs, not to mention joggers and cyclists.

As it happened, the weather had changed to what it is often like in late spring in England – that is, chilly with a blustery wind that threatened worse to come. By the time we were near our destination – I had been wondering if Patrick intended to call in on Greenway as he lives a short distance away but we didn't – big spots of rain were hitting the windscreen. Not a lot had been said during the journey.

'Good,' my husband murmured. 'This won't suit him at all. I'm hoping that he's contacted Wallingford and they'll both turn up. Or Wallingford might turn up without saying he's going to, which is even better.'

No, I don't chew my nails.

We came to a lay-by on the Ascot to Virginia Water road and parked. It was five fifteen. To merge into the local atmosphere of the sporty and affluent middle class we were wearing tracksuits and trainers with waterproofs on over the top and, turning my face away from a passing car, just in case, I went in for some stretching exercises. Patrick merely brooded and I knew he was worried.

'Right!' he said suddenly, making me jump. 'Are you ready?' And he set off back towards the road bridge we had just driven over. I jogged after him, feeling that I really did need some exercise that didn't just entail going up and down the stairs at home and trudging round supermarkets.

'Right,' he said again when we were on the bridge. He looked over the parapet and then moved on a few yards. 'Over you go then.'

Joking? No.

I looked over and immediately knew where I was. There

below were the ruins from the north African desert as set out
in English parkland. Even George the Fourth hadn't been able
to get the road moved so an embankment and bridge had been
built, the bridge constructed in roughly the same colour stone
as this section of the Roman temple. Where the embankment
rose up to road level was a drop of only a few feet.

'Go on,' Patrick said impatiently. 'There's around two
hundred years' worth of dead leaves down there to cushion
your fall.'

When I still hesitated he clambered on to the wall and
disappeared. This is no easy thing for him to do as to land
awkwardly could seriously injure that part of his right leg that
he can still call his own. But I just heard a loud crunching
sound and then a muttered oath. I sat on the wall and looked
down.

'Mind that fallen branch,' Patrick said, brushing bits of
countryside off himself and looking rather a long way down.

I heard a car coming, launched myself into space, landed
and then found that several of the said ancient leaves were
now in my mouth. I was hauled to my feet.

'Couldn't we have just gone in a gate like everyone else?'
I demanded to know having spat them out.

'Possibly a watched gate,' I was serenely told. He pecked
my cheek. 'Thank you. I'm glad you came.'

'You don't need me though.'

'I do. For moral support.'

I must have looked a bit baffled because Patrick added, 'I've
screwed this up so far and will probably carry on doing so.'

Sufficiently troubled by this, I grabbed his anorak with both
hands and said, 'Look, in the past most of the jobs we've done
have been fairly straightforward in the sense that it's been us
against criminals, mostly stupid ones at that. This time we've
been involved with powerful and corrupt cops who have turned
themselves into criminals. John Brinkley wasn't particularly
clever and he was no match for these people. All I can suggest
is that you put your MI5 hat on and get downright nasty.'

He smiled. 'I'll work on that. Do you have your little
binoculars with you?'

'In my pocket.'

'May I have them?'

I handed them over.

'The Smith and Wesson?'

'In the other pocket.'

The rain had eased off when we arrived but now started again, big spots thunking on to my hood. We slithered down the rest of the embankment, went through a free-standing archway and then under a pair of pedimented columns to reach the path under the bridge. There were low railings across it on the other side of the bridge and a gate that gave access to what lay beyond. When we had first come here the gate had been open as gardeners were working in the area but now it was closed and padlocked.

'I'll lift you over,' Patrick said, looking around to see if anyone was in the vicinity. 'Stay hidden in there until I turn up. Please don't move very far away and if you see anyone else just freeze.'

I had no time to think about this as I was picked up and heaved over the railings. Then he had gone off in the direction of the lake. Taking the lead, I hurried though the gap between a row of broken columns on my right and a wall with the remains of an alcove containing what looked like a small altar on the left. Beyond were mature trees and wild rhododendrons. The latter are quite good to conceal oneself among as they don't have prickles or tend to have jagged dead bits.

But not too close to the bridge, I thought, still walking and trying to do so quietly, not right here. Around twenty-five yards from where I had started from seemed reasonable. But there wasn't a good hideaway at that sort of distance so I went a little further. It soon became obvious that I was entering one of the wild corners of Windsor Great Park so I turned and went back for a short distance, reaching a point where there was a mound covered by rough grass and sapling trees, perhaps originally earth covering some chucks of stone that couldn't be incorporated into the reconstruction and now overgrown. From the top of it there was a view through the archway of the bridge of the lake and a short section of the path on this side of it. Perfect.

Having clambered up – it wasn't very big – I sat down on

what I thought was a log, mossy and wet, on the side facing the lake. It turned out to be a piece of broken stone. I had been careful to be just below the top of the mound in order not to be silhouetted against the skyline to anyone watching. My anorak was dark green in colour so I knew I would merge into my surroundings.

It was now five forty, the sky dark, even darker clouds looming in the west. I wasn't sure how my moral support could stretch to wherever Patrick was now and settled down for a long wait in the rain. It wasn't particularly quiet. Airliners taking off and coming into land at Heathrow flew low overhead and there was the distant sound of traffic on the A30 road that runs past the main entrance to the park. Sound carries over water and I could also hear voices on the other side of the lake.

Although vigilant, my mind wandered a little. That first meeting over the physics homework . . . the way Patrick had sat opposite me at my parents' kitchen table, not saying a word but conveying that he would much rather be somewhere else . . . I had remained coolly aloof, underlining the words Specific Gravity in my exercise book . . . then he had thawed and smiled and that was it . . . here was the man – he was eighteen and strictly speaking had left school – I wanted for ever and ever, right there in front of my eyes, the knowledge propelling me into womanhood in a matter of seconds. I was fifteen.

I was jerked back to reality: someone was rustling around in the undergrowth behind me, out of sight on the other side of the mound. Whoever – or whatever – it was came closer. Then, round to my right a Lycra-clad man wearing a bike helmet appeared. He was very skinny, his outfit in a hideous shade of luminous green, including the helmet, the former so tight that he looked as though he had been sprayed in high-viz paint. He appeared to be looking for something.

'Lost?' I asked.

He performed a nervous shimmy and whinnied like a frightened horse. 'Oh . . . you did scare me,' he said shrilly. 'Have you seen a bike? It's green . . . like me.' He uttered another weird snicker that I took to be a laugh.

'No,' I said.

'I–I must have gone the wrong way – no sense of direction at all – been walking for ages. I . . . I had to stop for a poo.'

'I haven't seen that either,' I told him, wanting to knock his revolting block off.

He just stood there staring at me resembling something weasel-like caught in headlights.

'Sod off!' I hissed.

Astoundingly, he bolted and kept on running until he got to the railings, which I could just see when I raised myself a little. After a couple of attempts he floundered over them and then disappeared at a leggy gallop.

Not one of Zeti Hiershal's mob then.

Just over half an hour went by during which I periodically checked on what was going on in front and below me. It began to rain harder. Although supposed to be waterproof and quite long my anorak wasn't preventing the sodden moss-covered chunk of antiquity I was sitting on from soaking my rear end to the skin. Murder, mayhem, arrests and God knows what could be happening elsewhere and here I was, soggy. I began to get a bit fed up about it.

Then, voices. I half stood again but it was only a couple jogging wearing waterproof jackets, a man and woman by the look of it. I was about to sit down again when three men came into sight. They were not dressed for any kind of fitness activity and slouched along in what looked like jeans and either hoodies or anoraks. They stopped when they got to the junction with the path under the bridge where one lit a cigarette and there appeared to be a short discussion, or even an argument, before they moved off again. I mentally filed them under Suspect.

Shortly afterwards I became aware of someone standing motionless among a group of trees over to my left. I stayed quite still as whoever it was moved slowly forward until they were roughly in front of me but were still around thirty yards away, a full view blocked by vegetation. Probably a man, judging by his deportment, his attention was fully on what was below him, the road bridge over the path and the lake beyond. He was quite tall and clad in dark green chinos and a matching parka with the hood up. There was something slightly familiar about him but I didn't know exactly what it was. Then I realized that it could only be because of the way he moved. My cat's whiskers then told me this wasn't any member of Zeti Hiershal's gang either. There was every chance that it was Wallingford.

He walked on, stealthily going down towards the padlocked gate over which he effortlessly vaulted. Then he turned sharp right and I could no longer see him. I remembered the alcove in the wall round there and wondered if he had concealed himself behind the remains of the altar, or tried to – it wasn't very big. It was more likely he had gone further along in the same direction to find somewhere more suitable. I filed him under Potential Hazard.

A few minutes later and with him staying out of sight – and he was still, in police lingo, an unidentified male – I decided to move closer and made my way as silently as possible down the mound and in the direction of the place I had first noticed him. The rain had eased off a little but it was getting dark, a rising wind gusting through the bare branches of the trees above me. I threw back the hood of my anorak in order to hear better, annoyed with myself for not doing it sooner.

Using the trunk of a large beech as cover I carefully surveyed the copse from which the man had emerged. No one else seemed to be there but it had to be borne in mind that if it was Wallingford he could conceivably have brought police personnel with him on some pretext or other. Then I abandoned caution and made my way to the copse where I concealed myself as best I could in an evergreen thicket but made sure I could move the greenery slightly to see what was going on. It wasn't safe here as I was only about ten yards from the bridge and I could no longer see through the archway.

Time dragged by and a thin mist began to drift through the trees. Then, making me jump, a man's voice said, 'Well, he can't be far away. Are you sure he said he'd meet you here as he'd had to change the plan?'

'Yes, an RTA by all accounts,' another man said, almost certainly Freeman. 'I resented having to walk all the way here though.'

'Do you trust him?'

'No. And when I contacted Greenway he said he'd acted against orders and he'd dismissed him from his team. I also have video evidence that Greenway sent me of Gillard pulling a gun on him and removing a file from his possession that was also supposed to contain evidence of our activities.'

The other man said, 'I went to the trouble of checking up on him before he and his wife called in to see me at the office. The man has a record of raising two fingers at authority.'

Yes, definitely Wallingford.

'And now he's offered you the opportunity to buy Brinkley's so-called evidence from him to get back at Greenway and the NCA,' Wallingford continued. 'What did he think, that we hate each other so much that you wouldn't tell me about the arrangements? On the other hand, he might have hoped you would so he could sell it to the highest bidder and we would just meekly turn up and he could hold an auction, the fool. I've never rated the military for intelligence.'

But that's exactly what the pair of you appear to have done, I thought.

'You've got Greenway where you want him then,' Wallingford said.

'Too right.'

'I made sure he had quiet warnings off.'

They both chuckled. But where were they? Not behind me, that was for sure.

'Pity Gillard didn't stay retired,' Wallingford grunted.

'Are you sure Brinkley actually had real evidence against us?' Freeman asked, sounding concerned.

'He said he did. That's enough for me. He'd been poking around in my affairs for years. The man had to be got rid of.'

'And Gillard?'

'I had a good look round just now and he doesn't appear to be here yet.'

'Did you bring anyone with you?'

'Cops? No. Use your head – how could I?' Then, after a pause, 'Did you?'

'Just a little back-up in case Gillard arrives with a private army. But, don't forget, he's unlikely to have brought the incriminating stuff with him.'

'So we kill him anyway and if he's hidden it then it'll probably stay hidden.'

'And leave his body here?' Freeman enquired.

'There's a deep ditch at the base of the embankment wall. We can dump him there and cover him with leaves and branches. You can chuck the gun in the lake.'

'What about his wife?'

'Oh, for God's sake! You ask far too many questions and worry too much. She writes crime stories and has to look after five kids. D'you really think she's a threat to us?'

'It's all very well for you in your ivory tower. What about that super, Judith someone-or-the-other who did the dirty work for you and grabbed Brinkley on the road to Bath? Is she still eating out of your hand?'

Wallingford chuckled. 'The silly cow seems to be besotted with me and just does as she's told. I have an idea you're a bit jealous of the way I've organized all this, getting the Hiershals on board too to snatch Brinkley from under her nose.'

'I am *not* jealous,' Freeman ground out.

There was a short silence and then Wallingford added, 'Are you a good shot with that thing?'

'Passable. I did a bit of firearms training when I served in Dalesland.'

'Well, Brinkley won't need it now.' Again, he chuckled.

Then they came into my view through the foliage. He and Freeman were standing beneath the bridge, perhaps to shelter from the rain, and had moved slightly to the side farthest away from me. I had an idea they had been speaking in little more than whispers but their voices were being amplified by the structure.

'I'm not sure that I trust you either,' Freeman said. 'You lied to me when you said Brinkley was in police custody. He wasn't – that bloody gang you're controlling had him.'

'It's a bit late to start moaning about things like that,' the other snapped back.

'No, I never have done really – right from the start. And if Gillard brings it with him I'm damned if you're going off with whatever it is that he's got hold of.'

'I shall have to as I'm the one who's still a cop. There might be details in it that are connected with cases the Met's still working on. And *you're* the one who ordered Zeti Hiershal to kill Brinkley, so that fact might come in handy one day too if the law catches up with you and you try to implicate *me.*'

I couldn't believe what happened next. Freeman yanked the gun from his pocket and fired twice at Wallingford from point-blank range. He then raced off, almost went full tilt into a group of cyclists on the lake path and disappeared.

I ran from cover and, having climbed over the railings, arrived at the fallen man at the same time as Patrick who had emerged from greenery nearby. He immediately left me with him and crouched, Glock at the ready, warily watching for the arrival of anyone else who might be coming towards us from the opposite direction. Nothing seemed to move but the cyclists had slowed and come to a stop and were clearly wondering what to do.

'Police!' Patrick shouted to them. 'I'm calling up help.'

A woman ran forward. 'I'm a doctor.'

'I think he's dead,' I told her. How could he not be with gunshot wounds like that?

She made a swift examination. 'Yes, sorry, he is.' She gazed at me sympathetically. 'Really sorry. Was he a friend of yours?'

Surprised at how shaky I felt, I said, 'No, thankfully he's the armed cop over there.'

'I've got it wrong – yet again,' Patrick whispered when he came to my side.

I don't like the expression and try not to use it in my novels but yes, he was gutted.

FOURTEEN

It would be easy for me to tell Patrick that he shouldn't blame himself for not having succeeded in arresting Freeman. The man would not have stopped if ordered to and to have risked a shot with members of the public in close range would have been madness. But Freeman's actions had been totally unexpected. Why had he killed Wallingford? As I had overheard him saying he wasn't sure he could trust him, and Wallingford's subsequent sly comments, the easiest answer was that he had feared he would 'sell him down the river'. And who would be believed, the serving assistant commissioner or the one who had changed his name having been kicked out of the Dalesland force in disgrace?

So I just gave Patrick a quick hug and said nothing for the moment.

The police arrived and, as was to be expected, the aftermath was protracted and we had to wait around, this author being on the wet side of damp, until someone more senior turned up to interview us and then we had to give statements. All this seemed to take half the night and Patrick's NCA ID didn't seem to cut much ice. He remained patient. The attending police had brought lights with them to enable scenes of crime personnel and others to do their work. Finally, at just after eleven, we were permitted to leave and I was pleased to learn that the park authority had opened a service gate to give the police access as I had no wish to climb the wall up to the road.

I was still haunted by the look of surprise on Wallingford's dead face.

What had happened was duly reported to Greenway and the commander was non-committal – Patrick got the impression he had woken him – which was surprising given the momentous outcome of the 'meeting'. Looked at cold-bloodedly, at least we had evidence against the two men, both of us having overheard what the pair of them had said, and even more cold-bloodedly there was now only one 'suspect' to apprehend. An initial search had been made for the three men I had spotted but no one was found and it was called off.

We stayed what was left of the night in London and very early next morning Greenway contacted Patrick to ask us to present ourselves at the NCA HQ. He had been brusque, if not abrupt, I was informed. When we arrived, almost half an hour after the time stated due to traffic chaos, I had an idea that he would be really angry and was all ready to protest as I had absolutely and utterly had enough. But he wasn't in his office and someone said he was in a meeting. We waited until, finally, the commander arrived.

'Well, he did a good job,' were his first words.

I thought it best to remain politely attentive and so did Patrick.

'He went home, shot the Woodlake woman dead and drove off,' Greenway continued, dropping into the swivel chair behind his desk. 'God knows why. What did you say to him?'

'Nothing,' Patrick replied. 'The pair of us had concealed ourselves nearby and I reckoned it was worth letting them chat for a bit to see what was said. You've seen Ingrid's report on the conversation as she remembered it and it tallied with what I'd heard. Freeman was going to kill me with the weapon he had – Brinkley's – and I was ready for him to try that. There was absolutely no indication that he'd planned in advance to kill Wallingford. He'd remarked that he wasn't sure he could trust him, which was borne out when Wallingford said that he wouldn't hesitate to drop Freeman in it if he tried to implicate him. That was what drove him to fire and from that range he couldn't miss.'

'Neighbours of Freeman's reported hearing a screaming row, which wasn't unusual apparently, and it demonstrates how loud it was as the houses are detached. Ms Woodlake was beside herself and shouting over and over again, "You've killed him! You've killed him!" followed by a lot of name calling. They got the impression he'd been responsible for the death of someone she was fond of. Then they heard what sounded like a shot but couldn't believe it was, thinking one of them had thrown something. They saw him drive off in his car and were still mulling over whether to call the police when they arrived.'

'Who called them?' I asked.

'She did herself. She managed to dial nine-nine-nine and speak a few words just before she died.'

Into the silence that followed, I wondered if Ms Woodlake had been 'fond' of Wallingford. Had she, having a way with words, written the file for him? We would probably never know now.

Possibly in an effort to lighten the atmosphere, Patrick said, 'You'd done a good job of convincing him that I was a wild card and you'd chucked me off your team.'

'Not difficult as it was mostly true,' Greenway observed briskly. 'But neither of us wanted this outcome, did we?'

'Do you have official protection *now*?' Patrick asked, not about to bare his soul on that subject.

The commander shook his head. 'No.'

'You're a fool. I reckon he's off his head. DCI Carrick told us he thought he was mentally unbalanced – and that was when he tangled with him quite a while ago.'

The commander merely shrugged and told us he'd also asked us to come in as he wanted us to make detailed statements while we were in the building – despite the fact that we'd done that for the Met already.

'So what do we do *now*?' Patrick argued. 'Freeman's still on the loose, Zeti Hiershal's literally getting away with murder, never mind his bunch of thugs.'

'I think you ought to go home, resume your new lifestyle, and we'll let the Met finish the job,' the commander said with a tight smile. 'You've endeavoured to fulfil your assignment but everything's been against you right from the start. I'll tell the director and you'll receive suitable remuneration.'

Everything had been against him? Greenway for one, notwithstanding any threats made to him.

'There's one snag to just dropping this,' Patrick said quietly to me when we had left the commander's office.

'What?' I asked.

'Carrick. I've been leaving messages on his phone but haven't heard from him.'

Behind us, Greenway's door opened. 'What did you do with the memory stick?' he called. 'I shall need it.'

'MI5 has it,' Patrick answered without turning round.

We didn't bother with making any more statements either.

'All I know is that James is in Barking,' Joanna said. 'He's trying to track down Freeman, or rather Rogers, through Zeti Hiershal. He rang me last night to tell me and said not to worry. Frankly, I could kill him.'

I was listening in to this conversation as Patrick had rung her – I had tried earlier but she must have been on duty as her phone was switched off – to bring her up to date with what had occurred at Virginia Water.

'Freeman will be hiding out somewhere like that,' Patrick said. 'Try not to worry, we're on our way there.'

I'd already had an idea we were.

'Trying to kill a DCI a few years ago didn't get him banged up but murdering one now and also a woman will,' Patrick said to Joanna. And to me after the call, 'Woodlake shouldn't have stayed around, should she?'

With Deepest Sympathy, I thought sarcastically and nastily and immediately berated myself.

'A few discreet enquiries,' Patrick murmured, an hour or so later as we walked down Axe Road in Barking looking for the Barking Mad Bar. It wasn't a long search because, as might have been predicted, it was at the end of the street nearest the town. Housed in a Victorian building on a corner where there was a meeting with another road, it had all the appearance of having at one time been a pub with a name along the lines of the Queen's Head. Now, the exterior of the ground floor had been ruthlessly ripped out and replaced with everything that was hideous in the modern design world.

'Being overcautious,' Patrick said, 'I'm going to ask if the Smith and Wesson in your bag is loaded.'

'Indeed,' I said. 'And it's actually in my pocket with my right hand on it.'

'The oracle is quiet,' he went on to say, scanning the crowded pavement.

'It goes like that when it's been banging on about murder and mayhem for around two days and I take no notice.'

'Would you rather wait for me somewhere else?'

'No, that's worse than coming along.'

'Nevertheless, bail out if things get difficult. I have an idea Hiershal owns the place.'

Patrick ploughed through the swing doors and I followed, wondering how the hell he intended to play this. The bar was quiet with just a few customers and more reminiscent of severe clinical depression rather than any mental state that could be described as madness. In other words, as gloomy as a crypt.

Very quickly it became obvious that the 'discreet enquiries' had been abandoned, as had one of his previous ruses of acting the aggrieved mobster. Neither was it the iron-gloved cop, nor any kind of out-of-work tradesman, chief cook or bottle washer. Here, perhaps for the first time since we had worked together, was Patrick Gillard as himself.

'I need to speak to Zeti Hiershal,' he said to one of the bar serving staff, not loudly, but he has a carrying sort of voice anyway, ex-choirboys and army officers usually do.

There was a brief hush in the hum of conversation and then people began talking again but not so loudly and I noticed a couple of men eyeing the arrivals narrowly.

'He's not here,' said the man to whom he'd spoken.

'I can see that. Get him, would you.'

'I told you, he's not here.'

'Look, I'm pretty sure he's out the back somewhere, so bloody go and get him!'

This demand must have been accompanied by a look that would have frozen the beer pumps solid for the man hurried off. He came back quite quickly.

'He wants to know who you are.'

'Tell him I'm here to prevent a very angry Scotsman from pulverizing him until he reveals where Kevin Freeman is.'

There was a longer wait this time, the barman finally reappearing to come through the flap in the counter and with a jerk of his head indicate that we should follow him. The same two men rose from their seats and endeavoured to come along too. They desisted when Patrick drew his Glock.

I supposed the room we entered was called an office but its contents were more like the leftovers of a jumble sale. Jammed in a corner was an exercise bike, seemingly broken, a large pile of what looked like old, and dirty, red velvet curtains which was rakishly topped by several wooden chairs, again broken. I did not notice the rest of the room just then, my attention on the man seated behind a metal desk which had a laptop computer on it, two brimming ashtrays and approximately a dozen dirty mugs.

Zeti Hiershal had gone downhill rather a lot since the carefree photograph taken somewhere or the other with his brother Lazno, John Brinkley and Ann Shipton. He had aged at least ten years, put on weight and was seriously unshaven. I am aware that the latter is the general fashion as modern man seems to think it makes them look trendy, cool, call it what you will, but the general effect with Hiershal was of something that had been forgotten when the bins were put out.

'A very angry Scotsman?' he queried in a deep, rasping voice with a mid-European accent, his gaze on the Glock, which Patrick now re-holstered.

The pair of us settled ourselves on chairs that didn't look as though they were on the point of collapse and Patrick said, 'Yes, in his bad old days when Freeman was a cop by the name of Rogers he banged up a DCI from Bath in an old industrial boiler and left him there to die. The cop didn't die though, and is now close by, and being a Scot, is determined to settle old scores.' And with a chummy grin, he added, 'You know what they're like.'

'No, tell me,' Hiershal said. 'I know nothing of these Scots.'

'D'you know where Scotland is?'

The man pointed vaguely towards the ceiling.

'Yes, north of here, cold and barbaric,' Patrick whispered. 'They let them join the police because they're merciless. Very good with small knives called *skean dhus*. If you don't tell him what he wants to know there'll be so much blood in here you'll drown in it – if you're not dead already.'

'How do you know this?' Hiershal asked.

'He told me – he's a chum of mine.'

'But why tell me? I don't even know you.'

'No, but I don't want my chum to end up losing his job and perhaps go to prison because he's killed you.'

'He wants Freeman.'

'Yes, he might kill him too and that's no good either.'

'So you want from me . . . what?'

There was a huge commotion somewhere outside and the door burst open. In dashed another scruffy, unshaven man who turned out to be James Carrick. He whipped round, felled one of the would-be bouncers who had been right behind him, caught a foot on the edge of a tattered rug and finished up sprawled on Zeti Hiershal's desk. Hiershal screeched in utter terror. To tidy things up a bit Patrick leapt up and floored the other bouncer who had run in, heaved him and his colleague back out through the door and slammed it. By this time Carrick had got back on his feet, walked round the desk and grabbed Hiershal by the front of his sweatshirt.

'What I want is the whereabouts of Kevin Freeman,' Patrick said to him as though nothing had happened.

'This . . . this is . . . is . . . is *him*?' Hiershal yammered.

'Absolutely,' Patrick drawled.

'Do I get anything in return for the information?' Hiershal, despite everything, wanted to know.

'Yes, it means I don't smash your face in!' Carrick yelled at him.

'All right! I tell you! I tell you!'

Carrick released his hold. 'We're listening,' he said grimly.

'Then you won't use your – your – whatever it is on me?'

When Carrick looked puzzled, Patrick said, 'Got your *skean dhu* with you?'

'No, not right now,' the Scot replied, even more puzzled.

Patrick produced his Italian throwing knife and sprang the blade. 'I have.'

Hiershal sort of withered back into his seat and then grabbed a memo pad and pen and wrote busily. Then he tore off the sheet of paper and smacked it on the desk.

Carrick picked it up, looked at what was on it, threw it back and said, 'Now write it so we can read it. If your writing's that bad print it.'

Hiershal glowered at him, then at the knife – which, I have to record, Patrick wasn't even pointing in his direction – turned over the paper and wrote again.

'And if he's not where you say he is we'll come back and skin you alive,' Carrick added. 'Not to mention burning this shit hole to the ground.'

'He went off and took some of my boys with him!' Hiershal shouted. 'Otherwise you'd never have got in here alive! I hope he kills you in this place Wemdale, wherever the hell it is!'

We left, walking fast and keeping up the pace for around two hundred yards whereupon Carrick took a sudden left turn down an alleyway, then a right into another and after going through a gate in railings and down stone steps we ended up in a subterranean wine bar. I guessed the thinking was that the two who had already been dealt with, who weren't feeling too well right now, represented the remainder of Hiershal's 'boys'.

'They have whisky,' Carrick reported tersely. 'Yes?'

'Absolutely,' Patrick said. Having indicated to Carrick that he would pay he turned to me and added, 'James was in the bar when we went in.'

I declined a drink and said to the pair of them, 'Just out of curiosity, how many police procedural rules did you break just then?'

'I lost count,' Carrick replied.

If Freeman really was in Wemdale it would be logical as that was where he had originated. I didn't think James would be very happy about going back there – although he had already made it clear that he would – but had made no other comments about it and there was every possibility that Hiershal was lying anyway. He was wired that way. The discussion that followed hinged on whether the search for the man should be made official – that is, involve Dalesland Police or remain off-piste. The latter was immediately ruled out as basically Patrick and James are good cops. The decision was made that Dalesland Police would immediately be told that a wanted murderer was likely to be on their patch, the information having come from an 'associate' of his. They also decided that Patrick would make it official with the NCA, stating that Avon and Somerset Police were on board in the shape of DCI Carrick who would liaise with DCI Sue Manning. The Met also would have to be kept in the picture as a priority – Patrick reckoned that Greenway could do that.

And were the three of us going to Wemdale? Of course.

When Patrick and I talked about it later we agreed that it was imperative James didn't go alone, notwithstanding any number of cops he might call upon to assist him. We owed it to him and Joanna to do that. I felt I owed it to Patrick to be supportive to him even if I ended up being banished to the touchline on account of the family if things got a bit hairy. Meanwhile we returned to our hotel – James said he would stay with an old Met colleague – where Patrick caught up with work that he could do 'at home' and I brought Commander Greenway up to date. I reckoned we had reached the stage with this case where anyone in authority would be reluctant to stop us on the grounds that they could throw the book at us if it all went wrong. I wasn't about to enquire of James what those in authority in the Avon and Somerset force might think about his self-motivated investigations.

Carrick left his car with the old colleague, we picked him up and all travelled in the Range Rover, which Patrick likes to call the 'battle bus' in such circumstances. It was a long drive, hours, and when we neared Wemdale any picturesque views of Yorkshire were blotted out by low cloud and curtains of wind-blown rain.

Someone in Dalesland Police called Patrick's mobile so I handed the phone to Carrick having explained that he was the senior officer present, which of course was true. The news was interesting in that they hadn't forgotten about Freeman, aka Rogers, the inspector on the line commenting that rogue cops – very few indeed in their force, he was at pains to point out – were always kept on the radar. It was known that Rogers had changed his name and had been living an ostensibly honest life in the south and he personally was delighted that the 'rat had come back to his nest' to enable him to be arrested for the murders of Wallingford and Alice Woodlake. He would arrange for covert surveillance to be carried out at a house which the man was known to still own. This was a different address to the one we had so we shared ours with him and he gave us the one they knew of. 'Do keep in close touch,' was the earnest plea from the DI who urged us to contact him immediately if we wanted back-up of any kind.

'It still rankles them,' Carrick said when he had related this to us. 'Wherever it happens it always does.'

Now late afternoon – we had stopped for a bite of lunch – the rain had not abated and heavy cloud ensured that it would get dark early. Aware that there probably hadn't been time for any surveillance to have yet been put into place, we located the house at the address 'that idiot mobster' had given us on the Internet, parked a couple of streets away and the men went off to have 'a quiet lurk'. It was now thumping down with rain so I didn't mind not being included in the lurk at all.

What I had seen of Wemdale so far – not a lot – had lived up to what James had told us about the place even though for obvious reasons he was very biased. All regeneration schemes seemed to have missed the town. I toyed with the idea that this was because it was situated in a narrow valley with the river Wem threading its dark way through the bottom and was thus almost out of sight from the surrounding countryside. You hardly knew it was there until you sort of fell into it down the steep hairpin roads that wound in and out between derelict mills and factories. I assumed this district was so awful it followed that it was thought no one would want to live here should any of these buildings be converted into flats.

Modern human habitation was strung out along the valley floor. This finally opened out into what had looked, from what I could see though the murk, like marginal farmland and a small lake. As we had travelled down most of this had been blurred into greyness by the present heavy shower. Orange street lights had flickered on, not improving the situation at all, least of all in this approach road to a business park where the Range Rover was now parked, the buildings just dark hulking outlines in the gloom.

The men returned after quite a long time, removed their dripping waterproofs, tossed them in the back, climbed in and for a few moments there was silence.

'Well?' I asked, always impatient.

'This place is like hell on earth,' James muttered.

'Nothing really of interest to us at the house,' Patrick said. 'It's in a run-down terrace and we're guessing that it's rented out. I had a quick look through the windows. There was an extremely sozzled woman and a clutch of kids in the living room, one bloke out of his skull on whatever in the kitchen bent over the sink, another one in a ground-floor bedroom watching TV. He was the one who answered the door.'

'You knocked!' I exclaimed.

'Yeah. I took back the baby sitting in the gutter outside. He had an idea it belonged there but was only the lodger.'

The thought of Mark sitting in a gutter in the pouring rain was horrible.

'Shall we have a snoop at the other place and then find somewhere to stay the night?' Patrick then suggested.

I said it might be a good idea to do it in reverse order and they agreed.

On the first occasion we'd had the misfortune of being in Wemdale we had stayed at a hotel that had been perfectly acceptable. It was situated in the old part of the town and overlooked a weir on the river. On arriving now we asked for, and got, the rooms we had used before, actually a so-called family room that consisted of a double and a single with an inter-connecting door. Patrick breezily mentioned that we were all on business in the area and Carrick was careful to register himself as just plain 'Mr'. Gossip travels fast.

The reason behind my wanting to delay our arrival at the address Dalesland Police had given us was a hope that they would put their surveillance into operation before we got there. For after all, if Freeman had gone off with several of Zeti Hiershal's 'boys', they would possibly be no match for the contingent from Somerset, but who wanted to risk a serious confrontation? Not only that, for all we knew the house was permanently lived in by people who had no love of the law either.

This property was a semi-detached house in an area that couldn't really be described as run-down, just tired. We drove by and although the road had quite a few parked cars there was no sign of life at all so whether any kind of watch was being carried out from one of them couldn't be ascertained. The local police had been given the number of our car so if anyone was on duty there we would be ignored.

'Please just tail us,' Patrick said to me when we were again parked a safe distance away. 'If you hear what you think is real trouble, call the number James was given.'

I had already saved it on my phone.

Well in the general mode of the area the pair, hoods up on their anoraks, hands in pockets, slouched off into the rain. I followed at a distance where I could still clearly see them. If anyone asked I was just a woman desperate for fresh air out for a short walk. I was, in fact, desperate for the fresh country air at home. Also hungry, we had postponed eating until later and it was no use telling myself that what I was doing was good material for my writing because it bloody well wasn't.

Ahead of me, Patrick and James paused for a few seconds, ostensibly to look in the window of a corner shop but I knew that in reality they were quietly checking their surroundings and, momentarily, Patrick looked in my direction to make sure that I was still there. I did the same: no one was in sight to my rear, the only movement just light traffic and a lone cyclist. Somewhere, a clock struck seven. We moved on, they turned right and when I reached the corner shop I saw that it was a newsagent's. A board in the window had faded and curled advertisements pinned to it along the lines of, 'Make Your Fortune in Three Weeks, Just Give Me a Call!', 'Linda Can Provide all the Relaxation Exercises you Require!' and 'Free Rats and Ferrets – Owner Giving up'. I found myself wondering if there was also a free terrier to deal with the former of these.

We walked the length of this road and then Patrick and James crossed over at the end of it at a junction with another and turned left. I caught up slightly as the distance between us had increased. We hadn't gone very far when, ahead, there was every indication that real trouble was happening to someone else. Some kind of silent and deadly turmoil was taking place in the road ahead in the general area of the house for which we were heading. Cautiously, the three of us hurried and it quickly became obvious that a man and a woman were being savagely beaten by several others. Amazingly, as soon as they noticed Patrick and James nearing, they launched into them too. But as will a ship when sent down a slipway at low tide, they soon ran aground and that's where three of them stayed – on the ground.

Mindful that I was in charge of communications I didn't want to get too involved but quickly saw that the woman was on her knees and crawling on the pavement towards the bottom of a neighbouring overhanging hedge. She appeared to be trying to yank something out of her jacket pocket at the same time. I ran to her. Even in the poor street lighting I could see that her face was covered in blood.

'For God's sake, call the cops,' she gasped, the words slurred and bubbly as she spoke. After another short struggle she finally managed to get her phone – no, radio – out of her pocket. 'Just press that button.'

'I know,' I said quietly. 'NCA.'

'Is Phil all right?'

'There are three, no four, blokes flat out in the road and one on his knees,' I reported.

'He'll be the one on his knees,' she whispered and collapsed.

I called the cops, emphasizing that an ambulance was needed and also contacted the number we had been given for good measure as I had an idea the DI might be the boss of these two. While I was speaking the man on his knees staggered to his feet and came towards us.

'Are you Phil?' I called before he got too close.

'I was when I got up this morning,' he groaned.

The little war was continuing and, seeing a couple of whoevers attacking James I grabbed the one nearest, who had his back to me, with two hands by the dreadlocks, a splendid handle, and swung him round in Patrick's direction. I've discovered that if you get even heavily built but unfit men off-balance they fall over very easily. Patrick provided the added impetus and he joined his friends in the road.

'Watch out, Ingrid!' Carrick yelled as a freshly anaesthetized yob came stumbling in my direction.

I leapt out of the way, tripped over my own feet and went flat. When I had picked myself up I was the only one standing but for Phil. Patrick and James had disappeared. The road was strangely quiet but for the muted sounds of traffic on adjoining roads and TVs in the front rooms of neighbouring property. No one appeared to have noticed what was going on outside and, if they had, were staying right out of it.

I went closer to the house. The front door was wide open, light streaming out. Another man was draped across a bush at one side of the garden path, thankfully no one I knew or was married to. As I got closer James Carrick appeared from within propelling someone at speed who was tottering in front of him and catapulted him through the door and into some unfortunate greenery on the other side of the path. The DCI didn't appear to notice me.

Hearing sirens in the distance – or was I imagining it? – I went in, prepared to step smartly aside should anyone else be evicted, and followed the sound of voices. They were coming from a room at the rear. I froze.

'Greenway told me he'd got rid of you. So what are you now, some kind of maverick cop?' a man, Freeman surely, demanded to know.

'I've always made a point of being a maverick everything,' Patrick's voice replied.

'Well, I have to thank you for rescuing me from this lot. They're Wallingford's gang of yobs come to get even after I threatened to expose him as the criminal he was. They even beat up the cop minders I'd been given. But I'm aggrieved that you didn't damned well turn up at the ruins.'

'I did let you know that there had been an RTA. It was serious and the road ended up being closed. By the time I got there the place was crawling with cops so I disappeared as it was nothing to do with me.'

'I reckon he'd planned to have me arrested. Did you let him know I'd be there?'

'Yes, I wanted to sell the evidence to the highest bidder.'

'You're a real bastard. He might have just killed you.'

'I've news for you. I've been stringing you along to see if I gave you enough rope you'd hang yourself. You're not only lying, you killed Wallingford.'

'I damned well didn't!'

'Why are you talking about him in the past tense?'

An arm shot out from my right and whisked me into very close proximity with someone.

'He hasn't seen me,' James hissed in my ear.

We stood quite still. I guessed the pair were talking in the kitchen, their voices carrying to where we were on account of the lack of soft furnishings that would have deadened the sound.

Patrick said, 'I happen to know that you shot him with Brinkley's gun. You talked under the bridge and were going to kill me and throw my body in a ditch under the wall. I was there and heard every word of it.'

There was a short silence and then Freeman quietly said, 'Just you though, no one else.'

'No, I was there as well,' I said, emerging from where I'd been standing and walking down the short hallway into the kitchen, the Smith and Wesson very, very handy. 'You shot him and I probably had a better view than Patrick.'

James appeared at my side. 'And I'm going to arrest you for the murders of John Brinkley and Alice Woodlake, and also for being an accessory to the murder of Tracy Adams – for a start.'

Freeman gawped at him. 'You! But . . . but . . . you're dead! We put you in that—'

'And I got him out,' Patrick interrupted sweetly.

Carrick continued, 'As you probably remember from your Derek Rogers days, all forces keep quiet tabs on their bent cops and Dalesland is no exception. They told us you might be here.'

Louder sirens.

Freeman let out a roar of rage and hurled himself at the Scot. Several years of bitter memories fuelled the jab to the jaw that caused him to crash to the tiles. When he recovered a couple of minutes later, having carefully been moved into the recovery position, Carrick formally arrested him.

Patrick, who had stayed right where he was rubbing the knuckles of his right hand, gave me a little smile.

The female colleague of Phil – we never discovered her name – was taken to hospital with a suspected broken nose and Phil himself, who had busied himself arresting the gang, went along with her in the ambulance for moral support. How the gang with Freeman had detected them was not revealed, if indeed anyone knew, so perhaps a refresher course in surveillance might eventually come their way. There were the usual statements to be made to the arriving police, one of whom was the DI Carrick had spoken to. He thanked Patrick and James for preventing the members of his team from being more seriously injured.

My one abiding memory of the end of the affair was Carrick walking away for about twenty yards to call Joanna, a few tears on his eyelashes when he returned, but also with a little smile.

FIFTEEN

The Barking Mad Bar was raided that night and Zeti Hiershal, discovered with two prostitutes in an upstairs room, was arrested. Trading Standards personnel alerted by the police closed the place the next morning having found the kitchen and cellars infested with vermin. Of the customers apprehended at the time, two were a little the worse for wear for at least two reasons, a handful of others taken into custody for carrying drugs, bladed weapons and wanted to help with enquiries anyway. Just about the only innocent party was a bone-thin cat shut in one of the cellars, perhaps with the hope that it would deal with the rats, which was handed over to the RSPCA. We discovered at a later date that the animal was found to have an identity chip and was missing from its home three streets away having probably been stolen.

A few months later there was still no evidence to suggest that one-time colleagues of Wallingford had been looking for John Brinkley, which led me to think that it was wishful thinking on his part. Perhaps he had thought it made his case against the one-time commander stronger and more credible, that others were working with him. Ultimately, Wallingford was found to have had a stolen identity, that of a police cadet with no surviving family who, years previously, had been tragically killed on a weekend expedition to Dartmoor. I think there were other details discovered about his past but at this point I'm afraid I lost interest.

It was very difficult for Patrick, but we had nevertheless attended John Brinkley's funeral which was held in London. It had been interesting and slightly humbling to see the number of people, police personnel by the look of them, who were present. Also there but very quietly was Charles Dixon. Afterwards, at a gathering in a pub near New Scotland Yard, he had made a point of seeking us out.

'I really hope you still don't think you failed in this matter,' he said to Patrick.

'Yes,' he was told. 'I do.'

'Sometimes one is literally outgunned,' the man had responded with a smile. When Patrick made no further comment, he continued, 'I understand Zeti Hiershal confessed to having killed Brinkley.'

'Freeman gave him five thousand pounds – which will be confiscated of course. Also, with a bit of luck, Freeman's house, car and any other crime-funded possessions.'

'That memory stick . . . I have an idea that some of the names mentioned on it didn't mean a lot to you.'

'One or two did.'

Speaking even more quietly than normal, Dixon had said, 'They meant an awful lot to *me*.'

Sarah Brinkley, who had been composed throughout the service, spotted Dixon and came over.

'Charles!' she had cried. 'How lovely to see you again!'

Sometimes it's best not to ask.

Normal family life resumed, if in fact there is such a thing. It might not exist any more than does 'the man in the street'. Patrick resumed his insurance company job and no one said anything about the extra days off he had taken, possibly because management still felt the company was partly responsible for what had happened. I asked him what remuneration he had received from the NCA following his 'contract', the quotes necessary as no one had signed anything.

'Two weeks' pay at my old rate,' he replied and then laughed.

'It probably came out of petty cash,' I raged. 'Tea bags, sugar, a birthday card and Patrick Gillard.'

'I can always flog the Glock.'

'Please *don't*.'